THE DEBUTANTE IS MINE

THE DEBUTANTE IS MINE

The Season's Original Series

VIVIENNE LORRET

AVONIMPULSE
An Imprint of HarperCollinsPublishers

Excerpt from "The Duke's Christmas Wish" in *All I Want for Christmas Is a Duke* copyright © 2015 by Vivienne Lorret.

Excerpt from *Serving Trouble* copyright © 2016 by Sara Jane Stone.
Excerpt from *Ignite* copyright © 2016 by Karen Erickson.
Excerpt from *Black Listed* copyright © 2016 by Shelly Bell.

EPub Edition APRIL 2016 ISBN: 9780062446275

Print Edition ISBN: 9780062446299

Avon, Avon Impulse, and the Avon Impulse logo are trademarks of HarperCollins Publishers.

AM 10 9 8 7 6 5 4 3 2 1

Our souls sit close and silently within,
And their own web from their own entrails spin;
And when eyes meet far off, our sense is such,
That, spider-like, we feel the tenderest touch.

~JOHN DRYDEN

CHAPTER ONE

The Season Standard—the Daily Chronicle of Consequence.

Lilah read no farther than the heading of the newspaper in her hand before she lost her nerve.

"I cannot look," she said, thrusting the *Standard* to her cousin. "After last night's ball, I shouldn't be surprised if the first headline read, 'Miss Lilah Appleton: Most Unmarriageable Maiden in England.' And beneath it, 'Last Bachelor in Known World Weds Septuagenarian Spinster as Better Alternative.'"

Lilah's exhale crystallized in the cold air, forming a cloud of disappointment. It drifted off the park path, dissipating much like the hopes and dreams she'd had for her first two Seasons.

Walking beside her, Juliet, Lady Granworth, laughed, her blue eyes shining with amusement. Even on this dull, gray morning, she emitted a certain brightness and luster from within. Beneath a lavender bonnet, her features and complexion were flawless, her hair a mass of golden silk. And if she weren't so incredibly kind, Lilah might be forced to hate her as a matter of principle, on behalf of plain women throughout London.

"You possess a rather peculiar talent for worry, Cousin," Juliet said, skimming the five-column page.

The notion pleased Lilah. "Do you think so?"

After twenty-three years of instruction, Mother often told her that she wasn't a very good worrier. Or perhaps it was more that her anxieties were misdirected. This, Lilah supposed, was where her *talent* emerged. She was able to imagine the most absurd disasters, the more unlikely the better. There was something of a relief in the ludicrous. After all, if she could imagine a truly terrible event, then she could deal with anything less dramatic. Or so she hoped.

Yet all the worrying in the world would not alter one irrefutable fact—Lilah needed to find a husband this Season or else her life would be over.

"Indeed, I do," Juliet said with a nod, folding the page before tucking it away. "However, there was nothing here worth your worry or even noteworthy at all."

Unfortunately, Lilah knew what that meant.

"Not a single mention?" At the shake of her cousin's head, Lilah felt a sense of déjà vu and disappointment wash over her. This third and final Season was beginning on the same foot as the first two had. She would almost prefer to have been named *most unmarriageable*. At least she would have known that someone had noticed her.

Abruptly, Juliet's expression softened, and she placed a gentle hand on Lilah's shoulder. "You needn't worry. Zinnia and I will come up with the perfect plan."

As of yet, none of their plans had yielded a result.

Over Christmas, they had attended a party at the Duke of Vale's castle. Most of those in attendance had been unmarried young women, which had given nearly everyone the hope of marrying the duke. Even Lilah had hoped as much—at first. Yet when the duke had been unable to remember her name, she'd abruptly abandoned that foolishness. And a good thing too, because he'd married her dearest friend, Ivy, instead.

The duke had developed a *Marriage Formula*—a mathematical equation that would pair one person with another according to the resulting answer. Then, using his own formula, the duke had found his match—Ivy. As luck would have it, both Ivy and Vale had fallen deeply in love as well. Now, if only Lilah could find her own match.

"I have been considering Vale's *Marriage Formula*. All I would need to do is fill out a card." At least, that was how Lilah thought it worked. "Yet with Vale and Ivy still on their honeymoon, I do not know if they will return in time."

Then again, there was always the possibility that the equation would produce no match for her either.

Juliet's steps slowed. "Even though I couldn't be more pleased for Ivy, I'm not certain that I want to put your future happiness in the hands of an equation."

Lilah didn't need *happiness*. In fact, her requirements for marriage and a husband had greatly diminished in the past two years. She'd gone from wanting a handsome husband in the prime of his life, to settling for a gentleman of any age who wasn't terribly disfigured. She would like him to be kind to her as well, but she would accept any man who didn't bellow and rant about perfection, as her father had done.

"A pleasant conversation with someone who shares my interests would be nice, not necessarily happiness, or even love, for that matter," Lilah said, thinking of the alternative. "All I truly need is not to be forced into marriage with Cousin Winthrop."

Lilah cringed as she spoke. This was the crux of her problems. If she did not marry a titled gentleman by the end of this Season, then she would have to marry Winthrop, as her father's will decreed. Like her father, Winthrop was obsessed with social standing. Perhaps even more so. And worse, whenever he'd witnessed one of Father's tirades, a dark, fiendish gleam lit his eyes and curled his lips into a smile.

Lilah did not need the gift of foresight to understand what the future would hold for her as the wife of such a man.

This union had not always been her father's demand, however. At one time, all familial expectations had lain on her brother's shoulders. Yet when Jasper was killed in a duel over a married woman and known courtesan, Father had been humiliated. His position in society faltered too, because Jasper's actions had tainted the family name.

As a result, Father had amended his will. He'd wanted to restore the family's honor by aligning with another noble bloodline. And since his only daughter was such a plain, unmarriageable creature, he'd added an incentive to ensure her success. Thereby, it was written that Lilah would have three Seasons to secure a titled nobleman or else be forced to *preserve* the family bloodline by marrying Winthrop Appleton, the new Baron Haggerty.

Lilah tried to expel her fear in an exhale, but all that came out was mist. She wished she could think of a worry that was worse than marrying Winthrop. Like the world suddenly opening up and swallowing her whole, for example. But still, that wasn't the worst possibility.

"I will not let you marry that conniving serpent," Juliet hissed. "We both know that if it weren't for him, your brother would still be alive."

Lilah nodded thoughtfully. True to his nature, Winthrop had been the one who'd told the Count of Montclaron that his wife planned to run away with Jasper. The French nobleman—and renowned marksman—hadn't cared about his wife's random affairs, but to abandon him would have caused humiliation. Therefore, he'd challenged Jasper to a duel.

"Though who is to say that another husband might not have stood in Montclaron's place sooner or later?" Even though she'd loved her brother dearly—loved him to this day—Lilah also knew that his roguish nature would have caught up with him eventually.

Her own experiences were completely opposite of what her brother's had been. While he had received so much attention that a constant selection of women had been at his disposal, Lilah could not tempt even one single man. And she was running out of time.

Pausing on the path to calm her nerves, Lilah noticed a spider's web draped over the boxwood hedge beside her. "I envy the lives of spiders. All they do is wake up, build a web, and wait. Likely, there is no concern involved. The spider knows that, eventually, the sticky gossamer threads will ensnare something."

Proof of that rested in a taut bundle of silk near the center of the web. In the bleary late-morning light peering through a soot-colored sky, beads of dew clung to the spiral, resembling drops of liquid silver. The spider herself was a dark beauty, marked with faint gray lines. She possessed a rather optimistic view of her future, busily repairing the surrounding area of her web, apparently anticipating more visitors.

Juliet leaned in to study the web as well. Then, with a shake of her head, she took a step back. "While I am not particularly fond of any eight-legged creature, I admire your rather unique perspective. Many a young woman would prefer to emulate a butterfly, gaining admiration and flitting from one gentleman to the next."

"Lying in wait for a *victim* seems to be my only option." Lilah laughed wryly. "A young woman of three and twenty with brown hair, brown eyes, and a forehead—which my mother has described as *vast*—is not likely to be compared to a butterfly."

"And for that, you should be thankful. Have you ever seen one up close? Absolutely terrifying!" Juliet kept her expression serious for a moment, until a smile gave her away and distracted Lilah from her worries.

And she appreciated her cousin's efforts. It had been a few months since Juliet had come to stay at Aunt Zinnia's townhouse. Only four years separated them in age, with Juliet the elder, and they'd become close.

It seemed strange, however, that for most of Lilah's life, she'd never known her second cousin. Many years ago, the family had fractured, severing ties with Juliet's parents and leaving them strangers. Then, a year ago, shortly following the death of Juliet's husband, Aunt Zinnia had reached out to her with an olive branch. And now it was as if they'd always known each other.

"Jest aside, however," Juliet continued, "in the past few weeks, I've suspected you have been hiding your best feature. Your milky complexion serves as a canvas for dark brows, warm eyes, and chimney-sweep lashes. Your nose is neither too long nor too pert. Your chin is nicely curved. And whenever you choose to smile—which is not nearly often enough—you look as if you have a secret. From what I understand, men are intrigued by women with secrets."

Lilah didn't know how to respond to such flattery. Other than her dearest friend, Ivy, Juliet was the only other person who said nice things to her. Mother had tried once or twice, but the efforts had been entirely too awkward and better left forgotten. "But I have no secrets. I believe in honesty."

"Yes! Don't you see? That *is* your secret. No one in the *ton* ever expects honesty," Juliet said with a light, conspiratorial laugh. Then, linking arms with Lilah, she turned and began to breeze down the path in the direction of their waiting carriage. "I can tell by the abundance of carriages on the street that it's nearly calling hours. If we fail to return shortly, I fear that Zinnia will unleash her severe stare upon the innocent parlor clock."

Aunt Zinnia's requests were always of an urgent nature. She was forever saying, *"Time is not our ally."*

Thinking about time was exhausting. It would be nice to enjoy a single moment without worrying about the clock or the calendar. "Aunt Zinnia is rather like my mother. Both sisters are rather *severe* about most things."

Lilah cast one last glance back at the spider, wishing that she too could spin a web to decide her own fate.

Juliet quickened their pace. "This is why we must return. Your future husband might very well call upon you this morning, flowers in hand."

With the clamor of carriages nearby, Juliet likely missed Lilah's snort of disbelief. "I do not mean to disappoint you, but there will be no morning callers."

It wasn't that Lilah was a pessimist. Not entirely. The simple truth was that during her first two Seasons, she'd never once had a gentleman caller. Therefore, the beginning of her third was likely to transpire as any other day would. Still, she felt a measure of comfort in her low expectations. There was no need to imagine a catastrophe awaiting her arrival.

"Last night's ball held little promise, I grant you," Juliet offered with a thoughtful nod. "However, it was only the *first* ball of the Season. There will be many other opportunities to make an impression."

"I think I would be content if a single gentleman had remembered my name." Lilah recalled every moment of the awkward evening. Standing between the perfectly poised Aunt Zinnia and flawlessly beautiful Juliet, Lilah had felt like a broom—out of place, uninteresting, and not meant to be acknowledged. "I was introduced to Lord Ellery three times last night, but each time he hadn't the vaguest notion of who I was."

"Some gentlemen have horrid memories."

Lilah appreciated the sentiment but knew that her cousin had no idea what it was like to be plain. After all, during Juliet's Seasons and before she'd married Lord Granworth, she'd been given the moniker of *the Goddess*. Even as a widow, now aged seven and twenty, it was still true. Juliet possessed a timeless beauty. "You have been away from London for more than five years and yet the viscount remembered *your* name."

"I'm certain it was only by chance."

That particular happenstance had yet to favor Lilah. "He was amongst several gentlemen who offered condolences over the loss of your husband last year."

As they neared the entrance where they'd begun their walk, Juliet lifted her hand, signaling their waiting driver to come around. "If the late Lord Granworth's name, or even my own name, is on anyone's lips, it only means that the gossips are in want of interesting topics."

"Or perhaps that you have always made a favorable impression."

Juliet stiffened but did not respond.

Lilah thought back to last night and wondered what it would have been like to have stood in Juliet's slippers. "If I had your beauty, then—"

"Do not make such a wish, dear Cousin, I beg of you," Juliet interrupted, turning toward her. Fine worry lines knitted her brow, and her mouth drew tight in a frown. "You have qualities that are far and above my own. You are lovely, sharp-witted, and approachable. I daresay the very makings of the Season's *Original*."

At this, Lilah could not contain her laugh. "The *Original*, indeed!"

Each year, an anonymous committee named the one person whose style and character shined above all others, the one person whom everyone wanted to imitate…the Season's

Original. No one knew which members of the *ton* comprised this anonymous committee. Nonetheless, at the end of the first month of the Season, the name of the *Original* was published in the *Standard.* Last year, the poor but beautiful Annabel Bronwyn was named and shortly thereafter had become the toast of the *ton.* Rumor had it that she had over a dozen offers for marriage.

Juliet stood in front of Lilah, hands clasped and eyes narrowed almost imperceptibly. A slight gesture but laden with immeasurable disapproval. The women in the family possessed a skill for such looks. "Do not make the assumption that a fashionable degree of beauty will guarantee your heart's desire."

Lilah chose not to mention that she'd abandoned any hope of fulfilling her *heart's desire* long ago. "But you married Lord Granworth. At the time, he was one of the wealthiest men in England."

"And renowned for his exacting taste in what he considered *beauty.*" Juliet closed her eyes for a moment and exhaled. "Nevertheless, even though he was thirty-four years my senior, I was fortunate to gain his interest. After all, you might recall a slight...*scandal* regarding the events that led to my sudden marriage."

Yes. Lilah had heard mention of it during one of her father's rants to Mother about the embarrassment of her bloodline.

"Lord Granworth saved me from ruin," Juliet stated, the dip in her voice hinting at a modicum of regret. "But had I been named the *Original,* my life might well have turned out quite differently."

"You mean to say that you *weren't*?"

Juliet averted her gaze, her attention on the slow progress of their carriage in the ever-increasing traffic. "No. In fact, the man I'd hoped to marry ended up marrying the *Original* instead."

Shocked, Lilah's lips parted on a gasp. "She could not have been more beautiful, of that I am certain."

"As I said, the *Original* possesses other qualities..." Juliet's words drifted off as her eyes widened, settling on a point over Lilah's shoulder.

Lilah pivoted on her heel and saw a handsome man on an ebony Thoroughbred, stopping on the street before them. Beneath a black hat, he wore an expression similar to Juliet's, though his was darker and somewhat angry. Lilah recognized him as Maxwell Harwick, Marquess of Thayne—or rather, the other party involved in Juliet's *scandal* from years before.

"You are still in London," Thayne said, gritting his teeth.

Juliet lifted her chin, her lips tight. "As you see."

"*Hmm*," he growled. "I'd heard a happy rumor that you'd returned to Bath."

The air surrounding them suddenly became weighted and tense. Even the horse must have felt it because he shifted and exhaled a harsh, steamy breath from his nostrils.

"I see things have not changed, Max. You've fallen behind on the latest gossip." Juliet smiled, even while her eyes narrowed. "I am living here now and staying with my cousins for a time. The townhouse where I once lived with my parents is looking for a new owner, and I plan to purchase it. This week, as a matter of fact."

"Impossible. That house is not four doors down from my mother's residence."

The incredulity and unleashed outrage in his tone caused Lilah's shoulders to stiffen. Ever loyal, she stood beside her cousin in a show of support. Not that the marquess would notice. As of yet, he had not once glanced in her direction.

Juliet squeezed her hand as she continued this heated exchange. "I have already been to see your mother, and she couldn't be more delighted about the news."

"She never mentioned—"

"*Thayne!*" A shout interrupted the exchange. "Are you accompanying me or not?"

Lilah's attention shifted to the commanding tone. As a coach and four ambled out of the way, she first noticed the chestnut Destrier. It towered over the bays and trotters on the street. Such a colossal horse was never seen in *town*. Hunting grounds, perhaps, but certainly not the teeming London streets. Was the rider prepared for battle? She nearly laughed at the thought. Then, tilting up her head, she wanted to see the man who would dare.

Yet when she did, something unexpected happened. She met his gaze. And, more important, *he* met hers.

Even in the shadow beneath the brim of his gray top hat, Lilah distinctly noted the uncanny brightness of his irises. His aquiline nose sloped down to a broad mouth that slowly arced upward at one corner. More smirk than smile. She tried to blink but couldn't. Breathing proved equally difficult.

Then, he inclined his head, touching two fingers to that brim. The gesture was meant as an acknowledgement, she was sure. She'd seen gentlemen salute similarly to other young women but never to her. And that was when she realized her error.

Likely, from this distance, she was confusing the direction—or *target*, rather—of his gaze. Clearly, he was yet another man caught by her cousin's beauty. She could not fault him for it. Even so, knowing it made her feel foolish for that single instant she'd thought otherwise.

Uncomfortable prickles of heat burned her cheeks. She couldn't be certain, however, if it was from embarrassment or a keen sense of longing. All she knew was that a man such as he would never tip his hat to her, let alone call on her.

With that final thought, their carriage pulled up, blocking her view. The marquess and her cousin's exchange concluded abruptly too, which was likely for the best. And now, it was time to return to Hanover Street and face the empty parlor.

At least there was a measure of comfort in knowing what to expect.

Jack Marlowe surveyed the flower market at Covent Garden with an appreciative eye. Not for the flowers but for the enterprise itself. He admired this horde of ragtag sellers, waving bundled blossoms in his face, shouting alliterative phrases to gain his attention. *"Penny posies, 'ere. Spare a penny for pretty posies!"*

Removing his hat to feel the cold morning mist on his face, Jack inhaled a potent combination of scents—the earthy, brackish stench of the gutters, the lingering odor of smoke and soot, and, rising above it all, the cloying perfume of flowers spilling from baskets in bright shades of pink, yellow, violet, red, and blue.

"Breathe it in, Thayne," Jack said to his friend, walking beside him. "This market is the epitome of determination. The very heart and soul of survival." He understood it well. He could even see a younger version of himself in a few of the faces of the errand boys and young hawkers scurrying about. Then, taking it all in, Jack raked a careless hand through his blond mane before donning his hat.

Beneath the black brim of a different hat, Max Harwick, the recently named Marquess of Thayne—*poor wretch*—furrowed his dark eyebrows. He'd been in a foul temper since encountering Lady Granworth and her blushing companion near Hyde Park a short while ago. "I see utter chaos."

"Precisely. A living, breathing entity born from hunger, cold, and perspiration. There is nothing more powerful." Jack still felt that invigorating chaos in his veins—that need for *more*. Even now, after he'd amassed a fortune through years of his own hard labor, he still craved it.

Thayne issued a grunt of acknowledgment as he scrutinized the market. Then he chuckled. "There might be one thing more powerful than chaos."

He gestured with a nod in the direction of the opera house, where a young buck dropped to his knees in front of a young woman in a feathered turban.

"Idiocy?" Jack watched the scene with a measure of loathing when the gentleman's signet ring fell onto the ground. Likely, the ill-fitting bauble was new to his finger from a recent death in the family. And as a holder of the title, his first order of business, clearly, was to procure a mistress. *What rot.*

But Jack expected nothing more from the aristocracy.

Scrambling to pick up the ring, the sap slipped it back on his finger before thrusting an audacious bouquet into the woman's arms. Yet she seemed not to notice. Her attention was fixed elsewhere. In fact, she appeared to be looking in *his* direction.

Jack held her gaze in return. He couldn't help himself. He enjoyed women, and they—by all accounts—enjoyed him as well. He made sure of it.

"Either idiocy or *lust*," Thayne amended with a scoff.

Suddenly, appearing out of the throng, a shaggy-haired errand boy rushed up, stopping just short of stomping on the toe of Jack's well-worn Hessians.

"Mr. Marlowe, sir?" the boy said, his thick Cockney accent nipping off the ends of each word. He stood no taller than a walking stick, his face lively and eager, though perhaps in need of a good scrubbing. He'd earn more coin with a clean face—a lesson Jack had learned.

"What can I do for you, my good fellow?" Jack asked, automatically reaching into his waistcoat pocket for a coin.

Surprisingly, the boy refused it with a shake of his head before lifting a yellow boutonniere into view. "Compliments o' Miz Raintree." He pointed to the woman on the opera house stairs. And, in turn, she offered a smile. A somewhat familiar smile.

"An acquaintance of yours, Marlowe?" Thayne asked.

Jack started putting the pieces together. An opera house likely meant an opera girl, and he'd entertained quite a number of them this past Christmas. He seemed to recall wanting to prove the common phrase of *the more, the merrier.* "Likely."

Jack looked down to the boy, who was still holding the flower. He knew that if he offered the coin again, the boy would be too proud to take it. So he thought of a better option. "Would you deliver this boutonniere for a half a crown?"

The boy's eyes went wide. "Yes, sir!"

"Very good." Jack handed him the coin and watched with pleasure as the lad bit down on it like a true entrepreneur. "Now, deliver this to the besotted fool in front of Miss Raintree, where it will be appreciated."

Grinning, the boy stowed the coin and rushed back to the opera house. He'd just earned half a crown for running forty paces. All in all, an excellent day's wage. After the exchange transpired, the kneeling gentleman leapt to his feet and embraced the opera miss. She, however, cast a wan smile in Jack's direction.

"I think she expected you to renew your acquaintance," Thayne remarked with sly amusement.

"Then, Miss"—her name was on the tip of his tongue, but he'd already forgotten it—"*she* wasn't paying attention when I gave her my speech."

Jack turned his attention to the flowers, wondering which blooms were the most suitable for paying a morning call. He'd never done this before, either buying flowers for a young woman or paying a call. However, a favor was a favor.

"Speech?"

"Yes, the one where a man explains that he's not looking for a wife or even a mistress, while stating that whatever they have together will be satisfying but of a brief duration." After paying for a handful of pink posies, Jack noted his friend's bewildered expression. "I believe in honesty from the very beginning. Don't you have a similar speech?"

Thayne chose not to answer. Though Jack assumed he did have one because it was too early for Thayne's new title to have turned him into a completely dishonorable cad.

Casting that thought aside, Jack looked down at the bouquet in his hand and found it on the small side. Then again, his hands were on the large side. When he was a boy, his mother had often called his hands and feet *lion's paws* and told him that if he finished his broth, he might grow into them. Although he doubted that the meager broth they'd supped on had helped, eventually he had grown. Even so, his mother still bade him to eat his fill whenever he visited her.

For good measure, Jack purchased two more clusters of posies and paid another woman for a blue ribbon to tie them all together.

"If you are not a romantic, then why are you buying flowers?" Thayne exhaled, seemingly impatient to end this errand as he glanced over to where their horses were tied.

"Because I promised Vale I would." Jack always kept his promises. Like *honesty*, this was part of his code of honor. The part that made him a better man than his father. "Our friend arrived at my country estate on Christmas Eve to ask about the validity of his *Marriage Formula*."

"The notion is ingenious," Thayne remarked as they maneuvered their way out of the market. "The *ton* is still talking about it. Using a mathematical equation to find a bride would obliterate the need for the standard methods of courting. There's no need to subject oneself to constant scrutiny by attending parties and balls..."

As his friend continued to list the horrors of what the aristocracy willingly endured, Jack thought back to the night when Vale had arrived. He'd looked like a man half-possessed. Jack had always thought his friend had a brilliant mind but one plagued with doubt.

Then, suddenly, something had changed. Vale had become sure and confident, boldly stating that his formula worked. And before he'd left, he'd handed Jack a card with the name of a woman and her address, asking him to send her flowers.

At first, Jack had thought that the woman was a paramour of Vale's, but his friend extinguished that immediately by stating that she was *respectable*.

Jack had wondered aloud why Vale was bothering with the flowers.

"Because I promised her friend that I would do whatever I could for her," Vale had said, keeping the full story to himself.

"You have me intrigued."

"No, Marlowe, I absolutely forbid you to be intrigued."

Forbid him? Oh, but there was nothing more decadent than forbidden fruit. And Jack, because he never refused a friend, agreed to the favor. Granted, that had been on Christmas Eve, and now it was March—business matters had called him out of the country. Nevertheless, he'd kept the card with him to serve as a reminder each day since.

Now that he was back in London, he was prepared to fulfill his oath. One reason was because it was the honorable thing to do, but the largest reason was because he was intrigued.

Apparently, Vale thought that sending this young woman flowers would help her in some way. But what genuine need could be remedied with such a paltry gift?

Jack had supposed that Vale could have been dangling this mystery in front of him for another purpose. Something that

had to do with the *Marriage Formula*. However, Jack readily dismissed that idea. After all, Vale knew that he had no
intention of marrying. He had an abundance of lovers and no
desire to produce offspring; ergo, Jack had no need of a wife.

Needing the answer inspired Jack not to simply *send* the
flowers by courier but to deliver them himself.

"I'd say Vale proved his equation well enough by using it
to find his own bride. And he wasted no time in marrying
her," Thayne continued, drawing Jack's attention.

"Uncharacteristically impulsive of him, if you ask me."
The entire episode struck Jack as odd. Normally, the Duke of
Vale was a stoic, rational man. Yet that night, his friend had
been so clearly in love that even a cynic like Jack had seen it
for what it was. *Poor wretch.*

It wasn't that Jack didn't believe in love. In fact, he often
quipped about falling in love. *True love*, however, was different. True love left carnage in its wake. And Jack wanted no
part of that idiocy.

Stopping near their mounts, Jack tied the flowers to his
saddle. Then he paid the boy who'd been watching their
horses before setting his foot into the stirrup.

Thayne mounted beside him. "I think Vale's hasty marriage displayed a sound belief in his work. I, for one, will use
it when it is my turn at the gallows. No messy courting for
me, thank you. I'd much rather have the assurance of compat-
ibility on paper beforehand, instead of learning of the lack of
it later."

Thayne clearly wasn't in his right mind this morning. His
encounter with Lady Granworth must have loosened a hinge
or two. Therefore, Jack—friend that he was—couldn't pass

up this opportunity to mock him. "Now that you have a title to uphold, do you plan to marry and produce a legitimate heir?"

Thayne gripped the reins and offered a solemn nod. "It is expected."

Having anticipated a jest in return, those words went sour in Jack's ears. The rules by which the aristocracy lived infuriated him. His own mother had been left with nothing because of these rules. And because of love. "By all means, you nobles must do what is *expected*."

Thayne jerked his head so fast in Jack's direction it looked as he'd been struck. "'Noble,' ha! You have more noble blood in your right foot than I do in my entire person. I inherited my title from a distant fourth cousin, whom I'd never met. You, on the other hand, are the Earl of Dovermere's son."

Careful not to spur Bellum to a gallop, Jack gritted his teeth and felt his jaw twitch. "No, I'm his bastard. There is a difference."

"Hardly. He's acknowledged you openly."

And what a happy day that had been, Jack thought wryly.

It wasn't until he was ten years old that he'd first met Dovermere. That day, the man had gone pale and still the instant he'd clapped eyes on Jack. Other than the sudden pallor of his countenance, an uncanny likeness—one that even a boy could see—had shined through.

"*Then it is true*," Dovermere had said, his voice gravelly and somewhat haunted. He'd looked past Jack to Mother but did not say a word before turning on his heel and disappearing into his carriage.

The day after, Jack had found himself in that same carriage on the way to Eton and, shortly thereafter, to a brutal initiation from a few of his fellow students.

"The only reason he has acknowledged me is because he has eight legitimate daughters," Jack said. "If he had a son—"

"And he does. Yet you cannot put your prejudice for the aristocracy aside. Lately, I often wonder how long it will be until you treat *me* like the enemy as well."

If nothing else, Jack was loyal to his friends. Had he not kept Vale as a friend after he'd inherited a dukedom? Or Wolford, when he'd become an earl? Jack was willing to overlook Thayne's unfortunate circumstance as well. "What has put you so high on your horse and turned you into such an arse, Thayne?"

"Forgive me. I've been on edge these past few months. And now it appears that I must see my solicitor about purchasing a house."

"I'm sure your ill humor could have nothing to do with Lady Granworth's return to London," Jack said, goading his friend with a lift of his brows.

"There." Thayne's tone sharpened to a razor's edge. "We have both drawn blood. Now we are on even footing."

Jack exchanged a glance and a nod with Thayne. All was forgiven, until the next time temptation got the better of them. "Good. I shall leave you to your errand. I have a call to pay."

He looked at the name on the card once more before tucking it away. Soon, he would uncover the mystery surrounding *Miss Lilah Appleton.*

CHAPTER TWO

A short time after arriving at Aunt Zinnia's townhouse on Hanover Street that morning, Lilah discovered that there was, in fact, something worse than having no gentlemen callers waiting in the parlor.

And that was having a room *full* of gentlemen.

And then witnessing their collective looks of disappointment when she entered the room. Naturally, those expressions altered to pleasure once Juliet followed.

Zinnia, Lady Cosgrove, rose gracefully from the jonquil-patterned upholstered armchair, which was the focal point of the violet parlor. She took great pride in her carriage and in keeping her figure well into her middle years. Her countenance and her precise coiffure conveyed elegance and composure. But her sharp bone structure and even the streaks of silver in her dark blonde hair conveyed an unmistakable edge of sternness underneath. Lifting a slender arm, she extended her palm in a wave toward Lilah and Juliet. "And here is my lovely niece and my cousin. Thankfully, they aren't *overly* tardy."

The mantel clock was only now chiming eleven. To Aunt Zinnia, however, being on time meant being a quarter of an hour early.

In the seconds that had transpired, neither Juliet nor Lilah made an excuse for their late arrival or mentioned the encounter with the Marquess of Thayne. Although every time Lilah closed her eyes on a blink, she could still see the man on the Destrier as if both were present in this very room.

Of course, that would make for quite a crowded parlor, she mused, almost smiling at her own jest. Her thoughts often vacillated from levity to worry when she was uncomfortable. And right now, facing a room full of men made her quite nervous.

The gentlemen all stood at once and bowed. It should have been thrilling. At last, it seemed possible that Lilah could escape the dire fate that awaited her. She might actually find a husband before the end of her third Season and not be forced to marry Winthrop.

Yet as she rose from her curtsy, she worried about all the things that could go wrong. She could trip on her way to the settee, bumping her knee and collapsing against the low table, effectively scattering dishes, spilling the tea, and toppling the biscuits and tarts from the tiered tray. Aunt Zinnia would be mortified.

Lilah blinked. Thankfully, she was still standing in the same spot. Collecting herself, she brushed the imaginary carnage from her skirts with one careful swipe. Her gaze drifted to the bouquets clasped firmly in the gentlemen's grips.

Flowers?

Oh dear…She could sneeze and have a dozen handkerchiefs presented to her at once. Which one would she choose?

Then again, she could sneeze and have *no* handkerchiefs presented to her—which seemed far more likely.

Best not sneeze, she warned herself.

Distracted by the cheerful blossoms, she allowed herself to wonder if it was possible that one gentleman in this very room might present *her* with flowers. The notion sent a tiny jolt of alarm through her. She thought she'd prepared herself for callers. Apparently not. Neither, it seemed, had she prepared herself for receiving flowers.

Did one merely say *thank you* and blush demurely? Did one praise the blossoms for their beauty or instead extend compliments to the gentleman on his keen eye for color? Did one remark on the size of the bouquet and compare it to the others? No, surely not.

After all, her brother had once told her that men were rather sensitive about comparisons. At least, that was the reason he'd given her when she'd asked why there were so many men who disliked him. She'd often wondered what object they'd been comparing.

"It is a pleasure to see you again," Lord Pembroke said, his nasal tone breaking Lilah away from her thoughts. He lifted a cluster of violets, a few of them wilting over his fingers. But that didn't matter. Until this moment, Lilah had had no idea that she'd made an impression on him. Then he pushed the flowers out of her reach, grazing her shoulder, and concluded his greeting by saying, "Lady Granworth."

Pembroke's actions started a melee of sorts. The gentlemen were eager to raise their bouquets and offer their effusive compliments to Juliet. Considering her cousin was newly back in London and past the period of mourning, this was to be expected. Only...Lilah wished *she* had expected it. An abundance of callers but apparently none for her.

She tried to step out of the way. Then suddenly, a bunch of fragrant white hyacinths appeared before *her* face. She gasped with pleasure. Which gentleman's hand held the precious gift? As they were all crowded into one space, she couldn't tell. However, that didn't matter. All that did were these pretty little blossoms. She reached up to take them. "Thank you so very much. I don't really know what to say—"

Abruptly, the flowers were tugged out of her grasp. "My mistake, miss," someone said and proceeded to nudge her out of the way.

Lilah stumbled back, the corner of a gilded milieu table striking the outer curve of her bottom. A hiss left her lips as she eased away. Not that anyone noticed.

"Gentlemen, if you please," Aunt Zinnia scolded. The austerity in her tone commanded instant respect, and the men, in turn, resumed their seats. "Myrtle, please see that the flowers find vases," she said to the maid who was hunched slightly forward and lingering near the door. And just when Lilah was beginning to wonder if her aunt had noticed that all of the bouquets were for Juliet, her aunt added, "And place them in the upstairs sitting room."

A room none of them frequented due to its poor lighting and lingering mildew odor. It was as good as banishing the flowers. Since her aunt was not an affectionate person—similar to her sister, Lilah's mother, in that regard—this likely was her way of offering support. Lilah's heart warmed.

Crossing the room toward the settee, she intended to sit between her aunt and her cousin. She needed to nurse her sore bottom on a soft surface. Unfortunately, once Juliet sat on one of the settee's cushions, Lord Pembroke quickly took the other. This left Lilah to take the only vacant seat remaining—the spindle chair near the door. Make that the *hard* spindle chair. She did her best not to wince when she sat down.

From that point on, both her cousin and aunt set about reintroducing Lilah to every man present. Lord Ellery was among them. He was the only one in the room who didn't require a wealthy bride. And, as luck would have it, his country estate in Surrey bordered her family's land.

After Jasper's death, her father's death, and the subsequent reading of the will, Lilah's primary hope was not only to find a gentleman to marry, but to marry one who could help her improve the lives of the tenants residing on her family's land. Viscount Ellery was the perfect candidate.

Now, if only she could get him to remember her for more than a single minute.

Juliet seemed to share the same thoughts, because she turned toward the viscount. "Did you know that Miss Appleton lives very near your country estate, Lord Ellery?"

When Juliet offered a smile, Lord Ellery's eyes went round and vacant. "Miss Appleton?"

Juliet gestured toward Lilah, her brow slightly, albeit prettily, knitted. Lilah imagined that her cousin, up until now, hadn't completely believed the claims of empty parlors and forgetful gentlemen. Blatant proof, however, was difficult to deny.

After another brief introduction, Aunt Zinnia and Juliet directed conversation in clever ways to ascertain each gentleman's interest in marriage, learning their family pedigree, fortunes, and so forth.

Lilah had observed this type of inquisition before from many of the *ton's* matrons in various ballroom settings and social gatherings. Yet Aunt Zinnia was one of the best. Once subjected to her subtle barrage of questions, a gentleman had no hope of withholding anything worth knowing. It was usually entertaining to watch.

This time, however, Lilah was feeling a bit overwhelmed and a bit wounded by the events of the past few minutes. Rising carefully, she excused herself from the room, stating a need to ensure there were enough tarts and biscuits to withstand the onslaught of callers. Even now, her words were accompanied by the pounding of the doorknocker. Soon, there would be more than twenty men crowded into the small parlor.

Lilah knew she wouldn't be missed.

After informing a vase-toting Myrtle of the low supply of refreshments, Lilah walked straight down the hall to the garden door and slipped outside to her walled haven.

Once in her favorite spot beneath the arbor, she drew in a deep breath and released it slowly. The air was chilly, but there was no breeze to make her too cold without a shawl. Overhead, clematis and rose vines were still brown and dormant. On the ground beside the stone path at her feet, a myriad of crocuses bloomed gaily, while tulip shoots were coming into their full height, hinting at their splendor. And halfway up, between the white arbor post and the slatted wooden bench, a spider's web fanned out, its occupant hidden from view.

She was just leaning closer to study it when she heard the door open and close with a quiet click. Assuming it was

Myrtle on an errand for Aunt Zinnia, Lilah didn't bother to turn. "You may tell my aunt that I will return shortly. I have need of a breath of air."

"Do you breathe better when you're bent at the waist?" a man's deep voice asked.

Startled, Lilah jerked upright, whipping around to face the stranger.

Only he wasn't quite a *stranger*. She'd seen him before. In fact, not more than an hour ago. And he looked just as out of place in this manicured garden as his Destrier had trotting along the London streets. She imagined, however, that man and beast would look perfectly at home galloping across an untamed moor or into battle. The man had a feral, warrior look about him. Especially with the golden, hot-ember color of his eyes beneath the arch of a tawny brow. And instead of walking with perfect pedestrian form, he *prowled* toward her—agile but controlled, as if always prepared for battle.

Beneath a gray tailored coat, his broad shoulders subtly rolled and shifted. The black buttons of his striped waistcoat were in a flat, straight line, suggesting a firmness, about which she likely shouldn't ponder. The same way she should not admire the storm-cloud gray shade of his riding breeches and the way they encased his thighs, displaying every gradation of his impressive musculature.

When her gaze dipped, she also took note of the large bouquet of pink and white primroses he carried, hanging carelessly by his side. The flowers were enough to remind her of why she was out in the garden. A fresh wave of disappointment hit her.

"I believe," she said, but when her words came out in nothing more than a whisper, she cleared her throat and began again. "I believe you'll find my cousin in the parlor."

He stopped just beneath the arbor, not two steps from her. As they had earlier, his lips curled into a smirk at one corner of his mouth. This time, there was no mistaking the direction of his gaze. He was, most assuredly, looking at *her*. "When I asked where I would find Miss Lilah Appleton, a rather frantic maid pointed in this direction. Was she mistaken?"

Lilah's breath caught in her throat. His voice was that of a warrior's too—sure and commanding but with an underlying edge. *Do not cross me*, that tone warned as much as it promised. *I will fight to the death for you.* She could easily hear him saying those words on a battlefield…or in a ballroom. *Of course, his attire would be different for each occasion…*

She shook the errant thought out of her head. *Bother.* Her imagination was conjuring all sorts of nonsense. Only this time, it wasn't about a catastrophe. She wondered what that meant, if anything. Distracted by the thought, it took a moment for Lilah's tongue and lips to find their proper placement. "No."

This man inquired after *her*…and by name? The notion was so outrageous that it refused to settle in her mind. Or in her stomach, it seemed, because it felt as if it were filled with the experimental effervescent wine that Vale and Ivy had served at their wedding, all light and full of bubbles.

The stranger flashed a smile of mostly even teeth, exposing a set of pointed canines at the top and bottom to complete his feral look. "I must admit you do look in need of a breath of air. If bending at the waist aids your intake, then by all means do not let my intrusion interfere."

A sudden flood of heat burned her cheeks. Just this moment, she was thankful that she'd not given in to the urge to rub her sore bottom. Otherwise, he might have witnessed that too. "You should not mention such things."

"Breathing?"

"No, the"—she made a subtle gesture in the general direction of her middle—"*other*."

"Am I not to know that you have a waist? *No*, of course not." He chuckled, mocking her with a shake of his head. "Oh, you highborn and your rules of conduct. Have you nothing better to do with your time?"

Lilah bristled. The euphoric bubbles inside her burst at once. "Pardon me, sir, but we are not acquainted. You know nothing of me, certainly not enough to warrant an insult."

"Ah, yes, your kind prefers inane flattery and flowers," he said, smugness etched in the set of his jaw. His gaze swept over her with apparent disregard. "That is why I'm here—with the flowers."

"But not with *flattery*," she scoffed.

"As you said, we are not acquainted." He studied her, leaning in a fraction and creating an intimate space between them. "I could provide compliments enough to make your blush return. However, it has come to my understanding that I should hold my tongue and pretend that I did not notice the nuances of your figure in the same manner that you'd noticed mine when I was walking toward you."

A breath of incredulity escaped her lungs. She wasn't certain if she was embarrassed, astounded, or insulted. Likely, it was all three. "Who are you, sir? I demand to know."

At last, he extended the flowers with one hand and doffed his hat with the other, revealing a mane of thick wheat-colored hair swept back from his forehead and ending just above his collar. "Jack Marlowe."

Jack Marlowe? The name was familiar to her but only through rumor. Apparently, he was one of the richest men in England and a rogue to boot. But what had earned him an ever-present marker on the lips of the *ton's* preeminent gossipmongers was the fact that he was the bastard son of the Earl of Dovermere.

His smirk returned. "I see my reputation precedes me."

"Perhaps, though it does not explain why you are here." Distracted, Lilah realized she hadn't accepted the bouquet of pink and white primroses. She reached out but hesitated when she noted the size of his hand. His grip enveloped the entire bundle of stems. As large as his hands were, there would be no way to avoid touching him. The flesh was darker too, as if he spent little time, if any, wearing gloves. Not a gentleman's hands. Most likely, they would be rough and calloused. At the thought, a peculiar sort of the thrill raced through her, quickening her pulse.

She took a half step toward him. Then she made the mistake of meeting his gaze. This close, she noticed that the color of his irises were more the golden brown of freshly nipped sugar than that of a glowing ember. His eyes were warm and clear but with a surprisingly alluring sharpness that spoke of intelligence and confidence. As any warrior should, he had a scar—a tiny S-shape of silver flesh just above his cheekbone, close to his temple. A strange temptation to ask him about it nearly rolled off her tongue. But in that same moment, she realized she'd been standing close to him for far too long.

Bracing herself now, she settled both of her hands just beneath the blossoms, cradling them. As she suspected, his hand was warm, his knuckles rough. So then why did a jolt of surprise rush through her?

A quiver vibrated through her at the slight touch. It seemed to hum in her ears, as if she'd plucked the longest string on her harp and rested her cheek against the curved frame. She pressed harder against his hand to quell this unexpected feeling. Slowly, he withdrew. The heated length of his fingers grazed the undersides of her palms, sending those vibrations to the very center of her body.

She let out a staggered breath and took a step back.

He stared at her, his expression nonplussed as he flexed his hand at his side, as if the brief touch had bothered him as well.

"Have you nothing to say of the flowers?" he asked after a moment, reminding her of the blossoms in her arms. "Or do you receive them with such frequency that you simply tell your maid to tend them with a shooing flip of your fingers?"

Had she been clear-headed, she might have laughed. Instead, she absently looked down and stroked the pink fan of a petal, her mind still contemplating the lingering reaction she'd had to his touch. "They are beautiful. It is a shame that they will be dead in two days' time, like all cut flowers."

"Would you have preferred a potted flower?"

"I'm not quite certain. These are the first flowers of any kind that I've received." When she realized what she'd just admitted, her sense returned with a snap. She looked at him, horrified that she'd revealed such a personal—not to mention embarrassing—detail.

When his gaze widened, she wondered if he would laugh at her again. Instead, he unfisted his hand and raked it through his hair before donning his hat. "Hmm...well, that adds to the mystery, doesn't it?"

She was almost afraid to ask. "What mystery?"

"The reason the Duke of Vale rode to my house in the dead of night on Christmas Eve, handed me a card with your name and address, and asked me to send you flowers."

Lilah recalled being at the duke's party that night. Ivy had been heartbroken and worried for the duke's safety. Fortunately, the following day had brought good tidings for both Ivy and Vale.

Looking down at the flowers cradled in her arms, Lilah calculated the time. "It is *March*. And you were given this task on Christmas Eve?"

When she remembered how lonely she had been without Ivy to talk to—but also abundantly happy for her friend—a handful of flowers might have been just the thing to cheer her. This man had been set with such a task, yet he'd chosen to wait for however long it suited him.

His self-important, tawny brows lifted. "*That* is the only thing you find noteworthy in all of what I said?"

"More than two months have passed. Surely a man of your..." Her words trailed off, and she blushed because it was inappropriate to mention money in polite conversation.

"Riches? Wealth? Well-endowed...fortune?" he supplied, mockery saturating those smug syllables. "You have permission to use any of those. *I* harbor no rules against stating the obvious."

In that moment, she decided she did not like Mr. Jack Marlowe. Not one bit. "An *affluent* man is bound to be in possession of a hot house, and therefore flowers at any time of the year. You could have honored your promise much sooner."

When Miss Appleton's wide brown eyes had first spotted the posies in his hand, she'd offered such a bland glance that Jack had assumed she didn't care for flowers. He still wasn't certain if he believed her confession about these being her first. What young woman of—well, judging by the enticing firmness of her figure, he'd suppose—*one and twenty* had never before received flowers?

While her nature was uncompromising—at least what he'd witnessed thus far—her lashes were as thick as bed curtains, softening even the harshest looks she fired at him. And even with that unflattering fringe of curls drooping over her forehead, she possessed a certain appeal. Her skin was creamy. Her posture, perfect. Her hands, elegant. Her mouth, however, was relatively unremarkable, seemingly without form or color...until she'd begun to scold him. Then her lips bloomed into a lush, inviting red. They were still in full color.

Were the men among the *ton* too blind to appreciate a subtle sort of beauty?

Then again, perhaps not *all* men were immune. After all, Vale had sent him on this errand. Perhaps he had noticed Miss Lilah Appleton. Which would explain why she had suddenly become interested in the flowers only after she'd learned of Vale's involvement.

Jack studied her closely. Did she harbor a secret *tendre* for Vale? Was there an attachment between them?

For some reason, the notion sparked his ire. "How quickly you alter. One minute you do not even look twice at the flowers, and next, you are directing me where I might find them in the future. No doubt, you'll be expecting a fresh bouquet each time we meet."

"No, Mr. Marlowe." She shook her head with superfluous enthusiasm. "We will not meet again. Your promise has been fulfilled, even though *quite* delayed." Concluding her reprimand, she stepped forward and angled herself as if to pass by him.

Jack, however, was too eager to solve this mystery. So he blocked her retreat. He'd been carrying her name on a card inside his pocket for the past ten weeks. Each morning, he transferred it, along with his pocket watch, from one coat to the next. And each morning, he was reminded of the promise he'd made, saying the name *Miss Lilah Appleton* aloud for good measure. It had become a matter of habit. Her name had been with him every day, under his care. In the very least, he deserved to know why he was here.

"And now we are back to the important matter," he said, standing close enough to pluck at the blue ribbon tied around the stems. "Are you not curious about the reason Vale would send me on such an errand? Or is the reason, perhaps, one you would rather not divulge, considering he married your friend?"

She gasped in swift understanding. Outrage widened those bed-curtain lashes. Then, she thrust the posies at him, crushing them against his chest. "You dare to insult me again! Ivy is my friend, and therefore *you*—blackguard that you are—should fear the scathing report on your behavior that I will send. *Then* let us see how quickly both she and her husband rally to my defense! If you do not recant your insufferable insinuations, you will likely find yourself labeled a dishonorable cad, even amongst your own friends."

He wondered if she was aware how red and kissable her lips were right now. In fact, he wondered what she would do if he slid his hand to her nape and kissed her here, beneath the shadow of the arbor.

For the moment, however, he cast those thoughts aside. He knew he'd crossed a line. There was no excuse for such slander. For the life of him, he didn't know what had possessed him. Or why he'd suddenly *needed* to know that neither she nor Vale shared any romantic inclinations—though her honest indignation convinced him just now. "You are correct. That was unforgivable of me. I cannot excuse my words just now. Please accept my humblest of apologies."

To make amends, Jack untied the ribbon around the stems and carefully rearranged the posies. Only a few blossoms were completely crushed and a similar number of broken stems. He did his best to tuck those toward the inside. Then, while struggling to retie the ribbon with one hand, Miss Appleton issued an exhausted sigh and shooed his fingers out of the way, taking over the task.

She liberated the flowers from him and rested them along her forearm. The pink buds nestled between the curve of her elbow and the generous swell of her breast. "Since we are not likely to meet again, I will forgive you so that neither of us is burdened by this encounter. It will soon be forgotten."

Jack frowned. "There still remains the mystery of why Vale would have sent me on this errand."

"I think it is obvious," she said, lifting her gaze from the bouquet, her lashes tangled at the corners.

Standing within arm's reach of her, he felt a peculiar impulse to brush his thumb across them. But he did not act upon it. Instead, he tugged on the ribbon once more. "Oh?"

"His Grace married my dearest friend. A gesture of flowers is a token of Vale's own regard, likely stating that whatever friends Ivy has, Vale would have as well."

"A possibility," Jack offered. "Yet this task was put upon me *before* their nuptials."

She lifted one softly rounded shoulder in a shrug, "Since he has a scientific nature, perhaps he thought it all out beforehand."

When her feet shifted on the path, and she began to step apart from him, Jack held the ribbon firmly between his thumb and forefinger. "There is the matter of his *Marriage Formula* to consider. You know of it, don't you?"

"Of course," she said, clear puzzlement wrinkling the bridge of her nose as she looked from the ribbon to his fingers.

"Do you think it possible that the reason Vale gave me your name was because he'd used his equation on the two of us?" Jack wondered why Lilah hadn't leapt to that conclusion. Women were always trying to marry him. "Though I must warn you that I have no intention of marrying."

Suddenly, she laughed, the sound as sumptuous as her lashes and those lush, scolding lips. Her cheeks lifted, turning her eyes into dark half moons of delight. The corners of her mouth tilted upward in pleasure, looking somewhat secret and hedonistic at once. "You needn't worry on that account. I would not marry you, regardless."

He found himself wondering again what she would do if he kissed her. Wondering what her laugh would taste like, which was odd, considering that laughter did not have a flavor. Though hers just might...

Then he reminded himself that he preferred women without nobility or innocence. "That is what most women claim, yet they play all manner of coy games to garner my interest—a drop of a handkerchief, a pretense of windblown debris caught in their eyes, a sudden stumble that puts them into my arms..."

"You are quite possibly the most arrogant man in existence. It almost pleases me to prove you wrong," she said, the top and bottom rows of her white teeth on display as her smile deepened. "Even if I were inclined to marry you—solely for amusement's sake—I *could* not. My father's will states that I have until the end of my third Season to marry a titled gentleman of noble birth."

"It is my experience that aristocratic families are easily swayed in their initial wishes, once a fortune is involved." He was approached daily with offers from desperate men of *nobility*.

She frowned. "Not my family. My mother still holds true to my father's wishes. We are loyal to each other."

Likely, he could prove her wrong. His fingers inched up the ribbon, drawing her closer. "And this is your wish as well?"

Either playing coy or unwilling to flirt, she withdrew a step, loosening the knot in the process. "Mr. Marlowe, I believe it is time for you to leave."

"I find you rather intriguing, Lilah," he confessed, twisting the ribbon around his finger until it came free from the stems. "I believe I will return during calling hours tomorrow."

"*Miss Appleton*, if you please. And I find you rather annoying," she said in a clipped but somewhat bored tone. It was as if she didn't believe him. Then she glanced at his shoulder. "*Oh bother.* You have a spider."

Jack grinned. He knew he'd charmed her. Her censure was quite the clever ploy too. She'd almost convinced him that she was completely unaffected. Even so, watching her take the initiative by reaching up to brush a hand against his collar surprised him. He hadn't taken her for such a bold chit. Not that he minded.

"You have an odd way of using your feminine wiles. If you wanted an excuse to be near me, then—" He broke off as a spider filled his vision. The creature was huge—as large as her palm. Black with yellow markings. He took an involuntary step back. "That is no spider. That's a rat, or the size of one."

"Hold still. I don't want you to frighten her," she crooned softly, her tone having a calming effect.

At least on him. He wasn't certain about the spider, which had become alarmingly still, as if prepared to attack. However, Lilah had a steady hand and eased the spider away.

"Rats do not have eight legs," she said.

He made a quick check of his shoulders to ensure that the creature didn't leave her mate behind. When all was clear, he let out a breath. It wasn't that he was afraid of spiders. It was the fact that—until this moment—none had ever dared trespass upon him.

Being caught off guard was a foreign sensation. *But not without a certain appeal,* he mused, watching Lilah bend near a web to allow her *pet* to disappear into the maze of vines climbing the arbor. Then, before he had a chance to truly admire the sight of her in that position again, she stood and situated her flowers securely in the crook of her arm.

Facing him, clearly fearless of both man and beast, she gave him—he was sure—her sternest look. Her eyes were sharp and soft at once, her lush lips pressed together. He wondered why he wasn't kissing her right this very instant.

"And to answer your declaration with one of my own," she began before he could answer that question, "*if you return during calling hours, I will not be* at home *to you. Good day, sir. I believe you know the way out.*"

Then she turned on her heel and strode away from him.

Damned if Jack didn't love a challenge.

CHAPTER THREE

That evening, Aunt Zinnia, Juliet, and Lilah attended an impromptu dinner at Harwick House. The day's turn of events demanded it.

Inside the modest foyer, Marjorie Harwick bustled toward them from the hall before the butler could take their hats and wraps. "Zinnia, I'm quite beside myself."

"We are all in a state of disbelief," Aunt Zinnia answered with a nod. Both she and Mrs. Harwick were close friends but opposite in appearance. While the former was pale, slender, and polished, the latter was dark, softly rounded, and possessed an all-around disheveled air, though more welcoming than unkempt.

"Juliet, my dear, after the news, I feared you would not accept my invitation," Mrs. Harwick continued, shaking her head in a way that caused her coral earbobs to sway and wisps of gray to escape her coiffure. "I do not know what has gotten into my son. I simply cannot believe that Maxwell purchased your house right out from under your nose."

Lilah was still reeling from the news. Only this morning, Juliet had informed the marquess of her intentions to buy that house. Considering the results, Lord Thayne must have rushed off to complete this despicable act, robbing Juliet of the home that had once belonged to her parents.

Through all this, however, Juliet appeared as collected as ever. Even earlier, upon learning the details from a solicitor, she'd never ranted or even hissed. Instead, she'd merely asked Lilah to play the harp, and all the while, she'd stood facing the music room window with her hands carefully clasped before her.

"Of course I came," Juliet said to Mrs. Harwick as she slipped the hood of her cloak down to her shoulders and bussed Mrs. Harwick's cheek. "I do not hold you responsible for Max's actions. In addition, I am here to demonstrate my resolve. I will not give him the satisfaction of seeing me bothered by what he has done."

Mrs. Harwick gasped. "My dear, you are not giving in, are you?"

After unfastening the clasp at her neck, Juliet revealed a flattering burgundy evening gown with a gusseted bodice trimmed in gold embroidery. The gown made a statement. She was not a woman to be manipulated. "No. I still mean to purchase that townhouse. No matter what."

"I am glad to hear it," Mrs. Harwick said but then clucked her tongue. "Alas, Maxwell has always been competitive. Always trying to prove himself—though I cannot imagine what victory he saw in this."

Smoothing a hand down her cream-colored gown, Lilah held her tongue. She was quite irritated at Thayne for his abominable treatment of her cousin. It was no wonder that he was friends with an arrogant, do-as-you-please man like Jack Marlowe.

"And Lilah," Mrs. Harwick said, patting her hand. "I pray that you have come with good news. Have you found a particular gentleman you favor?"

The question came so abruptly that Lilah still had Jack Marlowe's image stuck in her mind. It took a small push to clear him out of the way as she brought Lord Ellery to the forefront. Even so, she didn't think that her need of a husband surpassed her cousin's current predicament. Yet with Mrs. Harwick, conversations tended to circle back around eventually.

"I believe so, Mrs. Harwick," Lilah began as they walked from the foyer into the cozy blue parlor. "Viscount Ellery possesses the land and wealth that could aid my family the most. Unfortunately, he's also quite handsome."

Mrs. Harwick issued a surprised laugh. "Why should that be a hindrance? I imagine most young women would prefer a handsome husband."

"Precisely," Lilah agreed, frowning. Lord Ellery had the look of Jasper—fleece-like waves of golden hair, clear blue eyes, and a dimple in his chin. "I'm certain many of the debutantes are vying for his attention. It's only a matter of time before he settles on one of them."

Of course, she didn't know if his character was like her brother's. Jasper had been rather roguish and insincere when it came to women.

"One of *them*? My dear, he is just as likely to choose you." Mrs. Harwick gestured with a wave of her hand for Lilah to sit beside her on the blue chintz settee. "You have been introduced, have you not?"

Even though her *forgettable-ness* wasn't amusing, Lilah could not stop a wry smile. "Many times, my lady. Yet he never remembers my name. In fact, most of the gentlemen I've met suffer from the same form of amnesia."

"I've witnessed the very thing." Juliet, sitting in one of a pair of silver striped chairs across from them, shook her head. "I cannot understand it. Lilah is polite. She listens attentively. She is accomplished in many ways, not the least of which is that she plays the harp like an angel. A perfect companion and wife for any man."

With a delicate clearing of her throat, Aunt Zinnia commanded their attention. She was only now—ever so gracefully, of course—descending upon the other striped chair. Once she arranged her lavender skirts, she began. "I've been considering that Lilah needs to learn a new instrument. She should play something that demands attention, albeit in an *acceptable* manner."

Out of the blue, Lilah imagined herself in the front of an assembly, holding a pair of cymbals. *Clash!* "*I dare you to forget me now,*" she would say, inciting pandemonium, incurring collective gasps and, possibly, at least one person inhaling a feather from a turban...

Lilah coughed.

"Yes, but is there time enough for that? She only has a few months to find a husband on her own. After that, her only option is..." Mrs. Harwick slid a pitying glance in her direction and patted her hand once more. Neither Mrs. Harwick, Aunt Zinnia, nor Juliet were blind to Cousin

Winthrop's pompous and disturbing nature. Unfortunately, Mother was.

"True, very true," Aunt Zinnia agreed. "Nevertheless, she *must* make the statement of the Season—and soon."

Automatically, Lilah glanced at the clockstand in the corner of the room. It was painted bright white and trimmed in gold. Though to her mind, every clock might as well be shrouded in black and have a scythe for a pendulum. Time was running out, and a dire fate loomed not far enough in the distance.

"'The statement of the Season,'" Lilah mused aloud. "Only the one named the *Original* could do that." *No cymbals required.*

It wasn't until the room went silent that Lilah realized all eyes were upon her.

Mrs. Harwick clapped. "Zinnia, why didn't *we* think of this? It's the perfect plan."

"It isn't that simple, Marjorie." Aunt Zinnia unleashed her severe look upon her friend.

"*Pish tosh!*" Unaffected, Mrs. Harwick flitted her fingers. "We were once *Originals* ourselves. Because of that, we were able to gain the attention of the gentlemen we desired, just as Lilah will be able to attract Lord Ellery."

This news surprised Lilah, but it was Juliet who said, "I did not know that the two of you had been *Originals*."

"*Oh...*" Mrs. Harwick said, pausing to look at each of them in turn. "Yes, but a year apart and long ago. Zinnia and I were fortunate in that regard."

"How did you do it?" Lilah sat forward. At this point, she was willing to try anything.

Mrs. Harwick and Aunt Zinnia were tight-lipped, as if unprepared to divulge this secret. They engaged in a silent exchange of subtle shoulder lifts and raised brows. Then, after a moment, a nod.

"An *Original* must be confident," Mrs. Harwick began. "But, in the case of a woman, demure as well."

Lilah made a mental note to put more effort into the former.

"Good posture. Excellent carriage." Aunt Zinnia's cursory glance caused Lilah to sit up a little straighter.

"A degree of mystery," Juliet added, bringing to mind their earlier conversation in the park. Lilah smiled in response.

Mrs. Harwick nodded again, her earbobs swaying. "A style of one's own."

"Grace in the face of adversity." This wasn't the first time Aunt Zinnia had said this.

"A certain"—Mrs. Harwick opened her hands, splaying her fingers—"flair."

"And elegance in all things," Aunt Zinnia said with an air of finality.

Splendid, Lilah thought wryly. And she thought it was going to be difficult. She drew in a breath, absorbing it all. How exactly did one manage excellence in all things while being mysterious, stylish and…flair-some?

Before she could ask, however, Lord Thayne strode through the parlor door with none other than Jack Marlowe at his side.

"Good evening, Mother. Lady Cosgrove," Thayne said with a bow. Then, turning slightly, he acknowledged Lilah with a passing nod before his gaze settled on Juliet. "And Lady Granworth, how unexpected that we should meet again."

"'Unexpected'?" A look of resolve sharpened Juliet's features. "After what you did, I'm certain even *you* could have anticipated your mother's extending an invitation to dine here, even if only to make amends."

Thayne clenched his teeth in something of a smile. "Perhaps. Though I had expected you to decline or to flit away, as you are wont to do."

In the midst of the terse exchange, Jack Marlowe kept a steady eye on Lilah as he moved into the room. Briefly, she wondered if he was trying to remember her name.

He would not be able to, she knew. And for once, she wouldn't care a fig. Jack Marlowe was the one man whose amnesia would make her elated beyond measure. Nonetheless, she sat straighter, waiting for him to give up the attempt and for his gaze to leave hers.

His mouth quirked at one corner. "Miss Appleton. A pleasure to see you again."

A jolt of surprise snapped through her, causing the pulse at her throat to quicken. A flood of heat prickled her cheeks and her ears turned hot too.

"Mr. Marlowe, have you been introduced to my niece?" Aunt Zinnia asked, disapproval lacing her tone.

He inclined his head in something resembling both an answer and an absent gesture of greeting. However, everyone in the room knew that ladies of the nobility deserved *first* consideration, not last. "I took the matter upon myself, earlier today in fact."

Aunt Zinnia's gaze sharpened. "Do you mean to say that you introduced *yourself* to Miss Appleton?"

"Yes," he answered with a chuckle.

"Jack, that simply is not done in society," Mrs. Harwick added fondly but with a waggle of her finger.

"It is fortunate, then, that Miss Appleton and I did not meet in *society* but in the garden instead." He turned to Lilah, an unrepentant grin on his lips. "Unless you would consider our first meeting on the street this morning."

So he *had* seen her. The smile, the salute—those had been for *her*? Something warm inside of her fluttered. For an instant, she nearly forgot how much she disliked him. *Nearly.*

"*The street!*" Aunt Zinnia gripped the edge of her armrests. The subtle nuances in her expression that usually relayed her disapproval were now quite evident. "Marjorie, were you aware of this?"

"Of course not. Had I known, I would have made the proper introductions. After all, Jack has been Maxwell's friend since they were in school together."

This did not appear to appease Aunt Zinnia. "Lilah, you *must* think of your reputation. To be seen engaging in conversation with a man to whom you have not been introduced— and in a public square, no less—could endanger your options of finding a suitable match. We cannot afford to make any errors."

Lilah knew this all too well. "Aunt Zinnia, there was no 'exchange' in the street whatsoever."

"I beg to differ," Jack added, the certainty in his tone drawing far too much attention. "I distinctly recall your smile cast in my direction."

All eyes fell upon her. She clasped her hands to make sure she wasn't holding cymbals after all.

"No, I was laughing at the man who had the audacity to ride a war horse in the middle of town," Lilah corrected, forcing that errant fluttering to cease. "You must excuse Mr. Marlowe, for I believe he would like nothing more than to incite riots wherever he roams."

Jack's gaze dipped to her mouth. Absently, she wondered if there was something on her lip, such as an errant piece of fur from the lining of her redingote. Yet when she pressed them together, she felt nothing but her own flesh.

Juliet issued a short, hollow laugh. "Then he has chosen his friend well."

Lilah had to agree with her cousin. In fact, she wished the gentlemen had not come at all. She preferred knowing what to expect, even if it was all doom and calamity, but with Jack, she had not been prepared.

"What is done is done," Mrs. Harwick said as she stood and dusted her hands together. "Both with Maxwell and Jack. One cannot turn cheese back into milk, after all."

Juliet rose as well. Facing Thayne, she lifted her chin. "However, one can sign over the deed of a house that is not rightly his."

"I believe the *rightful* owner is the one who paid for it," he said, his hands fisted at his side.

Mrs. Harwick hurried around the grouping of chairs to stand between the two. "We have ample time to settle this matter. For now, however, we have an issue that is even more pressing. I'm certain you can cast your animosity aside for the sake of—"

Lilah winced with dread, hoping that Mrs. Harwick was not about to mention her own troubles in the midst of all this. *And* in front of Jack. The humiliation would be unbearable.

"Lilah," Mrs. Harwick said, her hands pressed together in prayer, as if knowing it would take a miracle to find Lilah a husband. "Directly before Maxwell and Jack walked into the room, we were speaking of ways for Lilah to gain Lord Ellery's attention."

Actually, Aunt Zinnia and Mrs. Harwick had been imparting secrets on becoming an *Original*. Not that such a topic would have been any less embarrassing to discuss in front of Jack. At the moment, Lilah wished that she had worn blue this evening so that she could disappear into the fabric of the settee. "There is no need to continue our discourse. The matter can wait."

"We do not have the luxury of waiting a moment longer. Besides, now is the perfect time, my dear, for we have two handsome gentlemen in this very room who can offer their assistance."

Oh, the mortification! Lilah did not glance in Jack's direction but felt his stare all the same. "I'm certain both Lord Thayne and Mr. Marlowe would rather adjourn to the study for an aperitif or even compete in a game of billiards."

"No, indeed," Jack said casually, moving deeper into the room. "Thayne has been too surly of late. I've no wish to spend any more time alone with him. The discussion and the company in this room are far more to my liking."

"Jack, you flatter us," Mrs. Harwick crooned, squeezing Jack's forearm as he passed by her. Then, she pointed at her son. "Maxwell, you should take his example and butter our bread instead of toasting it."

Thayne took the scolding well and bent down to buss his mother's cheek. "Then by all means, I am here to offer my assistance. Marlowe, what say you?"

All the while, Lilah had a sense of Jack's closing in on her. Moreover, she was all too aware of the lyre-backed chair nearest her, as if a beacon had been lit upon the empty seat.

"If Miss Appleton requires my assistance, then who am I to deny her?" Jack settled his hand atop the curve of that very chair. Taking the opportunity Thayne had provided, he sat down. Lilah had a feeling, however, that Jack would have done whatever he wanted to do, no matter what. Situating his muscular form, he flipped the tails of his coat out of the way. The process brought his thigh perilously close to her knee.

She shifted out of the path of danger—though why she assumed a mere brush of a limb would be dangerous, she did not know. There was no point in speculating, as it would never happen. "I do not require *your* assistance, Mr. Marlowe."

"Quite right, Lilah," Aunt Zinnia agreed with a nod before looking to Mrs. Harwick. "Mr. Marlowe does not exist in our circle and therefore can have little knowledge of our topic."

Lilah winced at the unmistakable censure. Even though she was not overly acquainted with Jack or fond of him in the least, she felt the need to soften her aunt's castigation. "It is somewhat of a private nature."

"Nonsense. Jack is a gentleman like any other. He can just as easily offer his opinion," Mrs. Harwick said absently, as she moved toward a footman waiting at the parlor door.

By the pursing of Aunt Zinnia's mouth, it was clear that she was not pleased by this. Jack, however, looked entirely too pleased—*and* smug.

A gentleman like any other? Hardly, Lilah mused. *A gentleman at all? Unlikely.*

"Zinnia," Mrs. Harwick called from the hall. "Might I bother you for your opinion on our seating arrangements for dinner?"

Aunt Zinnia hesitated, casting her disapproval over the group at large. "Of course."

As always, she took her time, perfectly poised in every movement as she rose and sauntered out of the room.

Thayne milled about, seemingly restless, picking up random figurines from tables as if to examine them. Yet his gaze often strayed to Juliet, a muscle ticking along his jaw each time. "The ways are innumerable to gain a gentleman's attention," he said absently to the room in general. "A glance. A laugh."

"A *smile*," Jack added, his voice low enough that only Lilah could hear.

The low hum vibrated through her once again. It was such a foreign, enthralling sensation that she didn't know whether to hate him for causing it or beg him to do it again.

"Women have dropped their handkerchiefs at my feet," Thayne continued, almost in a taunt. All the while, Juliet gave a good impression of ignoring him while she resumed her seat. "Or pretended to stumble into me."

Unknowingly, he'd confirmed what Jack had said earlier in the garden.

Arrogant as ever, Jack arched his brow at her.

"But there is only one sure way to guarantee notice," Juliet said. Gracefully perched on the edge of her cushion, she rested her clasped hands in her lap. "And that is by becoming this Season's *Original*."

Thayne laughed, the sound hollow and mocking. "I seem to recall that was a title you coveted at one time, Lady Granworth."

"I'm not certain I understand. What is an *Original*?" Jack asked, shifting to direct his question to Lilah, as if she were the only one in the room. "Another bit of nonsense for the highborn?"

She stiffened as he draped one arm over the back of his chair. He sat in a sprawled manner that seemed to take up every inch of space in front of her. There was no way to look anywhere but at him. His thigh swept near hers again, but she held her ground. This time, his eyes appeared darker, as if his pupils were made of treacle that slowly seeped into the golden brown. Along his jaw, she noted the shadow of whiskers that hinted at a darker shade than his blonde mane. And his mouth—even that arrogant tilt at one corner—was beginning to intrigue her.

Obviously, she wasn't thinking clearly. She was irritated, she reminded herself.

Taking the example of the women in her family, she attempted to gather her composure on a breath, and then she cleared her throat. "An *Original* is a person who possesses qualities that make her *or him* stand above all the rest. An anonymous committee of the *ton's* elite selects this person at the conclusion of the Season's first month."

"If they are anonymous, then how can you be certain they are members *on high* and not some footman having a laugh?"

"The editor of the *Season Standard* would know. After all, the naming of the *Original* has been happening for decades." Lilah huffed. "The point of the matter is that everyone takes notice. But most important, the *Original* would have a choice of whom she marries."

"As long as he has a title," Jack said, revealing that he'd been listening to her earlier.

Bothersome or not, it meant something to her that he remembered her name *and* their conversation. This was all new to Lilah. It felt so...*intimate*. She wasn't sure how to proceed.

"In my case, yes."

"Hmm," he murmured, his expression turning thoughtful. No smirk in sight. His eyebrows lowered, his gaze intent, as if he truly were contemplating ways to help her. "And you believe that this is your only avenue toward marriage."

Lilah considered ignoring his question. After all, the answer could very well gain nothing more than his ridicule. And she'd had enough of that already. Yet for reasons she couldn't quite explain, she wanted him to understand that this wasn't *nonsense* to her. This was her life, and there was a great deal at stake, should she fail.

Therefore, she decided to risk humiliation by being completely forthcoming. "Thus far, all other attempts have been wholly unsuccessful. You see, my father's barony has been entailed to my cousin, Lord Haggerty. Many women in such circumstances would lose their homes and depend upon the generosity of their relations to see to their welfare. Yet because of a codicil in my father's will, my mother and I have been allowed to remain in our home—but only until the end of this Season."

"By which time, you'll have secured your nobleman," Jack said with more confidence than Lilah had ever felt.

"Yes. Either of my own choosing or…my father's." And this was the most terrifying aspect of all. "The codicil also states that should I fail to marry a titled gentleman, then he has consented that I should marry my cousin."

Jack frowned. "You cannot be forced to marry your cousin if you do not wish it."

Unfortunately, her wishes had never been taken into account. "I have not reached my majority. My mother is depending on me to restore our family's honor. If I were to go against my father's last wishes, she would disown me. In disowning me, I would cause a rift in the family, splitting apart my mother from her sister, because my aunt has offered for me to remain with her. Believe me, I have thought of every possibility."

Jack's expression hardened.

"Yet as the *Original*, Lilah could choose the man she desires," Juliet interjected, before Jack could make further comment.

Thayne finally settled into a chair. However, it just happened to be the one Aunt Zinnia had vacated. The one directly beside Juliet. Although he appeared not to notice and faced Lilah across the table. "A surer path would be to enlist the Duke of Vale's assistance. With his *Marriage Formula*, you will be assured a true match."

Lilah glanced at Jack, recalling what he'd said about Vale's favor and how he'd wondered if it had something to do with the formula. Lilah was certain that hadn't been the reason the duke had asked Jack to bring her flowers. After all, the husband of her dearest friend would know about the codicil in Father's will.

Yet a measure of doubt crept into her mind. Could Vale have come to the conclusion that Jack and Lilah were suited?

No, she assured herself, all but shaking her head at Jack in the process. "With the Duke and Duchess of Vale away on their honeymoon, it would be impossible to calculate the formula."

"Besides, Lilah does not need to rely on an equation. That is something a cold and unfeeling man would want to do," Juliet said to Thayne, her gaze brimming with contempt. Then, as if she'd realized what she said, she looked over to Lilah. "Of course, I meant no offense to your friend or her husband."

Lilah reassured her with a smile. "None taken. Formula aside, Ivy is very much in love. I believe the duke is fond of her as well."

"See?" Thayne's hand swung out in a gesture of cock-sureness. "Neither cold nor unfeeling. Simply precise. In a contest, I'd wager in favor of the *Marriage Formula's* results against your notion of creating the Season's *Original*. After all, anyone can become an *Original*."

"Is that so?" Juliet's chin inched higher. Knowing that she had not been named an *Original*, Lilah knew this wounded her.

"Take Marlowe, for instance—"

"Not if you value your teeth," Jack interrupted Thayne smoothly.

Spoken like a true warrior. She could easily imagine his lithe body rising from the chair, shedding his coat, and issuing a challenge without saying a word. A man like him wouldn't need to do. A man like him likely never had cause to raise his voice either. In fact, Jack cared so little about propriety that he would be more likely to laugh than to berate his children for making a mistake. More likely to scoop his little girl in his arms after she'd fallen than to scold her…

Lilah shook her head, freeing herself of these errant thoughts. Why was she thinking about Jack's nonexistent children?

It must be because she was hungry. When her maid had brought up a tea tray earlier, Lilah hadn't wanted to eat anything for fear of spilling something on her dress. Now, she realized the hazards of being near Jack Marlowe on an empty stomach. She could not let this happen again.

"All right then, take the Earl of Wolford," Thayne continued. "Is there any man alive who spends more time in the gossip pages? Even with his fortune and title, matchmakers throughout the *ton* stay far afield of him. Yet it would take little effort to turn those scandals around and create one of the most sought-after gentlemen in society."

Juliet laughed. "Are you saying that you can turn Wolford into this Season's *Original?*"

"In my sleep."

"Be careful, Thayne," Jack warned. "You might have to prove it."

The marquess narrowed his eyes at Juliet. "Are you challenging me, Lady Granworth?"

Lilah had had enough of Thayne's overt intimidation tactics. It reminded her far too much of the verbal cruelty her father had unleashed. She stood and squared her shoulders in solidarity. "She is, my lord. In fact, she is going to transform me."

As soon as the words left her mouth, Lilah wanted to shove them back in, chew them up, and swallow, pretending that she'd never spoken. But she had. And now the words seemed like a dozen Destriers in the room, too intimidating to take back in one bite and too large to ignore.

Juliet's gaze darted to hers and held. "Are you sure about this?"

"Irrefutably." To her own credit, Lilah's voice barely trembled.

Juliet stood in front of her chair and extended her gloved hand toward Thayne. "The winner claims the house."

"The winner will keep *his* house," Thayne said, standing as well. "The loser must leave town and find another home."

"Agreed."

Lilah watched the two of them shake hands and wondered what she'd gotten herself into.

CHAPTER FOUR

"What the devil are you doing here, Marlowe?" Thayne asked as the butler escorted him into Wolford's bric-a-brac-crowded study. As of yet, Liam Cavanaugh, the Earl of Wolford, had yet to make an appearance.

Jack stood near the bay window that overlooked the street. Even before he'd spotted the carriage, he'd known Thayne would want to begin straight away. Apparently, however, they had both arrived too early for their friend to be awake. "I wanted to be present when you explained to Wolford that you were going to turn him into an *Original*."

"Of course I'm not going to tell him," Thayne replied with a dark scowl. "And I demand that you do not either."

Demand? Jack lifted his brows.

"All right then"—Thayne cleared his throat—"I'm *asking* you not to say anything."

After a moment of consideration, Jack inclined his head and walked past the mahogany desk, sidestepping a pair of Egyptian urns. "If Wolford doesn't know that he's to reform, then how will you accomplish it?"

Thayne paused in his study of an Oriental scroll under glass. "Since when have behaviors of those in society held your interest?"

"I don't know what you mean. The actions of your people are filled with such inane purpose that I find it tirelessly amusing." Yet honestly, Jack had been wondering the same thing. Why had he made a point of rescheduling his appointments so that he could be at Wolford's this morning? Curiosity, perhaps?

"*My people?*" Thayne mocked, shaking his head. "I'm not biting on your hook this time. The next thing I know, we would be in a brawl—"

"If you intend to brawl, please adjourn to the ballroom," Wolford said in a bored tone, his voice gravelly, as if he'd just woken. When he stepped into the room, his disheveled dark hair and heavily whiskered jaw confirmed it. He squinted his green eyes, either at the two of them or at the scant rays of morning light coming in through the window. "I would not want your clumsy skirmish to endanger my collection."

"Is that what you call all of this?" Jack asked with a chuckle. "I thought you were preparing an exhibition for a museum."

"Just a few things I've picked up over the years." Wearing a paisley banyan over his shirt, cravat, and trousers, Wolford trudged to the window and closed the curtains. Once the room was immersed in shadow, he released an exhale and opened his eyes fully. Then he poured a cup of tea from the service waiting on his desk, drained it, and poured another.

Thayne executed a chuckle and swept a hand through the air. "You have enough in this room to begin furnishing a new house."

"My other houses are equally full," Wolford remarked, as if the matter were mere happenstance. He had been born into a fortune and never wanted for anything in his life. While that fact had once irked Jack when they were schoolmates, the truth was that Wolford wasn't arrogant about it. He'd never once been a prig, flaunting his possessions. Moreover, neither Wolford, Thayne, nor Vale had labeled Jack a bastard and dismissed him, like most of the others had done.

"There are many elite who would enjoy a tour of your houses," Thayne continued. "I'm certain it would go a long way in improving your standing. Especially to those who disapprove of your hedonistic display of wealth."

Jack scrubbed a hand over his clean-shaven jaw, hiding a laugh. If this was Thayne's method for transforming Wolford, Jack needn't worry for Lilah's sake.

Abruptly, he frowned, distracted. He wasn't *worried* for Lilah Appleton. The outcome of her venture made no difference to him whatsoever. His being here was a means of satisfying a mere curiosity. Nothing more.

"And there is a salver piled high with invitations from those who thoroughly enjoy my hedonism, in every aspect. I am more of a mind to take pleasure in *their* company," Wolford said with a familiar, wicked gleam. His reputation for extravagance encompassed more than a steady acquisition of objects. Rumors of the salacious parties he attended kept his name from being spoken too loudly by those in society.

Leaning back against his desk, Wolford crossed his arms over his chest and looked from Jack to Thayne. "Have you come to admire my latest acquisitions or merely to scold me, as my housekeeper does?"

When Wolford looked to him, Jack jerked a chin in Thayne's direction. "I believe the *marquess* has something of a business proposition for you."

"I...*yes*. I do." Thayne shot Jack a look of warning before regarding Wolford once more. "I've recently acquired a new property, and I am in need of furnishings."

"I heard all about it at Lady Reynolds's party last evening. Your dealings with Lady Granworth have become infamous."

Thayne coughed. "You've heard?"

"By now, I'm certain everyone in town is aware that you practically stole the Widow Granworth's house right from under her nose." Wolford tsked.

"Oh, that," Thayne said on an exhale. "There was no thievery involved. I merely made a more handsome offer. I'm certain that is something you both can understand."

"There is nothing wrong with being a man of action, but I've never procured an object on which another person has laid claim," Wolford added, clearly to antagonize their friend. "Have you, Marlowe?"

Jack had learned at an early age that he had to fight for everything he wanted. The lesson had begun with a need to use his fists until he was old enough to learn that money and intellect held more power. Still, a man ought to know how to use his fists, especially when dealing with dockside merchants. "I enjoy a good challenge. Even so, I still have something of a code of honor."

"Sod off, the two of you. I'm making no apologies," Thayne sneered. "Both of you take what you want and never bother yourselves with what you don't. I merely wanted that townhouse."

"Hmm," Wolford mused with a sly grin. Then his gaze drifted back to Jack. "Though the statement makes me wonder why you are here, Marlowe, and not frittering away your day at the toil and strife you seem to enjoy. What has piqued your interest enough to bring you here, to an address that is at the very heart of the *haute ton* you so despise?"

The muscles along Jack's neck, shoulders, and arms flexed with tension. He wasn't overly interested in Thayne's bargain with Lady Granworth. All the same, he felt a need to be aware of the happenings surrounding Lilah Appleton. It was, he supposed, the aftereffects of carrying her card with him each day for so many weeks. His promise to Vale had been to send her flowers in order—he presumed—to assist her matrimonial endeavors. So how could he abandon his task without seeing it to completion? Clearly, Jack would have to stay in her life until she found a husband.

Satisfied with the answer, he relaxed and addressed Wolford. "I was wondering if you'd heard from Vale. Your cousin has been on his honeymoon for months."

"As a matter of fact," Wolford said. "I received a missive from him yesterday. I'll spare the two of you his lengthy sermon on the ideal marriage and how he acquired it. I will tell you, however, that he plans to return in a fortnight. And, no doubt, is prepared to encourage us all to find our own brides."

Jack couldn't help but notice how Wolford's comment landed neatly in Thayne's lap.

"For you to marry, you will need to learn how to please the *ton*'s matrons first," Thayne said to Wolford.

Wolford's harsh laugh ricocheted off of a nymph statue and reverberated inside a tall blue vase. "Now you truly sound like my housekeeper. As I have told her, I will marry when I am one and sixty, after I have lived a full life, just as my father did. And I need no one to nag me about my duties before that time."

Jack smirked. Wolford was not going to make this easy. Then again, helping Lilah might not be a simple task either. Already she'd stated a desire to marry one man in particular. *Lord Ellery.* Jack knew little about him. As of yet, there'd been no reason for him to find out more. Now, however, there was a reason.

"What about nagging you about a solid night of card play? It's been an age since the lot of us sat at a table," Jack said, needing an excuse to glean information from his friends on Ellery.

Thayne appeared to be waiting for Wolford's response.

Wolford shook his head. "Sorry, old chap. I've already given my word to Stapleton. He's hosting a soiree and a card game."

As Jack recalled, Stapleton had been a relative of Lilah's late uncle. Therefore, it seemed likely that she would attend this party. Perhaps Ellery would as well. In addition, Jack knew that Stapleton and Dovermere weren't particular friends. Which meant that Dovermere wouldn't attend. Which also meant that Jack *could* and without the risk of an encounter.

"I could procure an invitation for you, and we could have that game after all," Wolford offered.

"Though it may surprise you, I already have an invitation." It was true that Jack did not attend society gatherings. Yet that didn't mean he never received invitations. Quite the contrary. Jack received a slew of them every day. He supposed it was because, as Dovermere's bastard, Jack was a curiosity. Never before had he thought that it would work in his favor. "Gentlemen, it appears our game is on."

Lilah stared in the vanity mirror as Nellie finished curling the fringe that framed her face. The same face that had failed to tempt even one man to call on her in the past two Seasons. The same face deemed *forgettable*. And now, she'd promised to use this face to ensure that Juliet gained her home?

In fact, she is going to transform me...

"Nellie, what possessed me to make such a claim?"

Her maid's response was a shake of the head in the mirror. "I'm sure I couldn't say, miss."

Nellie had been her maid for over ten years but still harbored some skittishness from when Lilah's father was alive and browbeating everyone within hearing. She never spoke unless spoken to and rarely offered her opinion. In that way, Nellie was like Lilah. It was as if she was still afraid of bellowed demands for perfection. Afraid to fail.

Lilah was too.

So what possessed her to think that she could become the *Original*? She more resembled the wilting primroses in the vase by her window seat than a fresh-faced debutante with *a certain flair*.

"Juliet would need magical powers to turn me into this Season's *Original*." Certain failure loomed. Lilah needed a moment to figure out how to gently ease out of this bargain. Yet before she could think of anything, her cousin walked into the bedchamber.

"Pale-blue satin suits you well," Juliet said. Then, pressing her lips together, she tilted her head, as if in contemplation. "Though we must try something different with your hair."

Lilah held up her hand, protecting every curl that the maid had painstakingly set in place. "It took Nellie nearly an hour to arrange my hair." The maid in question said nothing but nodded.

Juliet displayed no concern over this news. "Do you want gentlemen to see *you* or to admire your maid's skill with the tongs?"

"To see me, of course," Lilah said, keeping her hand in place. "But as I mentioned, I have a rather *vast* forehead."

"Nonsense." Juliet picked up a brush, nudged Lilah's hand aside, and proceeded to undo an hour's worth of work.

When her hair fell across her eyes, Lilah began to panic. "Nellie shouldn't have to witness the loss of her efforts."

Juliet ignored her. "Nellie, please bring me a facecloth from the wash basin."

Lilah could only hear the sound of footsteps shuffling across the carpet. She couldn't see what was happening to her. Then, soon enough, she felt a slight dampness against her forehead.

"Now, Nellie, pull out the pins. We're going to start all over."

Start over? Lilah gulped. "We don't have time. Surely my aunt is already waiting for us in the foyer."

"Zinnia is only now leaving her room. Her practice of pedestrianism should give us ten minutes. Plenty of time." At that point, Juliet turned Lilah on the stool, away from the mirror, and brushed her hair forward and then back. "A simple twist this time, Nellie. We'll try something more elaborate for the Corbett Ball."

"Yes, my lady," Nellie said, her voice possessing more confidence and volume than Lilah had ever heard.

When Lilah could finally see again, her cousin smiled down at her. "I don't know why you had your hair styled in that fashion for so long. Why, your forehead is nicely sloped and adorned by the slight V of your hairline. With the way that your hair falls naturally, your face subtly resembles the shape of a heart."

"My mother is always saying that there's too much of my face"—Lilah tried to turn her head to see the results—"and that it would be difficult to find a girl with a larger head to stand beside."

"Uh-uh. Not yet. There is one more thing." Juliet clucked her tongue and then reached into a satchel. She withdrew an ornate brown jar with scroll work on the side, along with a round painter's brush with a fat cluster of long bristles. Lifting the lid, she dipped the brush inside. "Now, close your eyes, dear."

Lilah closed one eye. "What is it?"

"Pearl dust," Juliet answered, her soft breath sending a small flurry of luminescent powder into the air, each particle winking in the light. Then she tapped Lilah's nose with the brush. "Now, close both eyes."

This time, Lilah complied.

"That is how I see you—a pearl," Juliet said with the first stroke of the soft bristles. "Think of how they start as a grain of sand that, after a trial, becomes something beautiful. *Your* trials are behind you. You must emerge as nature intended.

Now, look closely at your reflection, and see what is truly there."

Lilah opened her eyes and grew nervous when greeted with Juliet's and Nellie's smiles. Suddenly, she was afraid to turn around and look into the mirror. What if they were just being kind? What if her forehead was peppered with freckles that formed the shape of a cow or something equally dreadful? Not that she wasn't fond of cows. She actually enjoyed cheese quite a bit. And butter on her toast. And yes, she realized she was stalling, but it couldn't be helped. After all, she might look hideous, and there was no time to warm the tongs and start over... *again*.

"Lilah, if you don't face the mirror this instant, I'm going to drag you out of this chamber and not even permit you to glance at your own reflection all night." Juliet failed to intimidate with her reprimand when she laughed.

Lilah's legs wobbled a bit as she stood. And then she turned.

She might have gasped if she could have drawn a breath. Her face was still her face. Her eyes, nose, mouth, and ears all in the same location. Only now, there was nothing to hide them. Had she been *hiding* them all this time? Hmm...she wasn't quite certain, but she felt a little more than exposed. Was this truly her face?

She took a tentative step closer. Even after all that brushing, some of her curl remained. With her hair parted down the center, the fringe that once covered her entire forehead now framed it in a soft wave of brown on either side. And strangely enough, instead of seeing the vastness of her forehead, Lilah saw her eyes, dark and bright at the same time. Her brows, too, were dark, but arched slightly where they tapered off to a soft point. This was a familiar face and yet new.

But was it enough to transform her into an *Original*?

Lilah began to worry, conjuring the most ludicrous scenarios for this evening.

"Well, what do you think?" Juliet asked, unknowingly putting a halt to a terrible, imagined disaster involving an apple, a wayward arrow, and a collective gasp from the entire list of attendants.

"To be completely truthful, I'm not entirely sure. It is as if another version of me is looking at me from the other side of the mirror."

Juliet reached down and squeezed her hand. "If that is true, then you are both going to be late for Lord Stapleton's party if we do not hurry."

In that same moment, a breathless Myrtle appeared at the doorway. "Pardon me, but her ladyship wishes me to tell you that *time is not—*"

"*Our ally?*" Lilah supplied with a grin, feeling a measure of relief in her aunt's predictability.

Juliet turned to Lilah. "I forgot my fan. I shan't be more than a minute."

Her cousin disappeared through the doorway. With Myrtle nervously shifting from foot to foot in the hall, Lilah didn't dally. Just before she left, however, she looked over her shoulder. "Thank you, Nellie. You were splendid this evening."

"Thank you, miss. So were you." Her maid's eyes turned liquid instantly as she bobbed a curtsy. Not wanting to be afflicted in the same manner, Lilah slipped away.

Downstairs in the foyer, Aunt Zinnia offered a rare smile. "My dear, you look beautiful. I knew your eyes were somewhere beneath that fringe."

With Juliet upstairs, Lilah was alone with her aunt. She gave into her fears. "I don't want to disappoint her, Aunt Zinnia. If I fail—"

"You are uncommonly brave." Her aunt touched a gloved fingertip beneath Lilah's chin and lifted her face, as if for inspection. Then she nodded. "I've no doubt that you will cause a stir this evening."

With so much riding on the outcome of this Season, Lilah was sure that any failure would be all the more catastrophic.

CHAPTER FIVE

"Marlowe, be a chap and spot me a hundred quid," Pembroke whispered, his voice slipping down through his hawkish nose in a high squeak. The man was all nose, arms, and legs, with an overblown cravat to hold him together. "Remember that time at Eton when I warned you about those blighters who were set on a tussle with you?"

Standing just outside Stapleton's game room, Jack looked at Pembroke with disgust. Not for the man's appearance—after all, that couldn't be helped—but because this viscount mistakenly believed he was entitled to *Jack's* hard-earned money. Pembroke hadn't even bothered to ask for it. Although the response would have been the same. An unequivocal *no*. "Your memory is faulty. I distinctly recall *you* leading the charge."

Pembroke averted his gaze as he withdrew a handkerchief from his sleeve and wiped his nose. "Yes...er...well, I did alert you nonetheless. And as I recall, you were successful in fending them off. Which might not have been the case, if it weren't for me."

"If anything," Jack began with a wry laugh, "you should be paying me for not pummeling you, as I did the others. Then again, I recall you were a rather fast runner. And you scream like a little girl."

Pembroke sniffed, then stormed away, leaving Jack with his memories. Those years at Eton had been difficult, but not because of the weekly threats of death and dismemberment. Having grown up doing odd jobs, from chimney sweep— until he'd grown too large—to errand runner and hawker, he'd become a scrapper. Ready and able in any situation.

Shortly into his stint at school, Jack had learned that he could use his skills to earn money. Some of that money had been earned through brawling and wagers, though most of it was in developing an enterprise. He'd started a small business, employing the village boys to shine shoes and buckles, before selling them at a higher price back to his fellow students. The aristocratic requirement to uphold appearances at all times was quite profitable, as well as educational.

By the time Jack left Eton, he'd begun other enterprises outside of school. It turned out that he was born with a knack for trade and investments.

And he'd be damned if—after all his hard work—he was going to *give* his money away to ignorant fools like Pembroke, who chose not to think for themselves.

"Tell me something, Marlowe. If you didn't come to play, then why are you here? You're as surly as Thayne this evening," Wolford said with a grin as he handed Jack a short glass of amber liquor. "I think Pembroke is off somewhere, cowering in a corner and biting his fingernails."

Jack tipped back his glass and downed the scotch in one swallow. "Have you ever seen him otherwise?"

"No. Pembroke is still as useless as ever. Though I did hear a rumor that he has called upon Lady Granworth."

Jack knew that already. Pembroke's carriage had been in front of Lady Cosgrove's house the day before yesterday. There had been no carriages today. When Jack had called, he'd been informed by the butler that Lady Granworth was not at home. Jack corrected his assumption by asking for Miss Appleton. The butler blinked as if Jack had made the request in Latin before showing him to the study. Shortly thereafter, he was informed that Miss Appleton was *not at home* either. But Jack knew that she would have received any other visitor, just not him. "Perhaps Pembroke was there to court Miss Appleton instead."

"Who?" Wolford's brow knitted for a moment and then lifted. "Ah, yes. She's a cousin or niece or something of Lady Granworth and Lady Cosgrove. Come to think of it, she might be a friend of Vale's bride. Do you imagine Pembroke is courting this Miss...Miss..."

"Appleton."

Wolford snapped his fingers. "Right. She must come from money, then, because Pembroke is as broke as a twig."

"As far as I know, she has nothing. Her father's estate was entailed to his nephew, Lord Haggerty." Jack had made a few inquiries on his own earlier today. The more he learned about Haggerty and his reputation, the more concerned Jack became for Lilah.

Wolford's countenance flashed disgust. "Tragic. There likely won't be an estate at all for much longer. The blighter is as dissolute as they come. I've no idea why Stapleton invited him."

"Haggerty is here?" Jack looked around the room, searching for a face he didn't know. "I've never met him." And, after Wolford's reaction, Jack wanted to learn more about the baron. Not to mention, more about the reason behind Lilah's bold declaration and willingness to transform.

"I saw him milling about, near the stairs above the foyer. You'll recognize him by the waves of superiority flowing from his greasy head."

Lilah's talent for worry had failed her this evening. Otherwise, she would have been prepared for the carriage to hit a rut, breaking the wheel, and causing them to arrive at Lord Stapleton's party late.

Aunt Zinnia was not pleased.

Juliet, on the other hand, still hoped for Lilah to make a grand entrance into the ballroom. "And when your name is announced, be sure to look straight ahead. Pretend that you are bored and could care nothing for their opinions. The *ton* will take notice if you are ignoring them."

"If that is true, then it is no wonder that I've had little success. I'm surprised anyone with a sense of decorum would." Lessons on how to act with perfect manners in society had been ingrained in Lilah since birth.

When a maid came up behind her, Lilah slipped off her redingote and adjusted the white satin sash beneath her breasts. As she stood in the foyer, she gradually felt a sense of being watched. A cold shiver slithered over the exposed flesh of her shoulders, throat, and modest décolletage. That was when she looked up and spotted Cousin Winthrop lurking near the minstrel gallery overlooking the foyer. With pursed lips and holding a quizzing glass to his eye, he surveyed her as one would livestock at the market.

Juliet made a sound and quickly pulled her into a room just off the hall. "That *horrid* man," she said, cringing. "And the way he looks at you...I can't bear it. I wish I could convince your mother of his *true* nature."

There were reasons why Cousin Winthrop had not found a bride on his own. First of all, while he'd inherited a barony, he also acquired barren lands, a crumbling estate, tenants who could not afford to pay rent, and absolutely no fortune.

Second was the man himself. He paraded around with a sense of self-importance, as if he was next in line to the throne. The few strands of hair remaining on Winthrop's round head were long and tended to hang limply over his brow. His fleshy face possessed a constant sheen of perspiration that no amount of patting with a handkerchief could remedy. He had a habit of licking his lips, which caused a buildup of froth at the corners of his mouth. Even worse than that, however, was the way Winthrop leered at her, that fiendish gleam ever present. The idea of being forced to marry such a man both sickened and terrified her.

Aunt Zinnia joined them, a frown upon her lips. "Haggerty's presence is quite unexpected. According to the maid with whom I just spoke, the only reason he'd garnered an invitation was because he told Lord Stapleton that an...arrangement had been settled with you, dear Lilah."

Lilah gasped. "How many others has he told?"

"There is no way of knowing." Aunt Zinnia shook her head and exhaled her displeasure. "However, I will speak to Lord

Stapleton straight away and correct the misunderstanding. Then, Juliet, you and I must set about doing the same with the other guests. We cannot allow Lilah's name to be tainted by such an association. Not many know about the codicil."

Juliet agreed with a nod. "If he approaches me at all, I will give him the *cut direct*."

There was so much at stake. Lilah felt a headache starting. She pressed her gloved fingertips to her temples. "He's waiting above the stairs. The moment we ascend, he will invite himself, unbidden, into our party. There will be no way to avoid the association. Then everyone will know." And all of her hopes of freeing herself from this dire fate would be for naught.

Thank goodness Aunt Zinnia was made of sterner stuff, for she adamantly refused to accept this outcome. "I know another way into the ballroom. It will be unseemly to traverse the servants' stairs, but we shall do what we must."

The moment Jack neared the arch leading to the gallery, he caught sight of a man who fit Haggerty's description. There was no doubt of his sense of self-importance. He stood—or posed, rather—near the rail, with one foot turned out, one hand on his hip, and holding a lens to his eye.

From the archway, Jack glanced down to the foyer to find the object of Haggerty's study. At once, Jack's gaze settled on Lilah. She was a vision in blue, her face radiant beneath the glow of the chandelier. Yet after a glance up toward the balcony, she grimaced. Before Jack could blink, Lady Granworth pulled her out of view, which was for the best because Jack didn't like the way Haggerty was looking at her.

"Pardon me," Jack said, pleased that he'd startled the man into turning away from the rail. "You wouldn't, by any chance, be Lord Haggerty?"

The man's lip curled as he looked Jack over. "The one and only. And you are?"

"Jack Marlowe."

"Ah yes, Dovermere's by-blow," he sneered, turning away.

Jack had heard all the insults. Such a *cut* no longer gained a reaction from him. This was a way for the nobility to indicate their superiority, snubbing their noses at him. That was…until they needed money.

Haggerty's head came up with a snap, like a man who'd just remembered something important. "*Marlowe*…rumor has it that you've amassed a rather vulgar fortune."

And there it was, the beginning of the beggary. Jack had heard it all. Some chose inane flattery. Some bragged about their standing in society, dropping the names of the people in their intimate circle, speaking as if it would be an honor to give a loan to a person with such high connections. Some made promises about repaying the loan tenfold. Some threatened him, making it known that they employed ruffians who would bring him harm if Jack did not concede. And some even offered the use of their own mistresses. Which was distasteful on many levels.

Jack wondered which method Haggerty would use. "*Vulgar* is an interesting word for this moment."

"Mmm…yes." Haggerty chortled. "You're a rather sharp fellow. I can see why Stapleton invited you. One must always have the best people at these parties, you know."

Flattery, Jack mused. Though not clever flattery.

"Of course, *I* was invited because of my close connection to Lady Cosgrove," the baron continued, tossing another component into the mix. "Her ladyship and I are related through marriage—my *upcoming* marriage."

The skin and sinew tightened over Jack's bones, a sense of dread washing over him, even before he was certain. When Lilah had spoken of this, it sounded as if she'd wished to avoid being forced into marriage, not that the matter had already been settled.

Needing clarification, he said, "My congratulations to you and…"

"My cousin, Miss Appleton. I inherited her father's paltry estate. Her welfare and her mother's reside squarely on my shoulders. Though it isn't too much of a hardship," he added with a wink. "My cousin, while having a poor showing at first, is now a ripe plum, just waiting to be picked."

The man was vile. Jack was sickened once more by the aristocracy. His disgust, however, had begun long ago, upon first learning how his own mother had suffered.

She'd been born into the aristocracy, with high expectations of marrying well. Even though she'd had no dowry, her parents had been certain her beauty would secure a fine husband. When a neighboring lord had asked for her hand, it had seemed her parents' dreams had come true. They had not known he was a dissolute cad.

Then, only a short time after her marriage, tragedy struck. Fever took the lives of her parents. Debts and a hanging took the life of her husband, leaving her without a farthing to her name. In her world, a young woman in such circumstances had limited options—find work as a paid companion, or find a protector. She'd chosen the latter and had become Dovermere's mistress.

At the time, Dovermere had been a young man—not an earl yet, but Viscount Locke. Then, a few years later, when he inherited, he'd had every intention of marrying his mistress—or so Jack had been told. Yet with the demands of an earldom came the need to marry an heiress instead. Dovermere had accepted this fate. Heartbroken, Jack's mother had chosen to end their arrangement, not knowing at the time that she'd been carrying Dovermere's son. His only son, as it turned out.

It had taken the earl years to find a wealthy bride and years to produce his first child. *A girl.* Now, eight girls in all. Jack was ten before his mother wrote to Dovermere, not asking for anything for herself but merely for an education for her beloved son.

Leaving her for Eton all those years ago, with nothing but the money she'd earned from sewing to keep her fed, had been the hardest day of Jack's life.

Standing in Haggerty's presence, it was impossible not to think of what Lilah faced for her future. It took Jack a moment to swallow down his bitterness. "And when is the happy event?"

"Well, there is a matter of her father's will," he hedged, adjusting his lace cuffs. "A codicil states that I should wait until the end of this Season; however, I may press my suit at any time. Though if you ask me, the delay only whets the appetite. Likely, I'll have an heir right off—*legitimate*, of course."

A final dig to make certain that Jack knew his place. But it didn't matter. Jack was too busy thinking about Lilah. It all became clear. No wonder she was willing to do anything to avoid marriage to Haggerty, subjecting herself to transforming into this Season's *Original*.

She didn't even realize that she needn't alter a thing. All she needed was a little more time to find the right man who would see her. The only problem was, her time was running out, and Haggerty made it all too clear.

"And while we're having this friendly chat, I may as well confess that I have all this land. More than I need," the baron continued with a grandiose chuckle. "Since the tenants aren't making good use of it, I could be persuaded to sell off a good portion. For the right price, of course."

Instead of taking a direct route, Lilah, Aunt Zinnia, and Juliet skirted through the private rooms of the family wing and made their way through a shadowed ingress at the far side of the ballroom. Thankfully, the Grecian design of the room provided an alcove concealed by a large column and ivory drapes, hanging from the vaulted ceiling and pooling on the mosaic stone floor.

"There is Lord Stapleton, near the gaming room doors," Aunt Zinnia said, still perfectly poised, as if taking the narrow servants' stairs was commonplace for her.

Decorum demanded they greet their host immediately. Yet after the disturbing news regarding Winthrop, Lilah didn't trust her legs to carry her across the room or her lungs to draw in enough air. She preferred to linger here. She was nervous and worried—without a ludicrous notion, this time—that all of Juliet's efforts would come to nothing. She might very well fail.

This fear resided far too close to the surface. She could feel it on her skin, making her so cold she shivered with it.

"Aunt," Lilah began, her voice breaking around the edges, "might I linger here for a moment or two?"

"Juliet and I cannot leave you here alone. And it would be unseemly for me to cross the room toward a gentleman unaccompanied," Aunt Zinnia replied automatically. Then she turned to Lilah and the sternness in her countenance softened. She must have seen Lilah's dread. "Very well, my dear. Juliet and I will greet him, clear up matters, and return to you shortly."

Juliet squeezed her hand. "In the meantime, take a deep breath and know that you are lovely."

Lilah followed her cousin's advice and drew in a deep breath as she took a step back. She wanted to stay out of the line of sight from the ballroom doors to avoid seeing Winthrop again. Or worse, letting him see her.

"You're late, Miss Appleton."

She jolted at the low, familiar sound of Jack Marlowe's voice. It vibrated through her, even as she pivoted around to face him. "What are you doing here?"

"Much the same as you, I suppose. I accepted an invitation." He grinned, flashing those canines in challenge as he emerged from the narrow passage as well. "I could have warned you earlier if you'd been *at home* for my call."

When the butler, Mr. Wick, had presented Jack's card on a salver, Lilah had been stunned at first. Since Juliet had been out shopping—and her potential suitors informed—there hadn't been a single caller. Aunt Zinnia had abandoned the parlor in favor of counting the silver with Mrs. Wick, the housekeeper.

This had left Lilah alone. But it was more pride than a matter of propriety that she'd refused his call. She didn't want him to see the empty parlor and make the correct assumptions about her lack of desirability.

Also, she was stubborn enough to keep her word. "I told you that I would not be at home. Although I suspect your visit was merely to test my resolve."

He didn't answer directly. Instead, he took a moment to study her, his gaze seeming to miss nothing. "Lady Granworth was correct, you know. You are lovely this evening."

Another breath stuttered into her lungs, warm and unexpected. She was sure she didn't need more air because now her stays felt too tight. She possessed a sudden urge to press his primroses between glass, so she could keep them forever.

"Though I'd expected to find you altered this evening," he continued, "given your declaration within Mrs. Harwick's parlor *last* evening."

A deflating breath abruptly remedied the tightness of her stays. His primroses might meet an early demise instead.

If the one man who had remembered her name did not notice the changes, then what hope did she have with the ones who had not? "I am very much altered. Can you not see? My hair has been brushed away from my face."

After spending her entire life with a thick fringe hiding her expansive forehead, this was quite a change for her. She felt vulnerable displaying—what she'd always thought was— her greatest physical flaw. And now, she had to endure an encounter that was doing nothing to settle her nerves.

"I feared making such an observation would lead me to compliment your eyes." His grin turned into a smirk. Then he leaned in marginally, his gaze dipping to her mouth before traversing her from head to hem and back up again. "And I'm not certain I'm supposed to know that you have eyes. Just like I'm not supposed to know that you have a waist."

The man was exasperating!

Even so, he smelled quite nice. *Sandalwood and a certain spice—clove, perhaps? Argh!* She shook her head. Distractions were not welcome at a time like this. She had to wonder at her misfortune this night. First Winthrop, and now him. Why, out of all the men in London, was Jack here? Was it merely to aggravate her? Clearly.

"I have a waist, Mr. Marlowe," she hissed. "There—are you satisfied?"

He pursed his lips as if mulling over his answer. "No. I'm not certain I believe you. I might require proof. Perhaps, if we were to dance a waltz…"

A sudden wash of heat stung her cheeks. Her imagination was far too vivid. In an instant, her mind misused her talent for contriving catastrophes and showed her what it might be like to be held in his arms. Her mind, obviously, had forgotten how much she despised him.

Refusing to let him see how he'd embarrassed her with his teasing, she turned around. "This is too small of a party for waltzing."

"Pity," he said, his warm breath brushing her neck. "Though perhaps I could call on you again tomorrow, and we could meet in the garden for a waltz."

Instead of answering, she intended to walk away. There was no use in speaking to a man who obviously delighted in making fun of her. From where she stood, she saw that her aunt and

Juliet were still conversing with Lord Stapleton. But in that same moment, she saw Cousin Winthrop enter the ballroom. He stood beneath the arch at the far side of the room.

Without thinking, she stepped back—colliding with Jack Marlowe.

"Careful." He steadied her with a hand. A hand *conveniently* located at her waist. He made no move to extract it either. In fact, he settled it more securely against her, his palm resting above the flare of her hip. His splayed fingers went all the way to her navel and up beyond the edge of her ribs, scant inches from the underside her breast. All the while, his thumb moved in small, distracting circles at her back. "*Hmm*...I suppose that proves your claim."

For a moment, Lilah's spine lost all substance, and she leaned back against him. She tried hard not to notice the warmth of his body. Or the feel of his superfine coat against the narrow expanse of bare skin at the crest of her shoulder blades. Or—*she swallowed*—the way her bottom nestled squarely against the hottest part of him.

She straightened, withdrawing enough to create some space between them but not far enough to risk being seen by Winthrop or by the guests who might happen this way. "Since I cannot move forward, the gentlemanly thing for you to do is to step back."

"Why can't you move forward?" His breath skimmed across her nape, teasing the tendrils that must have come loose earlier, when their carriage had hit the rut.

She shivered, closing her eyes. "I know very well that you do not care about my answer. All you are doing is delaying the removal of your hand from my..."

She'd said the word a moment ago. So why couldn't she say it now? Likely, because that part of her body had suddenly become the center of her world. It was now a place of intimacy and forbidden touches.

"*Waist?*" he supplied, moving his fingertips in such a way that it made her stomach quiver—not on the surface but someplace deeper inside.

"*Person,*" she corrected, yet noticed her thready word lacked censure. She tried again. "You really should not be touching me here."

"If I were assisting you into a barouche, I would have both my hands on your...person."

Both of his hands on her? She tried not to imagine it. When she felt an enthralling warmth spread through her, she knew she'd failed. "No. I mean here, in the ballroom. If anyone should see, the result would be catastrophic for both of us."

Her reputation would be ruined. He would be expected to marry her. They both knew, however, that he would not. His conduct indicated that he cared little for the principles of society. He didn't even like her. And more important, she reminded herself, she despised him.

"Indeed. The rules that govern your actions *must* be obeyed." With those hard-edged words, he dropped his hand and stepped back.

Lilah immediately missed his warmth and hated herself for it. She turned to face him, a reprimand at the ready. "If we didn't have rules, then society would be full of men like you who enjoy taking liberties."

He lifted his tawny brows. "You don't think society would be full of *women* taking liberties?"

She blinked, caught off guard by the question and by the very idea. Women taking liberties?

Spinning a web to decide her fate…

It was an unexpectedly intriguing proposition for a woman in her circumstances. Now, however, was not the time to ponder it. "I will not imagine such a thing. After all, if I were to have placed my hand on your person, then you would have removed it. Men do not wait upon politeness."

"I wouldn't have removed your hand…from *anywhere* on my person." He grinned, making her regret the example she'd used. Then he spread his arms out in invitation. "Please tell me you require proof."

She ignored the taunt. She only wished that she could force her pulse not to react. "Then the act wouldn't be taking *liberty*, would it?"

"I suppose not." He lowered his arms.

Feeling as if she had the upper hand, she intended to keep it. "If you choose to mingle with society and yet live outside of our strictures, then you should learn to govern yourself."

"I prefer to live apart from a society that marries for money and advancement and uses their daughters as chattel, leaving them with few paths to traverse."

In his direct gaze, she saw the loathing he must have gained over years through his own trials, but she also saw pity. She wondered, in that instant, if he was speaking of her fate, should she not find her own husband. "Did you happen to meet Lord Haggerty?"

"I did."

Lilah felt her spine straighten, one vertebra at a time. She did not want Jack's pity. "Then you understand my desire to find a husband of my own choosing."

He nodded. "Though I don't see why you need to find one of noble blood. Why not elope with a banker, merchant, or country squire?"

"My father's will states that any lesser marriage would not be validated."

"If you were to elope and prove that you were in a…delicate condition, any court would validate your union."

She blushed at the intimation. "The codicil addresses that as well. In such a circumstance, I would be cut off from any tie to the family. As I said before, my mother has already stated that she will honor my father's wishes. And if my aunt were to choose to keep our association, then she would lose a sister. I could not do that to her."

"These rules you live by are unconscionable," he growled, stepping away from her and deeper into the shadows. "And the worst part of all is that you accept it—the lot of you."

"Accepting implies that I am doing nothing to alter the outcome, when the contrary is true. Do you think that I enjoy subjecting myself to scrutiny? Being introduced to gentlemen who cannot bother to recall my name? Constant reminders of the calendar days slipping past? I can assure you that I do not." She huffed. Then, realizing she'd followed him, she stopped, prepared to leave his presence without even knowing what awaited her. "And I certainly do not need to be bothered by the likes of you."

"I know how to help you, Lilah."

The sound of her name on his lips shuddered through her. This time, she had to press her hand to her middle to quell the unwanted trembling. Unfortunately, it didn't work.

"*Miss Appleton*," she reminded. Again. "And I am already aware of my own requirements. I do not wish to hear your opinion."

"Finding a worthy husband will take more than revealing those dark eyes and donning a new gown. You need my help. In fact, I believe that's what Vale wanted when he wrote your name on that card. However, I can see that I've flustered you…"

"You are the most arrogant man," she interrupted, clenching her teeth. He was not even in society, yet he believed that he could help? Astounding.

He chuckled and continued. "If you find that the results of this evening have left you disappointed, then be *at home* for me tomorrow when I come to call. If I'm sent away, I'll have your answer and never bother you again."

At last, a bright spot in her evening. Smiling broadly, she mocked him with a curtsy. "Then this shall be our final meeting. Good-bye, Mr. Marlowe."

"Until tomorrow"—he inclined his head, letting his gaze linger on her mouth—"*Lilah.*"

CHAPTER SIX

The following day, Lilah had four callers. Though none of
them was a gentleman. In fact, they were all debutantes. Miss
Stapleton and Miss Ashbury were the last to leave.

"It was such a pleasure to meet you at my father's party
last evening," Miss Stapleton said as she tied the periwinkle
ribbon of her bonnet beneath her chin. Her smile appeared
genuine, the apples of her cheeks softly rounded and rosy.
"I'm still quite shocked that we hadn't met previously. Promise you will waggle your finger at me this evening if I even dare
to blink without acknowledging you?"

Lilah couldn't help but laugh. This was all very new and
strange to her. Had such a difference been made, simply by
baring her forehead to the world and powdering her face with
pearl dust? "If you insist."

Miss Ashbury clapped her hands, sending the tassels
dangling from the sleeve of her burgundy spencer in motion.
"Yes, you must, and to me as well. We who are in our third
Seasons must stick together, after all. By the way, which party

will you be attending—the Lewises', the Backstons', or the Smithfields'?"

Lilah suspected there was little sincerity in Miss Ashbury's abrupt affability. Her smile did not lift her cheeks. Instead, her hazel eyes narrowed ever so slightly as she tucked a lock of auburn hair beneath her bonnet. For some reason, Lilah felt as if she'd just made one friend *and* one enemy. The same had been true with the other two who had paid a call. One friend—*Miss Creighton*—and one enemy—*Miss Leeds*. Though if truth be told, Lilah had never been fond of Miss Leeds, especially after the way she'd abused Lilah's dearest friend, Ivy.

"I'm not entirely certain of our plans this evening. I forgot to ask my aunt," Lilah said, receiving a flash of annoyance from Miss Ashbury. The downy hairs on Lilah's nape lifted, filling her with a sense of caution. Though warned of what, she wasn't certain. Perhaps she said something wrong. Thankfully, Mr. Wick saved her from a further faux pas by opening the door.

After a few parting niceties, her new *friends* left. Juliet stepped out of the morning room down the hall. At the same time, Aunt Zinnia sauntered out of the parlor, where she'd been *chaperone* for Lilah's visits.

Her aunt and her cousin exchanged glances before Aunt Zinnia nodded thoughtfully. "An interesting turn of events."

"Quite promising," Juliet said with a careful smile. While she was not *at home* to callers, she had been listening to Lilah's visits from the adjacent room.

Lilah frowned. "Not a single gentleman paid a call."

Not even Jack Marlowe. Which didn't bother her at all. In fact, she'd barely taken notice and hardly even had glanced out the parlor window in search of a man on a Destrier. When she'd heard a knock at the door, she hadn't turned her ear, waiting for the sound of his low cadence. And she *certainly* hadn't been disappointed by its absence.

"A serious candidate will wait," Aunt Zinnia began. Her tone and countenance provided a confidence that few would disbelieve. "A sensible gentleman will think about what he has learned about you and the others. From there, he will consider his dance partners and with whom he would ask to stroll the perimeter of the ballroom."

"It may not seem like it," Juliet began, "but having four debutantes pay a call shows that you have already started to make a statement. They took notice."

"Then last evening was a...success?" Lilah had been thankful that she hadn't encountered Winthrop all evening. It was like her own small miracle. Two gentlemen had asked her to dance. Unfortunately, neither had been Lord Ellery, as he'd been absent.

Juliet nodded. "We will stay in tonight. That way, they will wonder what other party you attended. This will create an urgency about you. They will want to know more, and soon a tide of curious whispers will lift you high above the throng. And the next step is having your new *friends* ask what you will be wearing to the Corbett Ball and to the LeFroy's dinner. I imagine Miss Ashbury will be the first."

"Miss Ashbury already dresses at the height of fashion. I do not think my wardrobe would concern her."

"Dear Lilah, she is the one who cares the most. Be on your guard with her," Juliet warned.

A new frisson of trepidation stole over Lilah. She was out of her element. Her first Seasons had never encompassed such a variety of mannerisms. Thus far, she'd thought that pretending to be perfect had been difficult enough.

"I know how to help you, Lilah," Jack had said last night. Only now she wished she hadn't dismissed him so readily. As of now, Juliet's focus was primarily on Lilah's appearance, believing that these subtle alterations would make a difference. But what if Jack was also right?

Aunt Zinnia adjusted the seam of her glove. "Now, I must be off to tell Mrs. Harwick of the news."

"Might I share the carriage?" Juliet asked. "I will call upon my modiste and see about enhancing Lilah's wardrobe with just the right flair."

"I asked for primrose plants, Mr. Boone." Jack scrutinized the plant wrapped in burlap. Instead of primroses, however, little shrubs composed of sticks and small leaves waited on the flower merchant's cart. He would have preferred something with flowers already on it. He would have preferred for Boone to have been punctual. And since he was making a list, he would have preferred not to have lain awake all night, thinking about Lilah.

Even now, the card in his pocket felt as if it were searing a hole through his waistcoat and shirt.

"Azaleas are hearty. Perfect for spring," Boone replied with a quick nod of his head as he worried the brim of his black felt hat beneath his hands. He cast a nervous glance up at Jack's horse. "Mr. Marlowe, I know you asked for primroses, but they never would have survived the replanting, with frost coming. I didn't want to disappoint you."

When the man took a step back and appeared to shiver to the soles of his worn boots, Jack realized he was glaring at him. And standing beside his fearsome horse, both man and beast likely portrayed a rather ominous outcome for the gardener. Therefore, Jack made an effort to relax his glower.

The truth was, his surly mood had little to do with the flowers. "But you're saying that this *azalea* will survive, and you're certain it will bloom?"

"These are the buds, here." Boone pointed a shaky hand to a cluster of green teardrop shapes. "More will come and soon, blossoms so thick you won't see the leaves or the ground beneath."

Since Jack knew next to nothing about gardening, he had to take the man at his word. He held out the coin. When Boone reached out, Jack gripped his hand. "Should the claim turn false, I'll expect compensation."

Boone gulped. "P-please, sir. I would like for you to accept a second shrub as a gift."

Jack accepted the gift but mostly because he didn't want to be bothered anymore. And he was bothered a great deal. After spending the evening across from a card table from Haggerty, any man would be. In an effort to keep him from going into the ballroom, Jack had continuously lost more and more money to him. The more Haggerty won, the more he drank, and the more he drank, the more he revealed about his true nature, until Jack was certain he wasn't going to allow Haggerty anywhere near Lilah.

A perfectly reasonable reaction, he mused. Especially considering how close Lilah's story resembled his own mother's. He didn't want history to repeat itself.

Boone left two plants at Jack's feet before scurrying up into his cart and driving away. Watching the wheels disappear out of sight reminded Jack of sending Haggerty away in a hack last night. Afterward, Jack had wanted to return to the ballroom to see Lilah once more, but he'd abandoned the notion the moment it had filled his head.

He still wasn't certain what had possessed him to hold her in the ballroom earlier in the evening. Even he knew the rules of society. For some reason, he hadn't been able to help himself. She'd turned her back on him, and then, suddenly, she'd stepped into his arms. Instinctively, his hand had settled against her. Holding her close had felt natural. The curve of her body fit perfectly against him, igniting his blood. He was not a man led by errant desires. His actions had purpose. Yet it had taken all of his control not to pull her deeper into the shadows and discover the secrets behind her scolding mouth. He wondered if she tasted bitter or sweet.

Those thoughts kept him distracted as he tied the burlap bundles to either side of his saddle. Otherwise, he would have been prepared for the sudden intrusion that followed.

"Have you begun a new enterprise, son?"

Son. At the sound of the unwelcome though familiar voice of his father, Jack stiffened. Bellum's hooves shifted on the street, the muscles of his flank twitching as he sensed the tension. Jack brushed his hand over his Destrier to calm him without turning around to face the carriage that had stopped beside him.

"I have not, *Dovermere*. I'm merely delivering a favor for a friend."

"Interesting," he said, stepping out of his carriage and onto the pavement as if he'd been invited. "Though I wonder which one of your friends cannot see to the task himself. Thayne is in good health, as is Wolford. Therefore it must be Vale…since he is out of town."

On a slow exhale, Jack resigned himself to this conversation and met Dovermere's gaze. The shock he'd felt over their resemblance had lessened over time. Dovermere dropped in on him once a week, and Jack had grown used to seeing an aged version of himself—hair a shade lighter and salted; fanned lines beside amber eyes; creases beside a mouth that smiled too much and had been known to ask an endless amount of questions about the most inane topics. And clearly, Dovermere was also keeping track of Jack's friends.

"You are correct. This is an errand for Vale. He asked if I would send flowers to his bride's dearest friend." And before his father got the wrong idea about Lilah and jumped to the same conclusion that Jack had, he continued. "Apparently, he believes that flowers will help her find a husband. While I do not understand his method, *I* am a man of my word."

Dovermere stroked his jaw, scrutinizing the burlap. "A young woman who receives flowers can claim a certain desirability and gain interest from potential suitors. Perhaps that is what Vale intended."

"Perhaps."

"If I may ask," Dovermere began, even though Jack knew he wasn't waiting for permission, "if you are to send flowers, then what do you have here?"

"A flowering shrub. The young woman in question expressed sadness for the first posies I gave her because cut flowers only survive a few days." He pointed in an impatient gesture. "Hence, the plants."

Dovermere's brows shot up. "You've already called upon this young woman?"

"Yes." And after last night, Jack was determined to help her.

"Hmm…more than once?" Dovermere studied him with an uncanny shrewdness in his gaze. An instant later, he nodded, seeming to have read Jack's expression. "By chance, did she attend Stapleton's soiree last night?"

Jack despised Dovermere's unnerving skill of detecting the answer. "I have asked you before not to make inquiries regarding my affairs."

"You leave me little choice," Dovermere said with an absent shrug. Then, as if he had suddenly gained all that he required from this impromptu visit, he stepped toward the waiting landau. "If you were to come to dinner or join me at the club, there would be no need for other tactics."

Incredulous, Jack fisted his hands, watching the man calmly close the carriage door. "You made your choice. You already have a family."

"I know," Dovermere said through the open window. "And you are part of it." His steady gaze gleamed with challenge as the driver spurred the horses.

Jack hated that look. And the reason was because he'd seen it in his own reflection and knew what it meant. Dovermere wasn't about to give up.

Chapter Seven

Shortly after her aunt and cousin left, Lilah stepped into the music room. Her harp waited near the corner, the polished wood frame gleaming like amber. Pale sunlight caressed the curve of the shoulder, neck, and crown.

Moving into the room, she stroked her fingertips over the strings in a whisper of sound, like a secret told to a dear friend. And this instrument had been her friend, bringing light to the darkest times of her life. She remembered escaping to the music room at home, closing the door, and plucking the strings in order to drown out the constant bellows from her father. Sometimes, it had worked.

She was thankful that Aunt Zinnia had talked Mother into letting Lilah bring the cherished instrument to town. Otherwise, it would have been sold by Winthrop, along with most of the finer possessions the family had once kept. Her cousin was greedy and was not above using whatever means he had to make his own life easier. Which, apparently, now included spreading rumors that Lilah and he were already betrothed.

Lilah quickly pulled her hand away from the harp, not wanting to taint her usual enjoyment with thoughts of Winthrop. Typically, playing the harp settled her nerves. Unfortunately, not today.

Feeling restless, she slipped out to the garden. She didn't even have a chance to draw in a soothing breath before she heard a strange noise coming from the back portion, just past the arbor. Strange but somewhat familiar. The sound was sharp and broken, like a shovel striking earth and gravel. This was odd because her aunt's gardener came once a week in the spring, and this was not his day.

"Monsieur Bouton?" she called but received no answer.

Curious, she walked the path toward the arbor, passing the bench, and suddenly she stopped.

Those broad shoulders, dressed only in shirtsleeves and a green waistcoat, were not Monsieur Bouton's. The lean hips, firm backside, and thickly muscled thighs weren't his either. After all, the gardener was nearly sixty years old, short, and rather thin. And he typically wore trousers, not well-tailored buckskin breeches and fine leather boots.

Jack. His name spilled through her mind in the same unbidden tremor that rushed beneath her skin. She did not like it, she told herself. And she refused to admit to having had a secret desire to see him again. The compulsion was as strange to her as her actions had been late last night, when she'd pressed a few primroses between sheets of velum.

"Mr. Marlowe, I hate to repeat myself each time we meet, but *what* are you doing here?" She'd intended to sound forceful and displeased, but the airy quality of her voice lacked much force. Those were rather flattering breeches, after all.

He turned slowly to face her, smirking, as if he was not the least bit surprised by their encounter. Surely, he couldn't have expected her to come outside to the garden.

"This was the place for our rendezvous, was it not?"

Bother. Only now she remembered the challenge he'd issued last evening.

"I am not *at home* to you. You did not leave your card. Therefore, I had no way of knowing that you would be here," she said, needing a clear understanding between them. "Aside from that, why are you using a shovel in my aunt's garden?"

It was only then that she looked down and noted a shrub in the ground near his boots. In fact, there were two of them, one on either side of the path.

"You said you did not like the quick death of cut flowers, so I brought you these," he explained with a wave of his free hand. "Azaleas to bloom all spring."

She'd never blushed so much in her life as she had these past three days. Her hands came up to cool her cheeks. Had he listened to everything she'd said, every scold, every admission? This was unexpected and unfamiliar. She was used to being forgotten. How could she concentrate on her endeavors to transform if Jack Marlowe continued to keep her flabbergasted?

"Do not thank me, Lilah. I forbid you," he said, his voice commanding even as amusement lit his eyes.

What an absurd thing to forbid. Lilah was torn between gritting her teeth and grinning. With effort, she managed the former. "Thank you, Mr. Marlowe. They will remind me of you, especially when our gardener piles horse manure around them."

He laughed outright. The hearty rumbling sound plucked a thousand strings inside her at once in a wondrous glissando.

She did her best to ignore the sensation. The resonant hum made her heart, lungs, and stomach quiver. It would cease soon enough, however. At least, she hoped it would. *What a terrible ordeal it would be to suffer this way all the time. Simply horrendous and not at all pleasant.*

While she was busy convincing herself, his laughter died down to a low chuckle as he walked toward the slender wooden door—that usually kept the garden private—and propped the shovel against the ivy-covered wall.

"Tell me," he said, walking back to retrieve his coat, "do you unleash your censure on all the men you encounter?"

"I've had no need until recently. Most gentlemen behave as they ought in my presence."

He shrugged into the mink-brown garment as if dressing in front of her were a matter of habit. The fit of his waistcoat outlined the musculature of his chest and leanness of his stomach. His wide-legged stance pulled the buckskin indecently taut, displaying every component of his thighs, as well as...*other* parts of him. Parts she did not allow herself to glance at more than once or twice.

Thankfully, he didn't appear to notice.

"Hmm...that is what I'd assumed," he said. "Which leads us to the crux of your problem."

"*Us?*" she scoffed, ignoring the warm flush that covered her entire body and the foolish flutter of her pulse. Ignoring the wealth of intimacy in that small word. *Us.* "I hardly think you are involved. Only your supreme arrogance has thrust you into matters that are no concern of yours."

Adjusting his cuff, he pointed his finger at her and nodded. "You need to do more of that. Whenever you scold me, you come alive. Your eyes sparkle with vehemence, and your lips plump with crimson disdain. It's surprisingly alluring."

Alluring? Lilah stared at him in confusion. She swallowed, her tongue suddenly thick. She wished he would stop surprising her with the things he said. "You cannot say things like that to me. I have no idea what to think of them. And I am absolutely not going to begin scolding the gentlemen of the *ton*."

"Why ever not? I'm certain they deserve it."

His smirk did terrible things to her. She squared her shoulders against it and gave her best impression of Aunt Zinnia. "Because I would be known as a shrew."

The instant she finished, she saw a gleam of amusement in his gaze. But before he could utter a syllable, she narrowed her eyes in warning. "And if you dare lift those tawny brows even one inch, I will take that shovel and bury *you* in the garden."

He scrubbed a hand over his jaw, concealing his mouth and likely a smirk. "That certainly does not sound shrewlike. Not at all. I'm already envious of your future husband."

At this monotone declaration, a small laugh bubbled up Lilah's throat. She couldn't help it. This entire episode was absurd. With all her talent for worry, she never could have conjured Jack Marlowe. A man like him was unpredictable. He turned her world topsy-turvy.

"I'm not suggesting that you turn into a harridan," he continued, tilting his head as if studying a *curiosity* in an exhibit. "I'm saying that I know the secret to guarantee that you find a husband."

Now she laughed in earnest. "Indeed! A man with no wife and little interest in finding one would be an expert?" She affected a gasp. "Or is that your own secret? Have you been caught in a young woman's web? Are the banns to be read?"

He grinned and moved toward her in his easy-limbed manner, all fluidity and strength combined, muscles flexing, stones crunching beneath each step. He stopped within arm's reach, elbows slightly bent, those large hands of his—not fisted but not relaxed—ready. Always ready. She had no doubt that he could catch her if she stumbled. Or he could haul her against him in an instant.

His gaze dipped to her mouth. He made her all too aware of her proximity to him, and she didn't know what she would do *if* he attempted to kiss her. Well...she knew what she *should* do and that was to let decorum govern her actions. However, that wasn't what she wanted to do. And just the idea of what it felt like to have his lips on hers sent a jolt of trepidation through her. Her laughter died, and she blinked up at him.

"No, don't retreat," he said, his command so low that it felt like a caress. "Laugh more. Scold more. Passion is the secret."

"P-passion?" The stuttered syllables made her lips tingle. Unbearably so. She lifted her fingertips, absently brushing the surface to banish the sensation. "Proper young women do not think of such things."

He tsked as if he did not believe her. "Surely you've thought of kissing and of what happens afterward."

Lilah didn't appreciate the glimmer of amusement in his gaze. She straightened her shoulders. "Men do not remember my name. When do you suppose that any of them have desired to kiss me?"

"But you've wanted to be kissed."

She swallowed and decided not to answer directly. "A young woman does not intend to be kissed unless she is married. Women who kiss indiscriminately are the ones who fall in love with rogues. I know this because my brother was one, and he left his share of broken hearts in his wake." And that was what had gotten him killed by an angry husband. She sighed, missing Jasper's wicked laugh and even the way he would warn her against falling in love with someone like him. "Jasper was a romantic, always looking for a new love," she continued, abandoning her scathing tone for quiet resolve. "Since he was abused so abominably by our father, I can easily forgive him. However, his lesson has taught me caution."

"That is why honesty is important from the beginning," Jack said, stepping toward her until they were toe-to-toe. His gaze turned soft, as if they shared this understanding, and when he spoke, his voice was low and intimate. "I indulge in pleasure for pleasure's sake alone. I offer no pretense of love, and the women I bed understand this."

"I am not going to be one of those women," she clarified, knowing that she should have been offended that he would mention such a thing. And she was, of course. She was not inordinately curious about what it would be like to... *indulge in pleasure for pleasure's sake alone.* Not at all.

"I'm not suggesting your ruination, Lilah." In the shadowy recesses of his mouth, his tongue flicked over the two syllables of her name as if he knew the flavor of them.

"Then what"—she wet her lips—"*are you suggesting?*"

"Merely that there must be things you are passionate about—hobbies, outings, certain topics of conversation.

Unless..." He grinned and raised his eyebrows. "Unless scolding me is the only pleasure in your life. If that is the case, I will gladly continue to pleasure you."

She ignored the blatantly seductive double entendre. Ignored the warmth that tunneled deep inside of her. Ignored the slow, heavy pulse that began beating in the same place. "I thought you abhorred society."

"Correct."

"Yet you continue to encounter me intentionally. Surely the favor you promised Vale has been paid. It could mean nothing to you that I find a husband. Tell me now if I am merely a source of amusement for you."

He did not answer her right away. Instead, he studied her, his brow furrowed. "My mother's life mirrored yours," he said quietly. So quietly, in fact, it was as if the admission wasn't meant to be spoken aloud. Proof of that lay within the silence that followed. Then, after a few breaths, he spoke again. "She was married off to a dissipated lord on a neighboring estate. By the time his debts and cruel character were discovered, it was too late. At the same time, she lost the only family she'd had. And while her husband's debts mounted, he abandoned her and his responsibilities, leaving her to fend for herself."

A chill stole over Lilah, and she wrapped her arms around herself to ward it off. This account did mirror her own circumstances somewhat, especially the dishonor and cruelty. For her father, honor of the family name and upholding appearances had been all that mattered. He'd ranted about it ceaselessly until the whole house had quaked.

"Whatever happened to that man?" she asked Jack.

"His estate and property were confiscated to pay his debts. Months later, they found him outside of a gaming hell. He was then tried for his crimes and hanged."

Lilah let out a breath. "That is good. At least your mother escaped him."

Strangely, her own mother had accepted whatever Father had decreed and had stood by his side during whatever reprimand or punishment he'd given. Having witnessed affection between other married people—Ivy's parents, for example—Lilah had once asked her mother why she never said anything about the way Father treated everyone. Her mother had told her that a woman should never expect happiness as a requirement of marriage, only security.

Lilah had never told anyone this, but she'd been relieved when her father had died. There was sadness as well. She had loved him as much as their relationship allowed. But more than that, she'd felt despair over never having been loved in return. And after a lifetime of enduring cruelty, she'd hoped that his death had brought an end to his tyranny.

Unfortunately, he'd continued it from beyond the grave.

Jack stared at her with a peculiar intensity. "I had not thought of her circumstances in such a way."

"It is good that she did not suffer his cruelty for years or even watch her children bear the brunt. For myself, I cannot imagine anything worse." She realized she'd revealed too much when shock and something akin to anger altered his expression. Before he could ask her about it, she continued. "And Dovermere was kind to her?"

A muscle twitched above his jaw. "I've heard nothing to the contrary. In fact, she claimed to have been happy...until the demands of Dovermere's family coffers led him to abandon her as well."

Lilah saw a vulnerability within him that she'd never noticed. He'd been abandoned too, and the scar of it was now as clear as the silver S near his temple. She imagined her own scars were visible to him as well.

"Mr. Marlowe, I now possess a better understanding of your interference in my affairs, and I am willing to answer the question you posed to me about my"—she cleared her throat, refusing to say the word *passion*—"hobbies and interests."

He inclined his head, the ferocity disappearing from his countenance as he seemingly accepted their shift of topic.

There was a palpable intimacy between them now, forged from something deeper than mere attraction and curiosity. And because he'd revealed so much about himself, she was willing to give his notion merit. After all, by this point, she would consider any option. "I enjoy playing the harp."

He considered her answer without any mockery but with what appeared to be interest instead. "What appeals to you about it?"

"The sound, I suppose. It's soothing, beautiful." She closed her eyes, picturing herself situated on her stool. "I like the scent of the cedar wood, the coolness of the frame when I press my cheek against it, the bite of the strings against my fingertips, and the way my entire body seems to become part of the music."

Her eyes sprang open. She hadn't meant to admit that last part. While she hadn't heard his step on the path, it felt as if he were standing closer now, his eyes never leaving hers. They were sure and confident, and in that moment, she felt comfortable and secure.

"Don't be embarrassed," he chided softly. "Continue just as you were. I could almost see that passion in your expression."

This time, she didn't close her eyes. It was easier to continue looking at him. "I like how, with the barest touch of my fingertips, music fills the room... fills me."

"*Mmm*... I would very much enjoy watching you play the harp." His pupils expanded slowly into the flecks of brown and gold in his irises. "Have you played for anyone else?"

"My instructor, of course. Friends. Family."

"Are you skilled?" he challenged.

It was improper to be boastful. Nevertheless, she grinned up at him. "I am *accomplished*."

"And there it is—*passion*," he said, reaching up with one large hand to cradle her face. He tilted her chin upward, this way and that, his focus solely on her mouth. "Think of your harp the next time you are speaking with a gentleman."

The tingling returned, unbearable in its urgency. His thumb swept over the flesh of her bottom lip, not subduing the sensation but amplifying it. He leaned in. She thought he would kiss her. In that instant, she knew she would not stop him. All her professions from a moment ago abandoned her. She *was* a woman who would kiss indiscriminately. At least with this man. Right now.

Then, suddenly, he drew back—*one step. Two. Three.* He stopped to pick up his hat and raked a hand through his hair before settling it atop his head. And he kept walking. Near the garden door, he touched two fingers to the brim. "Never let it be said I am a man without honor, Miss Appleton."

And as he disappeared, shovel in hand, she wished he would have called her *Lilah*.

CHAPTER EIGHT

That evening, Jack figured out exactly what was wrong with him. The reason that he couldn't stop entertaining erotic thoughts about Lilah was because he'd been too long without life's pleasures. After returning to London earlier this week, he hadn't been to Lady Hudson's gaming hell or her private rooms upstairs since that first night back. Obviously, he required another visit before he did something foolish...

Such as kissing Lilah in the garden in the middle of the afternoon. And he'd almost done it. Even now, part of him wished he had. Jack never should have touched her.

And why had he come up with that ludicrous idea of asking her about passion? Their conversation earlier had unlocked something inside of him—a door, of sorts, the one that separated his world from hers. The one he kept locked from all of the aristocracy and the stupid rules they followed. Now, there was that open passageway between them, and he needed to close it—fast.

Releasing the thought, he exhaled into his glass of scotch and settled into the corner of a velvet-upholstered sofa in the empty room.

Lady Hudson's was an upscale gaming hell with a limited membership. One had to have great wealth in order to become a member. Wolford was one. In fact, on the way back to the lounge, Jack had passed Wolford playing *vingt-et-un* in the main gaming salon.

The proprietress prided herself on her exclusivity. Adorned in jewels and elegant frocks, many assumed, at first, that she was a member of the peerage. Actually, she was a widow of a wealthy merchant, and her given name was, in fact, *Lady*. Having a sense of wit, she refused to allow her patrons to call her either *Widow* or *Missus* Hudson. She would permit only "Lady Hudson," "my lady," or nothing at all.

Coming up behind Jack, Lady draped her arms and ample bosom over his shoulders and whispered in his ear. "Back so soon, Marlowe?" Her seductive purr was the sound men dreamed of as much as they did the skillful play of her fingertips, which were now roaming down his chest, flicking over his waistcoat buttons in invitation. "Did my new girl not satisfy you, or do you desire a woman of more experience? I bet I could show even you a thing or two."

He allowed her to continue, hoping that the desire plaguing him would rise up, ready to be sated. "Your girl was lovely and skilled, as you ensure that all of your girls are."

"And yet, in all the years of your membership, you have never returned twice in one week. As I recall, you've mentioned a reluctance to wet your wick too often in the same pot," she said with a saucy laugh, molding her hands over his chest beneath his now-open waistcoat.

"True. Though perhaps not as poetically as you've just put it." Jack never had a desire to keep a mistress, for obvious reasons. And tonight, he did not want an opera girl or even a comely widow. He only desired release.

When Lady's hands drifted down his abdomen toward the waist of his trousers, he kept his eyes steady on her progress. He wanted this, he told himself. He wanted her hands and mouth all over him. He wanted to be feted and worshiped. He wanted...

Bollocks. His lust was not stirred. Not in the least. The only hands he wanted upon him were those that never would be.

What a fool he was. With a gentle touch, he stopped Lady's progress. "Forgive me. You are all that is desirable, but I find that I am ill-tempered this evening."

"Hmm...a man who is truly ill-tempered seldom admits it. His grousing and grumbling usually make it clear. You, on the other hand, seem...preoccupied."

"Quite right," he admitted. "My thoughts have been carelessly committed elsewhere." Even now, he was thinking of his encounter with Lilah in the garden. The pain he'd witnessed in her gaze at the mention of cruelty had caused a surge of protectiveness to rise up within him. He'd had the sudden urge to dispatch anyone who'd ever brought her pain, even her own family. Then, an idiotic wave of disappointment hit him as well, for having presented her with plants that weren't in bloom. He'd wanted to give her flowers that would bloom all year.

"A woman?"

He shrugged. "A circumstance remedied soon enough."

"I shall wish it for my own sake, then," she said with a sigh. "Tonight, my bed will be as cold as the frost that gathers on my window."

Rising to his feet, he bowed and pressed a kiss to her hand. "Any man would be a fool if he did not warm you, as I am proving now. Good night, dear Lady."

Yet at the mention of frost, he thought again of the plants. Hardy or not, in this cold they likely wouldn't survive the night.

Staying in this evening had left Lilah far too much time with her thoughts. She'd come up with plenty of outlandish worries, which should have soothed her but instead seemed small when comparing them to her true fears.

She could fail—catastrophically. Not just herself but Aunt Zinnia, Juliet, and Mother. The stakes seemed higher, now that people were noticing her. Even if those people were debutantes like her. Calling hours today had jarred her and made this endeavor all too real.

In an attempt to relieve some of her anxiety, she'd taken a hot bath with a special selection of oils that Juliet had offered her. The rose and lavender relaxed her. The vanilla from the orchid pod was luxuriant. And the sandalwood made her think of Jack.

She'd submerged herself in the fragrance until she was out of breath, soaking until her fingertips and toes wrinkled. Then, with the help of Nellie, she'd washed her hair.

Her hair was still damp now as she paced her room in her night rail. She'd sent Nellie to bed and knew that Aunt Zinnia and Juliet had turned in as well. Beneath her feet, the floor was cold—colder than it had been for the past week or more. She'd become a well-practiced pacer in the past few days and could detect the subtle differences. Going to her wardrobe, she withdrew a pair of thick stockings and sat at her window seat to pull them on. It was only when she felt the draft through the window that her suspicions about the temperature were confirmed.

Her thoughts went directly to the garden and the new plants. The plants Jack had given to her. On such a night, they would never survive. Oddly enough, she'd grown attached to those flowers in a matter of hours, taking out several pitchers of water and admiring the number of buds she saw. While the garden was Aunt Zinnia's, those two small plants were Lilah's—and given to her by a man who both puzzled and intrigued her. She couldn't let the cold damage them.

Making a quick decision, she donned a wrapper and grabbed a lamp as she stepped out into the hall. Before she headed down the stairs, she pulled two folded bed sheets from the linen cupboard.

The house was dark and quiet as she padded down the hall toward the door that led to the garden. Through the glass, she could see there was enough moonlight to aid her quick errand, and so she left her candle behind. Lifting the latch, she was thankful that the hinges were well oiled and didn't alert the cook, who slept in a room not far from the kitchen, just around the corner.

A shock of cold air hit her, biting right through her wrapper and night rail and tightening her flesh. Wanting to stop the sharp sensation of the cotton against her taut nipples, Lilah clutched the bed sheets to her breasts and rushed down the garden path. She kept her steps light and quick, the ground frozen beneath her stockinged feet. And it wasn't until she breached the arbor that she, once again, stopped cold.

At the sight of Jack Marlowe piling hay around the plants, a sense of hilarity broke over her. She was forever encountering him when she least expected it. A strangled laugh left her. And when the sound of it caused him to start, jerking his head in her direction, she giggled.

"Why are you here?" he asked, mirroring the same question she'd asked several times since they'd first met.

The coincidence only increased her giggles. Who knew she was so easily amused? But she felt unaccountably giddy in this moment and inordinately happy to see him.

Jack stood erect, his greatcoat parting to reveal the whiteness of his shirt and the absence of a cravat. The sliver of moonlight offered a glimpse of exposed flesh at his throat, tapering down to the V of his open collar.

Abruptly, her giggles caught in her throat. "I came out to cover the plants." She could barely get the words out. Worse, she couldn't peel her gaze away from his bared throat, where the shadow beneath his Adam's apple formed an enticing hollow. She'd never seen a man's neck, except for her father's and brother's. Until this moment, she didn't realize how interesting they were. The sight made her want to walk the few steps between them and study his more closely.

"You're in your night rail," he said with a low growl that hummed inside of her.

A terrible sensation, she reminded herself. *Not at all pleasant.*

"And my wrapper," she corrected, as if the fact made all the difference between being decently or scantily dressed. Lifting her gaze to his, she realized he wasn't looking at her face. Not directly. She must look like...like she was prepared for bed. Which, of course, she was. But seeing his gaze take in every ruffle and ribbon as if he could see through them to her skin suddenly turned the notion into something less commonplace. "There are linens in my arms as well."

At that, his gaze lifted, as did one corner of his mouth. "Yes, of course, the linens. Otherwise, I might have assumed you'd rushed out to greet me for a tryst."

It was a chilly night. She could see her breath. So then why did she feel warm all over? "I am not a romantic moongazer, keeping watch over the garden. As you see, there is no balcony outside my window," she said with an absent gesture toward her window.

At the same time, she wondered what she'd have done if she had seen him. Until a few days ago, she knew she would have done the sensible thing. Now, she wasn't certain at all. Especially because she was still standing here with him and had no desire to return to her chamber.

He offered the house a passing glance. "The upstairs is dark, aside from your bedchamber. Why are you not fast asleep?"

She wasn't going to admit to being anxious about her transformation endeavors. Or confess to having a talent for worry. And she certainly wasn't going to tell him that thoughts of him settled the worrying part of her mind. So instead, she said, "I was merely allowing my hair to dry after my bath."

He groaned, shoving a hand through his hair as his gaze raked down her body again. "You're standing out here in your stockinged feet. You must be cold. You should return to the warmth of your chamber."

He was right. She should return. But she didn't want to. Not yet. "I still need to cover the plants."

"Very well. Then we will be done with this before irreversible damage can be done."

"Do you think it is too late for them?"

He stepped close to her. "I was talking about you, Lilah. Your reputation—your innocence—is not safe with me. Not tonight."

He reached up, his hand curling over the first sheet. Watching his long fingers slip between the folded layers caused a tide of warmth to rise up inside of her, and she wasn't even certain why.

"Why not tonight? Does the moonlight affect you strangely?" She tried to make a jest of it, but her words came out breathy.

As he whipped open the sheet and tucked it over the first plant, he shook his head. "Of late, neither moonlight, daylight, cloudy skies, rain, nor fog can make my thoughts predictable. The only thing they have in common is you. I fear my behavior will soon follow their path."

She frowned, concerned when he made no sense. He'd been thinking of her? No. Surely not. "Are you...unwell?" She moved closer, tempted to lift her hand to his forehead.

He released a hollow laugh and shook his head. "I should not be here. I should have stayed with a woman who could have helped to tame this alien need."

Stayed with a... He'd been with another woman tonight? Suddenly, every compulsion she had to feel his brow turned into something far less tender.

"Instead, I am here," he continued, prowling toward her again. "And you are standing in a bit of nothing, your dark hair in waves around your shoulders, your face lit up with moonlight, your eyes on my body, and your lips turning plump and crimson, as you are—no doubt—ready to scold me about being in the company of another woman. *Damn.* Even your jealousy is arousing."

She straightened her shoulders, clutching the last sheet like a shield and wishing she had a sword to match it. "I am not jealous. Not at all. Why should I be?"

He reached up for this sheet, his hand curling over the part that was directly between her breasts. Because his hands were so large, even grabbing the center of the sheet caused his knuckles to brush the inner swells. The flesh surrounding them drew tighter in response.

"Why, indeed. And why am I not half as tempted by another woman's charms as I am by the mere thought of you?" As he withdrew the sheet, the backs of his fingers grazed her nipple accidentally. Surely, it had to have been an accident.

The shock of it tunneled through her. She gasped but did not flinch or retreat. Instead, she lifted her gaze to find him looking back at her with dark, feral intensity.

Something inside of her tilted, drawing taut, warm, and liquid at once. A low, foreign mewl left her throat. She found herself nodding, even when he hadn't asked a question. And in answer, he dropped the sheet to the ground, snaked his arms around her, and hauled her against him.

He captured her mouth, his kiss hard and unapologetic. Lilah met him with the same force. Her fingers dove into his thick mane. His ears were cold beneath her palms, but his scalp was burning, inviting her closer.

She practically crawled up his body, wanting to be nearer to his mouth. Her head slanted instinctively, her nose pressed alongside his. She could hardly breathe. Opening her mouth, she inhaled at the same time he exhaled, and in that instant, she could taste him on her tongue. A sweetness of liquor, an enthralling heat combined with an unnamed spice, created an elixir that filled her lungs, flooded her veins, and incited her curiosity. What if she pressed her open mouth to his? She didn't know why she wanted to do so, but she needed the answer.

She didn't waste any more time with breathing. After all, time was not her ally. Hadn't she heard that enough? This moment would be over too soon, and she needed to make the most of it. And *oh…what a sensation.* Open-mouthed, their lips pressed together, and then together, their mouths closed, their lips tangling one over the other, nibbling each other like candied fruits, again and again, gorging themselves.

"I should not kiss you," he said on a growl as he kissed her again. His tongue slipped between her lips, gliding over the sensitive inner flesh, tracing the ridge of her teeth, brushing against her tongue.

She broke away on a gasp, unsure, panting for breath, wondering if he'd meant to do that, wondering if she was supposed to allow such an intimacy. "You are teaching me…about passion. Therefore…a kiss is completely acceptable."

"Mmm…irrefutable logic," he said, nuzzling the corner of her mouth. "Now give me your tongue, Lilah. I want to claim it."

Any hesitation she might have had evaporated in the steam they exhaled as their open mouths fused once more. She gave him her tongue—an offering more than answer to his command. Although at the moment, she would have given him anything he asked. Never in her life had she felt this secure. Nothing bad could happen while here in the shelter of his arms. The solid strength of Jack's body, his arms tight around her, ensured it. She was so certain of this that she curled her legs around his waist, her night rail migrating upward.

He groaned—a delicious vibration against her tongue and lips. Apparently, her new position forced him to alter his hold because his hands slipped from her waist to the swells of her bottom. Even through the fabric, his hands were hot. He squeezed her flesh, his fingertips splayed, skimming the sensitive underside. "You're making me forget my code of honor."

Dropping her hands to his shoulders, she wriggled closer, seeking the hottest parts of him while nipping at his lips. "Code?"

"I am honor bound not to bed a virgin," he said, even as his fingers kneaded her flesh and pulled her closer, sliding her against a rather hard, hot, and lengthy part of him.

Lilah blushed. She might be inexperienced, but she wasn't a simpleton and understood what he was saying. Yet her mother had informed her—in a vague, general sense—that a husband and wife would *lie down together*, and it was the wife's duty to bear it as best she could. "Surely that is nothing to worry over now. Not while we are standing in the garden."

"*I* am standing. You, however, are perfectly situated to make it possible."

I am? She wondered how that could be true...

He growled, his dark pupils expanding as he shook his head. "And you must stop staring at me with such blatant curiosity, or I will ask you to reach between us in order to show you."

"It's hardly my fault. You're the one who involved my imagination," she scoffed but only half-heartedly.

His gaze dipped to her mouth. "If you scold me once more, I will not be able to control my actions. I will rob you of your innocence here, in this very garden, and then carry you up to your chamber, bolt the door, and continue until I've satisfied every curiosity you could ever conjure."

She wondered if he realized that he was terrible at issuing threats. And for that she was thankful, for she'd overheard too many in her life. "Then kiss me again, and I won't have cause to scold you."

He did kiss her but briefly and far too chastely. "I cannot do that either. Your sinful mouth has the same effect on me, no matter what it is doing." And this time, it was clear he meant it.

Disappointed, she uncurled her legs from around him. Gradually, he lowered her so that her feet could touch the ground, but the journey—her body sliding against the length of his—was pure, wondrous torture.

Lilah kept her hands on his shoulders, unwilling to release him. "Are you going to return to that woman?"

"I should. You and I would be better off if my desire was slaked. Then I would not be—even now—contemplating all the things I could do to you. Things that would leave your innocence intact but only by the strictest definition," he said, making her blush again. His hands lingered at her waist, as if he was equally as reluctant to let her go. "However, it would be unfair to her if I could think only of you."

"I agree." She nodded, earning a low chuckle from him. "It would not be fair to any of us."

"Including your future husband," he reminded. This time, he was able to set her apart from him, and she instantly shivered from cold. He shrugged out of his greatcoat and settled the heavy garment over her shoulders. It was still warm, and his scent rose up to fill her nostrils, filling her with a sense of comfort. "Come. I'll walk you to your door."

They walked the stone path in silence, the weight of honor and expectation between them. Lilah was the first to speak.

"I do not think that I will sleep at all tonight," she said, facing him.

The muted glow from the candle just beyond the door glass caught the heat in his gaze. Lifting a hand, he brushed her cheek softly with his fingertips.

"Nor I." Then, slipping that hand to the back of her neck, he lifted her hair free, letting it fan out over her shoulders. "I like the look of you, wearing my coat over your nightclothes."

She grinned and offered a small curtsy. "I shall tell that to Juliet's modiste when she arrives tomorrow morning before calling hours." She hesitated. "Speaking of which, do you think perhaps…"

She let her question trail off, hoping that he would issue a command for her to be *at home* for him. And she would let him know that she would consider receiving him, all the while hiding her eagerness.

"I have business matters that I have been neglecting since my return to town," he said instead, his brow lined with regret. "I never imagined that the aristocratic practice of *calling hours* could be something I would find so distracting and so tempting. And by the by, what you referred to as *tomorrow morning* is actually only a few hours from now."

Lilah sighed. "Juliet will likely murder me if my eyes are shadowed with bruises before the Corbett Ball in the evening."

"You will look lovely, of that I am certain," he said, stepping near enough to gently grasp the lapels of his coat.

Feeling wistful but not wanting to let on, she smiled up at him. "Knowing that you will not attend in order to confirm your claim, I will tell you in advance that I will be at my loveliest. It will be a pity that you will miss such an awe-inspiring sight."

Without warning, he tugged her close and kissed her once more, making her forget what she was saying.

Before removing the warmth of his coat from her shoulders, he whispered, "Don't dream of me, Lilah. I forbid you."

She caught sight of his smirk just before he turned away and strode down the path. "I will not, Mr. Marlowe. After all, it would be unfair to all the *other* gentlemen I have parading around in my dreams already."

The sound of his knowing laugh warmed her through. *What an arrogant man.*

CHAPTER NINE

" 'And as for the newest name to grace our humble pages, we are all wondering which party the mysterious Miss A— attended last evening,' " Juliet read, beaming over the edge of the morning's *Standard*. "You see? Just as I said, your name is on everyone's lips."

Lilah bit back a yawn, hoping that her efforts resembled a smile instead. She stood in her bedchamber upon a crate, her arms lifted and straining at her sides, as the modiste set about pinning her gown. "*Miss A* could be Miss Ashbury, Miss Amherst, or even Miss Ainsworth. I'm not so quick to suspect that my forgettable-ness has altered from one evening."

"Gossip travels swiftly, my dear," Aunt Zinnia said from a chair near the hearth, a cup of tea waiting on the rosewood table beside her. "Be thankful it is in your favor."

"Indeed," Juliet added, that one word holding the weight of experience, both favorable and censorious. "If horses fed upon gossip instead of hay, then we could all travel to the Continent and back before luncheon."

"Since we are on the topic, I wonder what Lord Thayne's reaction was to the column in the *Standard*." Aunt Zinnia offered a pointed glance in Juliet's direction.

Juliet smiled sweetly. "Choking on a bit of egg in the breakfast room, I hope."

"Marjorie and I were not pleased at the bargain you struck. And to involve Lilah?" She pursed her lips an instant before she exhaled her displeasure. "She already has quite enough to worry over."

Strangely enough, Lilah hadn't worried at all this morning. Not even once. Likely it was because she was far too exhausted. Then again, her mind had been so agreeably engaged with memories from last night that she may not have had time to worry. "Actually, Aunt, I volunteered. Thayne was antagonizing her so much that I had to do something."

"Well, you certainly have no lack of bravery, much to your credit."

"And I have complete faith in Lilah," Juliet interjected and then turned to the modiste gesturing to the pins in Lilah's bodice. "Claire, perhaps we should maintain a little more mystery. We don't want our efforts to be obvious—just a few hints here and there."

Thank goodness! If Lilah were to lift her arm during a quadrille, she would likely spill out. Then there would be no mystery, and gossip would soon turn ill favored. Of course, that was only if she were asked to dance. According to the letter she'd received from her mother this morning, it was next to impossible.

"Be sure to thank my sister for all she's done. And should you attend any balls, be sure to stand beside a girl with a bad complexion and poor posture. That should improve your prospects of finding a gentleman who is willing to dance with you."

Mother hadn't meant to be awful. She simply spoke with her own brand of honesty, believing that her opinion and desire for perfection was universal. Yet even having come to this understanding over the years, Lilah still felt a twinge of sadness.

Juliet surveyed the reinvented gown, tapping her fingertip against her mouth. "Now you need a signature, a statement, something that is unmistakably you, my dear Cousin. And I think I have the perfect thing."

Stepping over to the vanity, Juliet lifted up a small wooden box and carried it back. When she opened the latch, Lilah gasped. Dozens of pearls of all shades and sizes filled the cavity. Each one glowed, transforming the gray morning light into satiny spheres.

Then, when her cousin pinched one in between her thumb and forefinger and raised it to her gown, Lilah suddenly understood the reason. "You cannot mean to use—no, I won't allow you to waste such a beautiful treasure."

"And what use have I for them? As you know, Lord Granworth left me very wealthy indeed," Juliet said matter-of-factly. "These pearls make me think only of you. So why shouldn't they be yours?"

Lilah wasn't sure what to say. She still wasn't used to her own reflection in the mirror. But at least she knew it was still her. "I don't know. It just seems as if I'm misleading everyone, pretending that I have pearls of my own."

"*You* are the pearl. Remember that."

"Have you seen it, Marlowe?" Thayne barged into Jack's study and slapped down a copy of a society newspaper. "Lady Granworth is a bold one, indeed. She must have had this entire charade planned even before our wager."

Jack brushed the paper aside. Beneath it, the ink smeared on the letter he'd been writing to his groundkeeper in Huntsford on the topic of the proper care for azaleas. "I've no desire to read about frippery and nonsense. As you see, I'm quite busy. Or perhaps you don't know what an occupation looks like. I can give you an example. There are some men, you see, who sit at desks, much like this, quill in hand, ledgers open, a stack of letters to be read and answered..."

"And it's all there, the curiosity about a certain *Miss A*," Thayne continued as if he hadn't heard Jack speak. "One can only assume that '*Miss A*' is Juliet's cousin, Miss...Miss..."

"Appleton?" At this, Jack took the paper by the folded edge and scanned the page.

One mention of Lilah, and curiosity got the better of Jack. Then again, it wasn't as if he'd spent any time *not* thinking about her. Especially not after last night. He'd been so close to losing complete control that it frightened him. Her kiss, the soft, hungry sounds she'd made, and the way she'd surrendered kindled a primitive chant within him. *Mine...mine...mine...* He'd been tempted to throw her over his shoulder and carry her out into the night with him.

That was all his mind had been able to think of since then as well. He couldn't sleep anymore. He had no appetite. His work was suffering. He had an unopened stack of letters from various men who farmed his many landholdings. He spent little time paying attention to negotiations in his investment endeavors. Earlier today, he'd handed over ten pounds to a wine merchant for a case of rotgut. And worse, he looked at the card in his pocket at least once every hour. He was turning into a buffoon.

"Yes, that's it—Miss Appleton," Thayne said, with a level of bitterness in his tone that made the hackles on the back of Jack's neck rise. "The ingénue who will doubtless make me feel guilty for keeping my house and forcing Juliet out of town."

Jack dropped the paper and stood, pressing his knuckles to the desk. "What makes you think that she won't succeed? If there is already a measure of curiosity, then Miss Appleton may be on the path to becoming an *Original*."

As far as he was concerned, she already was. It was an odd notion to him that the *haute ton* considered themselves experts on who was the most original. After all, the lot of them behaved in the *same* manner and followed the *same* rules.

Apparently, Thayne was too busy pacing in front of the desk to notice the note of warning in Jack's tone. "She will not succeed because this is not the year for subtlety. Last year's *Original* was all smiles and politeness. The *ton* quickly grew bored of her by the time her betrothal was announced. This year"—he pointed a finger to the ceiling—"is the year for audacity. The year for a man. Wolford is bold enough to cut a swath through the *ton* and leave them all gaping behind them."

At the mention of the betrothal of last year's *Original*, Jack automatically placed a protective hand over the card in his pocket. When he realized what he'd done, he felt the flesh around his eyes tighten and his brow furrow.

He should be glad, for Lilah's sake. The marriage she needed was within her grasp. Yet he couldn't help but wonder if there was a better solution. She shouldn't have to marry to satisfy her father's will. She should marry because it was her desire to do so.

Wasn't Jack always railing against the *haute ton*'s inane rules? Then why was he helping her follow them? Instead, he should be finding another solution.

Yes! He sat down again, taking up a fresh page and jotting a note to his solicitor. He would have Mr. Quince conjure a way to study the will and see what could be done.

"Tonight is the Corbett Ball. According to my mother, every notable will be in attendance. Therefore, if Wolford is to have a shot at becoming the *Original*, he must attend as well. The problem is, I've asked him, but he absolutely refuses. He claims to have been invited to view a private collection of antiquities at Ruthersfield's, along with Dovermere and a handful of other collectors."

Again, Thayne managed to pique Jack's interest. Dovermere was going to be absent from the Corbett Ball? Hmm...Jack had received an invitation to Corbett's last week. He wondered if he could still find it.

"Perhaps there might be a way to entice Wolford. You could always forbid him to go." After all, Vale had used that tactic on Jack on Christmas Eve, when he'd handed him the card with Lilah's name on it.

"No, Marlowe, I absolutely forbid you to be intrigued."

Suddenly, Jack realized that he'd been using the same tactic on Lilah. He grinned and then wondered if it would yield a similar result.

Chapter Ten

Standing between two pilasters and slightly behind a potted palm, Lilah opened her dance card and smiled. Four names in various scrawls stared back at her. Four! Among those was Lord Ellery's, and what's more, he'd remembered her name. In fact, each gentleman had remembered. She could scarcely believe it.

A little overwhelmed, she took a breath. Closing the card, she tucked it inside her elbow-length glove. Earlier, she'd worried that Juliet had planned to cover her with pearls. Yet that hadn't been the case at all.

This evening, Lilah's hair was pinned in place with a pearl comb, her face powdered with pearl dust, and a single pearl sewn into the center of her bodice, anchored by delicate silver threading. Since her gown was ivory satin, the pearl was hardly noticeable. However, Juliet said that true beauty was never obvious. Which was an odd thing to hear from the most beautiful woman Lilah had ever seen. Nevertheless, the end result left Lilah somewhat relieved. She didn't have to worry about feeling like a fraud. At least, not too much of one.

"I do not see what all this fuss is about." Lilah heard the words from a young woman passing by. When she saw that it was Miss Leeds—talking to Miss Ashbury, no less—she stilled and hoped they would not see her. "There is nothing at all uncommon about her."

Lilah cringed. The words struck her as similar to the worried thoughts inside her own mind. She only hoped that Miss Leeds wasn't speaking about her. A part of her held onto doubt that this plan would work. Part believed she wasn't pretty. Of course, the note she'd received from Mother today hadn't helped either. This transformation was still new and fragile. She was still learning.

She felt as if she were held together only by a fine silver web. One misstep, and she might begin to unravel.

"And there is nothing remarkable in her wardrobe either," Miss Ashbury remarked. "Of course, how can you improve such a plump figure?"

"My father told me that they are hoping to lure her cousin to marry her. Can you imagine?" Miss Leeds giggled. "She's so undesirable that even Lord Haggerty would have to be forced."

Lilah swallowed down a rise of bile up the back of her throat. They were speaking of her. And they knew about her father's will. What they'd heard was not accurate—but it was close enough to ruin her chances. It was all too much. Her brief moment of euphoria sputtered out like a taper at the end of a night.

"Oh, Miss Appleton," Miss Ashbury began, lifting her hand to her mouth and affecting a look of innocence. "We didn't see you there."

"Dear, you really should try to do something to draw attention to yourself," Miss Leeds added with a smile.

Lilah expected to feel small and worthless as one of her worries came to fruition. Instead, she was shocked by the amount of anger she felt. Not on her own behalf but for Juliet, who'd sacrificed her time and treasures for Lilah's benefit. And perhaps there was a small amount of anger for herself because...well...how dare they try to belittle and demean her. Hadn't she suffered enough of that at home?

Abandoning the principle of *grace in the face of adversity*, she opened her mouth to offer a scathing response in return. Then, suddenly, another young woman came along and bumped into Miss Leeds, albeit gracefully, sort of like a carefully choreographed push.

"Oh, do forgive me. I didn't see you there," said the young woman, who Lilah only now recognized as Lady Piper Laurent, the Earl of Dovermere's eldest daughter. She and Lady Piper had met at the Duke of Vale's Christmas party. What Lilah had not known at the time was how similar her coloring was to Jack's. Like her half-brother, her hair was the shade of winter wheat, and her speckled brown eyes gleamed with challenge.

"*How dare*—" Miss Leeds began in outrage before she turned to see who had bumped into her. Then, abruptly, the simpering began. "Oh! Think nothing of it, Lady Piper. We had merely paused for a moment. How fortunate for us that you happened along to join—"

"How clever you are, Miss Leeds," Lady Piper said, cutting her off, "to blend into the walls so well."

Miss Leeds's lips parted as she glanced down at her gown and then to the ivory pilasters. Before she could comment,

Lady Piper continued. "And Miss Ashbury, how sweet you look this evening. I believe my youngest sister has a gown just like that for one of her dolls."

Lady Piper grinned rather mischievously at Miss Leeds and Miss Ashbury and then slid a look to Lilah. It became instantly apparent that Lady Piper had heard the exchange. A giggle escaped Lilah as she realized what was happening. Jack's sister was quite clever and sly in her wit.

Miss Leeds and Miss Ashbury squinted their eyes in unison.

"What a pleasure it was to see you both again," Lady Piper said to the pair, essentially dismissing them from her presence.

As it appeared many guests were beginning to leave the great hall and traverse the golden-lit gallery toward the ballroom, neither Miss Leeds nor Miss Ashbury offered a comment. Instead, they turned on their heels and walked off in a huff. Battle lines had been drawn.

"I cannot thank you enough, Lady Piper," Lilah said. "I was quite at a loss for words. At least, any proper words."

"Please, you must call me Piper." With an easy smile, she splayed her gloved fingers beneath her throat. "As the eldest girl of eight, I'm hardly ever at a loss for words. And most likely to my younger siblings' regrets. Besides, this is my first official ball, and I want it to be fun, without any stuffy formality or odious persons." She slid a perturbed glance to the retreating pair. "Father has been restricting my exposure to society through dinner parties alone. Though I believe the truth of the matter is that he finds balls rather dull and chooses only the invitations that appeal to him."

Lilah seconded the need for informality between them. "And I have the opposite problem. Last year my aunt typically accepted more than one invitation per night. The memory of that entire Season is now a blur of turbans and feathers."

"I hope to have such a memory," she said with a laugh. Then, as her father neared their party by the potted palm, she raised her voice. "So far, all I've seen are a bunch of old men sitting around their drawing rooms, speaking of antiquities. Ghastly dull."

The Earl of Dovermere cleared his throat, and Piper's gleam of mischief returned once more. "Sorry, Father, I meant to say *elderly* gentlemen instead of *old*. Forgive me?" She squeezed his forearm and rose up on her toes to peck him on the cheek.

"Many of those gentlemen are younger than I am," Dovermere said, his tone eerily recognizable, though with less of an edge than that of his son's.

"Well, that makes *all* the difference." Piper turned her head to make a comical face before addressing her father once more. "I should amend my declaration by describing the lot of you as *stately*."

"Hmm..."

"*Distinguished?*"

"Better," the earl said with a nod. "Now, behave yourself and introduce your friend, or I shall demand reimbursement from your decorum instructor."

"Do forgive my father, Miss Appleton. I have heard that a man's memory starts to fail him when he reaches a certain age," she said in a stage whisper, cupping her hand next to her mouth. Then to her father, she added, "This is Lilah Appleton. We met her at Vale's Christmas party."

"Miss Appleton, a pleasure." He inclined his head. "I recall our introduction perfectly now. Lady Cosgrove is your aunt, and Lady Granworth is your cousin." Then he lifted his eyebrows in a familiarly challenging way to Piper, earning a small laugh.

"It is a pleasure to meet you again, Lord Dovermere." Lilah dipped into a curtsy.

When she rose, however, she caught sight of an unmistakable pair of broad shoulders and blond head at the opposite end of the room. Her breath caught.

Jack Marlowe was striding through the massive doors of the hall. He looked dashing in his black evening attire and snowy cravat, his hair brushed back from his forehead to reveal those chiseled features. Her lips tingled at the memory of his mouth on hers. Then, when his gaze met hers and he grinned, a warm ache filled her, making her long for another stolen moment in the garden…or anywhere. She just wanted to be in his arms again.

It wasn't until Lilah heard Piper speaking to her father about a dinner party and adding Lilah to the guest list that she realized calamity was about to ensue.

From their position near the fronds of the potted palm trees, it was likely that Jack couldn't see those with whom she stood. Even if she were determined to risk rudeness, there wouldn't be time for her to abandon her party in order to intercept Jack before it was too late.

To him, she offered a discreet shake of her head in warning. But with his long strides, he was already to her.

"Miss Appleton," he began, in his typical fashion of focusing solely on her without paying attention to those around her. "You are indeed looking lovely this evening, as promised."

It was up to her to warn him, but when she saw the heat in his gaze, every sensible thought vanished. She blushed and tried to think of a bland response. Tried to pretend that she had no idea what it felt like to have his tongue in her mouth and that she wasn't thinking about that right this moment. "Mr. Marlowe, you flatter me. At the moment, however—"

"Jack!" Piper said with a burst of enthusiasm, stepping into view. She reached out and gave a brief squeeze to his forearm, much the same way she had with her father. "How wonderful that you are here! The last time Father and I dropped in on you, you declared never to attend a societal function, but now, here you are."

Jack stiffened, his easy manner turning to granite. "Piper." He inclined his head. "Dovermere."

"How fortunate that our earlier engagement ended, and we were able to attend this party," Dovermere began, clearly having noticed Jack's reaction. "And what a coincidence that you are acquainted with Miss Appleton. Piper was just testing my memory. Now, I seem to recall that Miss Appleton is particular friend of Vale's new bride. Is that correct, Miss Appleton?"

"I am, my lord," Lilah affirmed, not understanding the knowing, smug grin Dovermere passed to Jack, nor the glower Jack passed back to his father. Well, perhaps she understood the glower. Nevertheless, all at once the entire hall had gone silent. Even those in the gallery paused to cast discreet glances over their shoulders.

"Miss Appleton, did you know that Jack and Vale met at Eton and that the two of them competed for highest marks?" The pride in Dovermere's voice and in his expression was unmistakable.

Even so, she swallowed, nervous that the remark was made in such a nonchalant fashion. It was almost as if Dovermere suspected that she and Jack were more than casually acquainted. Then again, her rush of nerves could simply be her worrying self catching up with her.

"I did not, my lord, though it is easy to imagine." It was only when Dovermere's gaze sharpened that she realized what she'd said. To compliment a gentleman in the presence of his family was to indicate interest or a reciprocation thereof. "That is to say…he *appears* to be a competent individual, though I have no way of knowing."

Oh, but those words weren't any better. Now, because of their association, it sounded as if she meant to slight Jack, effectively labeling him a simpleton.

Jack shifted beside her, a nearly imperceptible movement of his shoe on the polished floor, but she guessed he wasn't pleased. She could sense the tension rolling off him. Yet when she chanced a sideways glance, his expression surprised her. He was smirking at her. It was a small lift of one corner of his incredibly talented mouth, but it was still a smirk all the same. Knowing him, he was enjoying watching her discomfort.

"Appearances are often misleading, Miss Appleton," Jack said, his gaze dipping to her lips for one hot second. How dare he make her blush again and leave her no way to scold him for it!

"A circumstance only remedied upon further acquaintance," the earl interjected. "Surely you would consider that an accurate statement, Jack?"

In turn, Jack's nod was more of wariness than agreement. Even Lilah felt a sense of apprehension. Piper, however, nodded vigorously, as if she knew exactly what was about to be said.

"Good. Then it is settled. You will both attend the dinner party that Gayle has arranged. Four days should give you ample time to come up with a plausible excuse for your absence, Jack." Dovermere's words were said more in challenge than invitation. Yet because his fondness was clearly evident, Lilah nearly found herself hoping that this method worked in his favor.

Piper chimed in, turning her full attention to her half-brother. "But you wouldn't do that to us again, would you? After all, it will only be a dinner and then a small gathering in the music room for entertainment. I play the pianoforte, and I should like you to hear it."

While there were definite similarities between father and son, there was also a measure of hardness in the latter that was missing in the former. Which made it all the more startling when Jack's stiffness suddenly left him.

He lifted his brows, glancing at Lilah before responding to Piper. "By any chance, would you happen to have a harp?"

After an hour had passed, Jack wasn't sure why he was still at the Corbett Ball. It helped, he supposed, that Dovermere had kept a discreet distance after their initial encounter.

However, that did not stop the constant curious glances from the guests in his direction, the whispers behind fans, or even the blatant comments made within earshot.

Jack had learned a lot about people in his life and his business dealings. Even when he was a boy, he'd realized that people were all the same. At one point or another, they either wanted to buy something or sell something. They wanted to believe they weren't paying too much for what they wanted or receiving too little for what they were parting with. And most of all, both buyer and seller wanted to believe they were in complete control of any negotiation.

Jack could say the same for the people in this room. After all, wasn't this party just an elaborate venue to negotiate marriages? The debutantes and their chaperones were the sellers, and the unmarried gentlemen the buyers. Lilah was here for the same purpose. She was the commodity on display, eager for Lord Ellery's attentions, while Lady Cosgrove and Lady Granworth were here to oversee the transaction.

Jack was the only one present who was neither buying nor selling. Although, perhaps he too wanted to ensure that Lilah received the best offer and did not give up too much in return.

Yet that did not explain his primitive urge to storm through the line of dancers and haul her off with him. He would take her by the hand, of course. But he wasn't above throwing her over his shoulder either. Besides, anyone could tell by the paleness of her complexion that she wasn't enjoying herself.

"I see you've donned the same expression as your friend this evening," Juliet Granworth said, sidling up to Jack, her hands clasped before her as she watched the procession of dancers. "Max took his glower into the card room. You, on the other hand, appear contented to cast yours upon the dancers. Do you dislike the amusement so greatly?"

"I neither like nor dislike it." But if Markham didn't stop ogling Lilah's décolletage, Jack would have to rip out his eyes, one at a time, and cram them down his throat.

"That makes me wonder, then, why you are here at all." Juliet remained as she was, perfectly poised and appearing as if standing beside him was a matter of happenstance. "There are whispers abounding that you came to reconcile with your father."

"Until I arrived, I had believed Dovermere was engaged elsewhere. Otherwise, I would not have come." Jack tasted a lie upon his tongue. He suddenly wondered whether Dovermere's presence would have influenced his decision in the end. Knowing that Lilah was going to be here had been all the persuasion he'd needed. "Or rather, I would have had second thoughts about attending."

"That is quite the alteration from what I've learned from Mrs. Harwick. She said that you unequivocally refuse to be in his company."

It was true. When he'd first arrived, Jack had been tempted to walk away without a word and never look back. The entire tableau had been altogether too cozy for his tastes—Dovermere standing in a public forum with his eldest daughter and his bastard son, as if everything was bright and gay. As if the entirety of Jack's struggles to survive as a boy had never happened. As if Dovermere had never abandoned Jack's mother in favor of society and aristocratic expectation.

"I am not one to turn on my heel like a coward," he said, the words gritty in his throat.

For a moment, Juliet was silent. Her lack of response left him with the hope that he'd satisfied her questions. Unfortunately, such was not the case, because she continued.

"Yet until now, you never have attended a ball, regardless of the company."

"Not true," he said, evading her question and her insinuation that there was another reason he was here. "In school, we were obligated to attend two similar events per annum." Likely, it had been the schoolmaster's only way to validate the torture of dancing lessons.

"You are missing my point," she said, exhaling a sound of frustration.

No, he understood her perfectly. Turning his head, he offered a smile of reassurance. "You have also heard that I spoke with Miss Appleton, and while in Dovermere's presence, no less. I have heard the gossips nattering away all evening, the speculation, the intrigue…but know this—I would do nothing to hinder her efforts. I know what is at stake for her all too well."

Juliet scrutinized him, her blue eyes sharp. "You have offered no direct answer to any of my queries."

"Haven't I?" He chose not to laugh when her gaze narrowed.

"I can see why you and Max are friends, and that is no compliment to you, sir," she said, though lessened her censure by adding a wry grin and a shake of her head. "I know the *ton* still calls me the *Goddess*—and some even, *Hollow Goddess*—believing that I am nothing more than pretty wrapping over an empty package, but I'm rather fierce when I need to be, and I protect those for whom I care the most."

Jack was actually relieved by this. Knowing that Lilah would be looked after, even when he couldn't, smoothed the frayed edges of this newfound disquiet. "A trait we have in common."

"Then we have an understanding?"

"We do." He inclined his head.

With no more apparent concerns, Juliet slipped away into the crowd, just as the set finished. Markham delivered Lilah to her, bowed, and then left. From the corner of the room, Lilah's gaze skimmed the crowd, searching, until it settled on him. There was a certain frailty in her expression, making him want to go to her. Before he could, however, her cousin drew her away, and they walked together toward a hallway leading off the main ballroom.

"I should have wagered on you, Marlowe," Thayne said with undisguised bitterness as he stood in the same place that Juliet had vacated a moment ago. "The gossips are all atwitter on your sudden forays into society. Hell, I even saw one young buck finger-comb his hair straight back and then tell his friend that he was *in the style of Marlowe*."

Jack laughed. "What do you expect me to do about it? These idiots are your people. I cannot control their level of foolishness."

"Damn it all, you could have warned me." Thayne lifted his glass to his lips, only to find it empty. He muttered a curse and dropped his hand to his side. "You know what is at stake."

"A house." Jack shrugged. "You have others. Surely it would matter little if you kept this one in particular."

"You know better than anyone that it's about more than a house," he said with quiet vehemence.

Yes, Jack knew, and he'd promised Thayne more than five years ago that he would keep those reasons a secret. "I'm not here to undermine your efforts with Wolford."

"Then why would you be here, if not for the wager?"

Jack couldn't answer that—or rather, *wouldn't* answer that. "Perhaps I thought it was time I saw what all this fuss and frippery was about."

"I hope that is true, old friend, because—" Thayne broke off. Then, before he turned toward the terrace doors, said, "I need a breath of air."

In that moment, Jack knew that Lady Granworth had returned. Automatically, his gaze sought Lilah. Yet when she was not beside her cousin or her aunt, a measure of alarm shot through him. He waited, milling about the crowd, lingering on the outer seam. He spotted Piper and Dovermere, but Lilah was not there either. Then, when the musicians were beginning to return to the gallery above, Jack went to find her.

The hallway where she'd first disappeared was virtually empty, with most of the guests waiting in the ballroom. A pair of debutantes exited a room, giggling and blushing when they saw him. Many of the other doors in the hall were open, the rooms dark. Yet the door from where they'd appeared was closed, the glow of candlelight coming out from beneath it.

Supposing that this was the retiring room for the ladies, he waited in the shadows in case anyone else appeared. No one came, and he could hear the musicians tuning their instruments. Taking a chance, he rapped his knuckles quietly against the door. "Lilah?"

A familiar gasp was his answer, and he felt a measure of relief. At least he knew where she was, but he didn't know the reason she was still here—and without her aunt. Because of that, his sense of alarm would not dissipate.

In the next moment, the door opened a crack but not enough for him to see her clearly. "You cannot call to me through the door *and* use my Christian name," Lilah hissed. "You are not even allowed in this corridor. It is designated for women."

"You disappeared from the ballroom during the last set. I wanted to be certain you were not taken ill," he explained, the excuse sounding perfectly reasonable to his own ears.

"Even if I were at death's door, you would not be permitted in this—"

He opened the door. Taking the room in at a glance to ensure that she was the only occupant, he drew closer. Lifting his hand to her face, he angled it toward the light from the sconces. Her face was cold, a stark-white oval broken only by her dark eyes and brows. She looked haunted instead of like a young woman who was having a night she'd always hoped she would. "You are pale. Tell me—did that cad Markham say anything to upset you? If he did anything to you…"

His words trailed off when she laughed at him. "Such a fearsome warrior, even when you're not on your Destrier. Somehow, I knew this about you from our first meeting. How terrible it must be for someone of your nature to be in between battles. No wars to fight. No enemies to slay."

Her words kindled a warmth inside of him that helped to soothe his anxiety. She must feel well enough to tease him. And surprisingly, she understood his nature. Then again, perhaps it wasn't too much of a surprise, considering he felt as if he knew her too. Well enough to know that she was warrior as well, brave and loyal to a fault. That didn't mean, however, that she didn't need someone to watch over her. And he—*a warrior in between battles*—needed an occupation.

"You forgot to mention women to capture and then carry off as the spoils of war." He shifted closer in the narrow doorway. His gaze dipped to her mouth just as color began to bloom. His lapels brushed the edge of her bodice, reminding him of the ruffles of her night rail and how it had felt to have her body against his. It took all of his control not to put his hands on her and continue where they'd left off. "Now tell me, why are you hiding in here?"

"I am not—" She stopped when he arched his brows in disbelief. "Very well. I am hiding, but only because I promised Lord Ellery the quadrille."

"And you don't want to dance with him?" A light sensation of pleasure filled him. Perhaps she hadn't truly set her cap for Ellery after all.

Lilah shook her head. "It is that I *want* to dance with him, very much indeed."

That light sensation swiftly turned into a scuttle of coal, dark and weighted. Jack shifted back a step. "Then what is preventing you?"

"There is so much at stake," she said, her voice trembling. "There were rumors tonight regarding Haggerty and me. Knowing that I am so close to failing fills me with a sense of desperation that churns in my stomach. I am all too aware that I need to make a favorable impression on Ellery. I need to say something that will entice him to call upon me or perhaps offer to take me for a drive through the park. Yet I can think of nothing to say. My mind has gone…vacant."

For the first time, Jack was reluctant to offer his assistance. Which made no sense because that was the reason he was here. He was honoring his word to Vale. Yet already, Jack had contributed more than he'd promised. Granted, kissing her hadn't solely been for her assistance. Nor a lesson in passion. It had been pure, raw desire.

And now, he wasn't certain he wanted to continue to help her woo Ellery.

"Well, what are your thoughts?" she asked, taking a step closer and placing her hand in his.

When he felt the coolness of her hand, even through her glove, and the gently imploring squeeze of her fingertips, he couldn't deny her. Resigned, he exhaled. "You are neighbors in Surrey. Perhaps you could speak of that."

He'd discovered this fact upon his initial inquiries. Since Ellery's property was in close proximity to her family's, Jack imagined that was the reason Lilah had set her cap for him. He hoped that was the *only* reason.

"Yes. That is correct," she said, nodding. Her eyes brightened. She pressed his hand once more before releasing him and reaching up to pat her cheeks. "Am I still pale? A moment ago I was imagining myself standing at the edge of the ballroom, my skin and gown so white that I blended into one of the pilasters. Then, I imagined Lord Ellery stopping to search the faces of waiting debutantes, looking for mine. Yet because of my camouflage, I would have been invisible. And he would have asked Miss Leeds to dance instead." She drew a breath and then looked sheepish. "I might as well confess to you that I worry…on occasion."

All the worries she possessed found a home inside him, twisting and turning. He had the urge to banish them all for her. If only he could.

"I worry about you as well," she said softly.

Jack went still, her statement affecting him strangely. A knotted sensation—born of an unnamed longing—filled his stomach. He lifted their linked hands and pressed a kiss to the gloved fingers twined with his. "Why me?"

"When we were standing with your father and sister, I knew it must have been uncomfortable."

He suddenly wanted to tell her about his life, about the bitterness he carried with him. Instead, he issued a hollow sound, resembling a laugh. "Do not worry about that. Dovermere is constantly intruding in my life. It was time I repaid him." He glanced out into the hall to ensure the way was clear before he pulled her with him. "Come. You will be missed."

She followed without argument, which was refreshing for a change. But then, halfway down the hall, her steps slowed. He looked back over his shoulder and motioned her forward. Up ahead, the bright glow of the ballroom spilled onto the blue-and-gold runner. People stood facing the dance floor, their backs to the hall.

"Do you never worry?" she whispered.

He took two strides back to her and further away from being seen, should any of the guests turn around. "No. I take control. I take what I want."

A wry grin curled her lips. "That is fine for you, but I simply cannot walk up to Lord Ellery and tell him that he is going to marry me."

A new twist and pull in his stomach made him realize there was another unwelcome emotion in the knotted mess. Jealousy. He'd felt it plenty of times throughout his life. Especially whenever word reached him about his father's happy family. This was the first time he'd ever been jealous over a woman. "You can if you have no doubts that it is he you want to marry."

"How can I have anything other than doubts?" she asked, not knowing how much of a balm her words were to Jack. "All I know of him is that the land of his country estate borders my father's. I'm hoping that he would be willing to help our tenants, even though the land would never belong to him. I'm counting on a great deal from a man with whom I've never conversed."

"Then, with any luck, Ellery will be a complete simpleton…" *and you will despise him as much as I do.*

"That does not sound *lucky* to me." She laughed softly, all trace of worry gone from her countenance as she lifted her gaze to his.

His heart stuttered. The nervous, uncertain pulse was foreign to him. It was far too tremulous for a fearsome warrior. Jack swallowed. "You should go. It would not serve you well to be seen exiting the hall with me."

She hesitated, her soft eyes flitting over his face before she nodded. "Thank you, Jack."

He inclined his head. "My pleasure, Miss Appleton."

After finishing their dance, Viscount Ellery had kindly escorted Lilah to Juliet's side. He lingered long enough to ask if she would like a cup of tea, but she declined. Then he inquired about her calling hours before bowing and walking away, leaving her with the first kindling of hope she'd had all Season.

She didn't know why she'd been worried. Ellery possessed an affable nature that would put anyone at ease. More than that, he was already aware of their families' adjoining properties. He spoke fondly of his time in the country and even confessed a regret that he hadn't met her there.

She couldn't wait to share the news with Jack.

"What a fortunate turn of events," Juliet whispered from behind her fan. "Those dreadful rumors were quickly forgotten when Marlowe arrived and created a buzz."

Surreptitiously, Lilah searched for him in the crowd. "I am certain it was not his intention. He cares little for what society thinks, let alone what amuses them." And to encounter Dovermere at a public venue? Lilah knew it bothered him. She hadn't believed his earlier assertion to the contrary. Not when that stark vulnerability had crossed his gaze.

"Whatever his reasons, I am glad he chose to attend," Juliet said.

Lilah was too. And if she could find him, she would tell him so.

Then, just as the first strains of the waltz began, she caught sight of him walking out of the ballroom. He was leaving?

Juliet closed her fan. "Is there a name on your card for the waltz?" Lilah stared at the back of Jack's head, willing him to turn around and see her. But he didn't. "No."

She never had the chance to tell him that she'd saved this dance for him.

CHAPTER ELEVEN

"The gossip hounds are frothing at the mouth over the news, my friend," Wolford said, striding up the steps of Jack's townhouse behind him. "The *ton* is positively mad about the notion that you will be joining Dovermere for dinner tomorrow evening."

Wolford's carriage had just pulled up as Jack returned from his solicitor's office, and he was in no mood for a friendly chat.

The news he'd just received had left him bitter and angry. According to the solicitor, there was nothing Jack could do to alter or argue against the stipulations of the late Baron Haggerty's will. By all accounts, Lilah was listed as one of her father's assets. Because of that she had no rights of her own and no legal ability to free herself of her circumstances. Her husband, however, could do so. Should she marry a titled nobleman, said gentleman would have the right to breach her father's contract with the current Baron Haggerty. But an ordinary man, even one with an extraordinary amount of money, could do nothing. Well, next to nothing.

Such a man *could* marry her and then get her with child in order for the courts to validate their union. Not that Jack had given the notion any thought. It had only been a supposition. Nothing more. Well, nothing more than his constant consideration.

Regardless, Jack also knew that under such a circumstance, Lilah would lose ties to her mother, her aunt, and her cousin. A man who truly cared for her would never cause her such grief. A man who truly cared for her would be willing to enter her world, not force her to be part of his.

"I'm not going to Dovermere's dinner party," Jack said to Wolford as he tossed his hat and gloves on the cluttered demilune table in the hall. Unlike Wolford's, Jack's townhouse was sparsely furnished. He didn't believe in wasting money on objects. "Let those gossip hounds gnash their teeth instead."

Jack had made the decision shortly after having left the Corbett Ball three days ago. He had no desire to pretend that all was well and forgotten. For years, he'd been avoiding all association with Dovermere. By leaving Jack's mother and making a life for himself, Dovermere had made his choice. Obviously for Dovermere, the foolish rules governing the *haute ton*, the disgrace of marrying his mistress, and a desire to pad the family coffers had been far too important to cast aside.

Besides, why would Jack want to see inside the house where Dovermere had made a life with a woman other than his mother?

Though Jack hated to admit it, he'd driven past the Mayfair townhouse a time or two. Occasionally, he'd wondered what it might have been like to have lived there and never to worry about money or food. Never to feel rage at watching his own mother go without for his sake. Or use the fabric from her own clothing to sew him a new shirt or pants.

"No," he said again. "I will not be attending Dovermere's dinner."

Wolford tsked at the news. Either that, or he was tsking at the state of Jack's study, which was a mess of crumpled papers, broken quill pens, stray nibs, and ink spots. And that was just his desk. He really ought to think about hiring a housekeeper. His house in the country existed with a small staff, primarily serviced by the caretaker and his family. But it was far enough removed from his primary life in London that he didn't have to think about how aristocratic it seemed to have live-in servants. He'd never wanted his life to resemble that of the nobility. Since he was gone for months at a time, however, his country estate had required more care than his townhouse.

"Still have not hired Mrs. Swift, I see," Wolford said, sitting on the arm of an overstuffed chair, which also overflowed with accounting books that he'd failed to return to the shelves.

Jack paid Mrs. Swift to clean three times a week, but perhaps he should cross the Rubicon and hire her to live here. Permanently. At the thought, an instant headache assailed him. Thankfully, there appeared to be a bottle of brandy on the mantel. "This isn't her day."

"Likely, you make her ever eager to return, never knowing what to expect," Wolford said with a sardonic laugh as he waved off a silent offer for brandy. "What about a cook, or a man at the door, in the very least?"

"I have hired men for the door in the past. All of them were pretentious and looked down their noses at the merchants and other business associates who came." Jack swallowed the brandy, feeling the burn of it all the way to his stomach and fighting to loosen the knots there. "As for a cook, I'm hardly here to warrant one. And when I require hot water, I light a fire in the stove myself. Besides, I can take a meal anywhere in town. In addition, my larder is always full." He never had to go hungry again.

Wolford twisted his gold-handled walking stick beneath his palm. "If *anywhere* suits you, then why not sup at Dovermere's?"

"Because I have no desire to *sup* there," Jack growled in warning.

Wolford tsked once more. "Then you have lost me a goodly sum. The betting book at White's is primarily in favor of your not attending. I, on the other hand, had thought you would have risen to the challenge Dovermere issued."

"It was another tactic of his, nothing more. He merely took advantage of a more public venue," Jack said after one more drink. "Usually, he brings one or more of his daughters to see me, where they then unleash their pouts and pleading gazes. Trust me. If I can refuse that sight, I can refuse anything."

His friend's green eyes widened. "You say that as if you are fond of your...sisters."

Jack rolled his shoulders. "Whatever I hold against Dovermere is not their fault. I am not so angry that I would be rude to them or ever turn my back on them if they were in need." They were blood relations, and in being so, they shared a bond. If Dovermere were ever to abandon them, for whatever reason, Jack would ensure they did not suffer.

"And what about Miss Appleton?"

In the midst of returning the bottle to the mantel, Jack stilled. "What do you mean?"

"From what I heard, she was one of the few people to whom you spoke for the duration of the ball. I thought there was a measure of significance in your association."

"Nothing more than a favor I'd promised Vale," Jack said and went into the details of it in order to make his *association* with Lilah perfectly clear.

Of course, it did not help that Jack was having a hard time staying away from Lilah or keeping her off his mind. He couldn't trust himself when he was near her. His acquaintance with Lilah was enticing him to do things he would never dream of doing. Worse, he didn't like this possessive need to keep her from other men. It made no sense because he knew that he would never be with her.

Even so, he'd been tempted beyond imagining to see Lilah during calling hours this week. But it was for the best that he'd stayed away. Yesterday, he'd even refused Thayne's invitation to dine at his mother's house. He'd known Lilah would be there…and he'd wanted to see her so badly that it frightened him.

"Hmm…then you are decided against attending?"

"Quite."

"Well, since you have made me lose money, I demand recompense," Wolford said with false vehemence. "What say you to a friendly wager and a race at Rotten Row tomorrow morning?"

Lord Ellery came to call.

In fact, this was his third visit in as many days since the Corbett Ball. On the first day, Lilah's worries of catastrophes had prevented much conversation, but thankfully, the viscount's amiable manner helped her to overcome many of them.

Today, with Aunt Zinnia embroidering a handkerchief in the corner, Lilah and Ellery had fallen into easy conversation, which mainly consisted of their favorite things about Surrey.

"As always, it has been a true delight to visit with you, Miss Appleton. Conversing about Surrey makes me eager to return. Perhaps one day we might take a tour of Leith Hill together." Ellery stood and bowed at the waist. Ever punctual, he arrived at eleven each morning and left by a quarter after, as it was commonly determined that calls should last no more than fifteen minutes. It was rude to remain, unless asked.

Lilah never asked.

"There is nothing more enjoyable than conversation about the most beautiful countryside in all of England," she said, offering a curtsy before walking with him to the foyer for his top hat, gloves, and walking stick.

Little by little, gentlemen had seemed to be remembering Lilah's name. At the Corbett Ball, they'd signed her dance card and even looked for her in the crowd when it had been their turn, seemingly eager. During the days, she received calls from Piper, Miss Creighton, Miss Stapleton, and even Lord Markham. Although Markham seemed more interested in the way her fichu was tucked into her bodice than he was in actual conversation.

The past two evenings, she'd attended dinner parties, where she'd been seated in a place of honor near the hostess. Her gowns had all been altered to have a single pearl sewn into the bodice. And it had not escaped her notice that the wardrobes of the other young women were being adorned similarly.

These should have been the best days of her life. At last, a future without falling prey to Winthrop seemed within her reach.

So then why couldn't she stop wishing to see Jack?

She hadn't seen him since the ball. Not by chance in the park. Not when she'd attended another dinner at Mrs. Harwick's. Not during calling hours. Not even when she'd slipped out at night to cover the flowers in the garden.

She tried not to think of him because thinking of him made her feel empty, like she was all alone in the world. Which made no sense because she had more attention than ever. Daily mentions in the *Standard* assured her that she was no longer forgettable.

So why did Jack's absence cut through her? She feared she knew the answer.

"I hope it is not too presumptuous of me to ask, Miss Appleton," Lord Ellery said, breaking into her thoughts, his pale brows furrowed. "But are you quite well? Your usual vibrancy seems to have dimmed. I hope I said nothing to offend."

Drat. She'd forgotten her first lesson from Jack—to think about playing the harp when speaking to a gentleman. But since she was trying not to think about Jack, it made perfect sense that it had slipped her mind.

Trying now, she visualized herself playing a beautiful melody. Though of late, playing the harp hadn't given her the same pleasure because it only made her miss Jack. In fact, everything she did made her miss Jack. It was absurd. The man was making it abundantly clear that he did not feel the same way about her.

"I am well, thank you. I fear the heavy rain today has dampened my spirits. My cousin and I did not have our walk this morning."

He nodded. "Ah. Then that explains your frequent glances to the window. You were hoping for a glimmer of sunlight. I must admit, however, that I feared you were hoping for another gentleman to call."

She felt her cheeks grow hot. Her surreptitious glances had been noticeable. "No, indeed. Your visit has been the brightest part of my day. Forgive me if I made you feel otherwise."

Ellery smiled broadly, his chest expanding on an inhale. "I am pleased to know it. And, if you will permit me to say— eleven o'clock has become my favorite time of all. Perhaps, if the day is bright tomorrow, we could drive through the park."

"I would like that," she said, summoning a smile. After all, her dreams might very well be coming true. She just had to keep reminding herself of that.

"Until tomorrow."

The following morning, Jack stopped on the path at the mouth of the Serpentine. Leaning forward, he stroked the neck of his flea-bitten Thoroughbred. "Good girl, Araneae."

Purely by chance and shortly after his challenge from Wolford yesterday, Jack had encountered a merchant who'd planned to ship this mare to France, hoping to fetch a higher price than he could here. Apparently, almost everyone at Tattersall's had thought she was too large to race and too young to be in foal. Jack, however, had taken one glance at her and felt a sense of kismet. On the spot, he'd offered the man his asking price without any negotiation.

"Jack!"

At the sound of his name and Piper's familiar lilting voice, he lifted his head, expecting another encounter with Dovermere. Instead, he saw her sitting in a glossy black phaeton with the second eldest of his half-sisters, in addition to Viscount Ellery and…Lilah.

His gaze fixed on her for an instant. He almost feared that if he blinked, she would disappear in the same way she had in his nightly dreams. Then again, his fantasies had never included her sitting snugly beside Ellery on the driver's perch. The reason Jack had left the Corbett Ball was because he hadn't wanted to see her with him. And now, he had no choice but to look at them together.

"Ellery." Jack inclined his head. "Piper. Lark"—Lady Dovermere had taken to naming each of her eight daughters after birds—"Miss Appleton."

Lilah feigned aloofness, her countenance somewhat disapproving, yet her blush gave her away. He wondered if she was happy to see him.

"Good day, Marlowe," Ellery said with a broad grin. "How fortunate that I should have your sisters, in addition to Miss Appleton, in my carriage when we happened upon you. You have met Miss Appleton, have you not? I believe Lady Piper made mention of it."

Jack felt his shoulders stiffen, his pulse escalating, ready for battle. He didn't like the way Ellery intimated a degree of guardianship over the women in his carriage, as if they were rightfully his to look after. But they weren't. Jack's blood tie to Piper and Lark certainly proclaimed him their protector, if ever the need arose.

As for Lilah, Jack's regard for her was unrivaled. "We are acquainted."

"Jack, is that a new horse?" Lark asked, her ebony curls practically spilling out from beneath her pink bonnet as she leaned over the side to see more of the mare. "I certainly hope you have not gotten rid of Samson."

"Samson?" Jack's brow furrowed.

"Your Destrier. We never knew his name, so we gave him one ourselves," Piper explained, tilting her chin down and gazing up at him in a way that always made him feel guilty. He was certain she knew exactly what she was doing too.

"Bellum is his name." He slanted another look at Ellery. *Bellum* was Latin for *war*. And right now, Jack felt eager for a skirmish. "Do not worry. He is being pampered and fed at the stables this very moment. However, I could not ride him in a race against Wolford's stallion and expect to win."

"This one is very pretty," Lark crooned. "What's her name?"

"Araneae. Which is Latin for—"

"Spider," Lilah finished for him, her voice barely above a whisper as her gaze collided with his. There was a measure of uncertainty in her soft brown depths, almost as if she was wondering if he remembered their first meeting and the spider in the garden.

"From the first moment I saw her, I knew she possessed something special, a determination to win at all costs. I admire that trait. And the reason behind her name is because of her markings, here." Jack pointed to the horse's shoulder where the flea-bitten patches of red hair formed a cluster. "It rather resembles a garden spider. Wouldn't you agree, Miss Appleton?"

Her mouth bloomed with color as she smiled. "She's beautiful."

"I think so," he said, without looking away. At least, until Ellery spoke again.

The viscount shifted in his seat, turning his shoulders as if to block Jack's unobstructed view of Lilah. "And did your horse outrace Wolford's stallion?"

"She did." Jack hands fisted, every tendon tightening, readying. He didn't like the way Ellery's body language imitated that of a buyer who'd found an object he wanted. In fact, Ellery was behaving as if he had already set his sights on Lilah. And in such a short time too. The notion disturbed Jack more than it should have done. "Would you care to race? Test your finest against mine?"

Ellery's grin didn't falter. "Not today, Marlowe. I must see these young women home safely and then prepare to meet them again this evening. I am most fortunate to have the privilege of escorting Lady Cosgrove, Lady Granworth, and Miss Appleton to your father's house tonight." The viscount's gaze sharpened. "Though I'd heard rumors that you've decided not to attend."

"No. That cannot be true." This time Piper displayed no pretense of manipulation. In fact, she looked stricken, her pale brows drawn together. Jack felt like a heel.

"You must come. Father has decided that I am old enough to attend," Lark said, pouting prettily and batting her long lashes. "I have a new dress with Belgium lace trim."

"I imagine you will be lovely," he said, humoring them as he always did. Evasion was the only defense. Besides, Jack had already made up his mind. He wouldn't be attending Dovermere's party.

"I have been practicing on the pianoforte all week," Piper said, heaping on the guilt. "And when you mentioned wanting to hear the harp, Father had ours restrung. And not only that, just today, Miss Appleton has confessed her skill and agreed to offer a performance."

Ellery turned to Lilah, his arm brushing hers. "Indeed? I am most eager to hear it."

And that was all it took.

Fire blazed through Jack's veins at the thought of Ellery witnessing Lilah at the harp. "Of course, I will attend. Nothing could keep me away."

CHAPTER TWELVE

"Mother, this is Miss Appleton," Piper said to the Countess of Dovermere.

They stood in the middle of the octagonal drawing room of the Earl of Dovermere's townhouse on Mayfair. Decorated in the Oriental style, silk wall hangings, jade figurines, and bold shades of red and gold accented the room.

"I cannot tell you how delighted I am to meet you. As my two youngest were ill, I was unable to attend the Corbett Ball. However, I am so very glad that John and Piper persuaded you to come to our little gathering." The countess smiled warmly. She blended into the room's exotic décor perfectly. Her ivory complexion was only marked by the hint of age in the subtle lines beside her eyes. Her coiffure of raven hair had yet to see a single silver strand. Piper's delicate features were there as well, but for the most part, Lark was an exact copy of her mother.

Currently, Lark was standing beside her father, a few steps away, while speaking to Aunt Zinnia, Mrs. Harwick, Juliet, and Lord Ellery, who'd been their escort this evening.

"I could not imagine being anywhere else this evening."
Though with at least four dozen in attendance, this was hardly
a *little gathering*. "I hope your children are feeling better."

The countess issued a small laugh. "Indeed they are, and
lively enough to needle me about making an appearance at the
party. They are too young, however, and are hosting their own
private ball upstairs."

Piper grinned, shaking her head. "Neither Lark nor I
were invited. And from what I have heard, the third eldest
of us has borrowed Mother's pearls for the event in an effort
to emulate a certain *Miss A* she reads about in the *Standard*."

"All the girls are caught up in the excitement of the Season," the countess added.

Lilah felt a spear of nervousness at this announcement.
At least, that was what she assumed when a tremor rushed
through her.

But then she glanced at the door in the same moment that
Jack entered the drawing room.

Conversations stopped midsentence, and the hushed
swivel of every head turning at once was the only sound. More
than the crowd's reaction, however, she sensed his nearness
inside—a deep vibration, as if her soul was made of strings
that he'd strummed all at once.

He stood centered in the double archway, feet planted, arms
bent and ready, shoulders back, expression hard, gaze…on her.
And within it, she saw his promise to battle if need be, but there
was also a trace of that vulnerability she'd witnessed before.

It had to be difficult, coming here after having spent
years estranged from his father. This wasn't the family he'd
known as a child, after all. She knew from bits and pieces of

conversation with him, and also through rumor, that Jack's childhood had not been idyllic. Far from it. She could easily imagine there would have been bitterness on his part, and rightly so. Yet despite it all, he'd transformed himself into the man he was today. And she'd grown rather fond of that man.

A fiercely tender sort of desperation stole over Lilah without warning. She wanted to cross the room to him and throw her arms around him like a shield. All the disappointment she'd had over the past few days evaporated. She was willing to forgive him for not calling on her and even for bruising her heart with his absence.

Piper turned to her mother. "Do you think Jack would be willing to go upstairs to visit my sisters, if I asked?"

"In time, perhaps. We do not want to overstep or rush him," the countess said with compassion that Lilah appreciated for Jack's sake.

The earl appeared beside his wife, taking her arm without a word. Yet they exchanged a look of such joy that no words were needed. Clearly, they were glad Jack had come. Piper gave Lilah one more squeeze, while Lark bit into her bottom lip as she beamed, the two sisters following their parents.

Lilah stayed where she was, though the pull to cross the room was almost impossible to resist. Out of the corner of her eye, she watched Juliet leave Aunt Zinnia, Mrs. Harwick, and Ellery and come to stand beside her.

"Cousin," Juliet whispered, "is there an understanding between you and Mr. Marlowe?"

The words were so out of the blue that Lilah started, her gaze disconnecting from Jack's as she faced her cousin. "Of course not. Why would you say such a thing?"

Yet even as she made the declaration, her pulse quickened, jumping with excited little leaps at the notion. She suddenly envisioned a different life than her own—a life free to marry any man of her choosing, and Jack's was the only face she could see.

"Because of the way he looks at you. There's a primitive sort of possessiveness in his gaze, as if he thinks of you as his. I witnessed this at the Corbett Ball as well."

Nervous and giddy all at once, Lilah laughed. "Surely not. Mr. Marlowe looks at everyone in the same manner, like a man determined to take on the world. I am merely in his line of sight."

Her gaze slid back to the grouping near the doorway, watching as he greeted his father with a handshake and the countess with a bow. Then, one corner of his mouth twitched at something Lark said as she laughed. Piper laughed as well, squeezing Jack's arm and taking her father's hand, linking them.

Lilah's heart ached with gladness. Jack could have come here determined to be cross and ill mannered. Instead, he was cordial and displayed an evident fondness for his sisters.

"Hmm…so you say, but I do not think I'm the only one who has noticed." Juliet's gaze surreptitiously alighted on Ellery. He was standing only a few steps away and wore a pointed frown as he watched the figure in the doorway. "Just be cautious. Right now, the whispers are in your favor. However, there is nothing more damaging to a reputation than the wrong sort of speculation. Not to mention, a member of the anonymous committee might be in attendance, prepared to change the course of your life."

The Season's *Original* was usually named at the end of the first month. There were only a handful of days left in March to make a favorable impression.

Lilah nodded. "I understand, but truly, there is no cause for worry."

The moment the words left her lips, Lilah wished to take them back. She knew better than anyone not to make *worry* prove itself. And in that same instant, Jack inclined his head and said something to his family, just before he left them and started to cross the room, his steps aimed in her direction.

Out of the corner of her eye, she saw Ellery nod at her aunt and Mrs. Harwick, just before he too started in her direction.

Lilah's breath hitched.

Juliet did not miss a thing. "The choice is yours, Cousin. Be sure it is the right one."

With Ellery only two steps away, he arrived in front of her first. He bowed. "Miss Appleton, would you do me the honor of allowing me to escort you to dinner this evening?"

Lilah's gaze skimmed past the viscount's shoulder to see Jack slow his step. Then, after looking from her to Ellery, he turned and headed in the Marquess of Thayne's direction.

Apparently, the decision was not hers after all. "Thank you, Ellery. Yes."

Jack had come here, determined not to give the *haute ton*'s gossip hounds any meat for their dinners.

To ensure that outcome, he'd had a glass or two of brandy beforehand. Upon arriving, he'd greeted his father, met the countess, and conversed with his half-sisters for a suitable amount of time, by his own standards. When he could no longer take seeing Lilah across the room, instead of standing beside him, he'd politely excused himself from the welcoming party and made his way to her.

Unfortunately, Ellery had arrived before him. Jack's first impulse was to separate Ellery from Lilah. Yet when all eyes seemed to track his progress across the room, he could not. And seeing the conflict in Lilah's expression compelled him to think about what his actions might cost her.

Therefore, Jack had paused only long enough to find Thayne, who'd been accepting a fresh glass of sherry from a waiting footman. Jack had taken one as well, smiled to the wolves blatantly staring at him, and then tossed back the dark crimson in a satisfying swallow.

He'd hoped that by the end of the evening, they might even have become bored of him.

Dinner had been a torturous affair of polite conversations and glimpses of Lilah sitting next to Ellery for the duration. Did she have to smile so much at him? Surely the viscount couldn't have been that amusing. Of course, Jack had no confirmation either way, as he'd been obliged to sit near the head of the table beside Dovermere, half the distance of the table away from Lilah.

Dovermere had asked if the wines were to his tastes. The question held just enough of a warning note to cause a spark of rebellion to rise up, encouraging Jack to have another glass. And perhaps another after that.

However, now that he was standing in the music room— or rather, leaning against the archway leading to the music room—he wasn't certain how many glasses he'd had.

Enough, he supposed. There was only the faintest of knots in his stomach. The rest of him was warm and pleasantly numb.

One of the guest debutantes was singing before the assembly, elbows out and hands clasped in front of her bosom as if she were praying not to screech on all the high notes. Her prayers were not heard. Jack was tempted to clasp his own hands in prayer—or over his ears—but just then, Dovermere came up beside him.

"Are you not fond of music?" he asked, keeping his voice low.

"I'm quite fond of music, actually. I'm looking forward to hearing some," Jack said, tasting the words on his tongue. They were a little slurred and slow to come out. He'd choose faster words next time.

Dovermere lifted a cup and saucer into view. "Here. Drink this."

"I do not have to do what you say," Jack said but took the cup and lifted it to his lips. After the first sip, he decided that the coffee was hot enough to mix well with whatever else he had inside his stomach. When Dovermere lifted his hand, and a servant poured more into his cup, Jack said, "Clever trick. Does he appear every time you do that?"

"Only when I say the magic words first," Dovermere quipped. The footman pressed his lips together to hide a grin before standing off to the side, pot and tray in hand.

Jack blinked in surprise at his father. "You have a wry wit."

"I find that a sense of humor is an essential part of any gentleman's character." He slowly exhaled. "Especially during moments like this."

"I've embarrassed you." Jack wasn't so drunk that he could ignore the shock of remorse that hit him. Yet why should he feel remorse at all in the presence of Dovermere? He wasn't the one who'd abandoned his father, after all. Dovermere was the one who'd left—

Jack stopped before finishing that thought, knowing that he wasn't drunk enough to continue. Besides, the coffee was beginning to taste bitter and unsettling. He placed the cup onto the saucer and handed it back to the footman.

"No. Actually I am thrilled that you are here in any capacity," Dovermere continued, after the applause died down for the first debutante, and another one began to sing as well—or as poorly, depending on whether or not you enjoyed music. "Though I hope there is a time in the future when you will be able to tolerate being in my company without any…assistance."

Damn. Now Dovermere was just making Jack feel guilty. And he didn't want to feel guilty. "What is it that you're trying to sell?"

"Sell?"

"There are only two kinds of people in the world," Jack began, ticking them off on his fingers. "Everyone is either trying to buy something or sell something. Since you're not using coercive tactics to buy me, that must mean that you're selling. You're hoping to have something I want."

Dovermere nodded thoughtfully and clutched Jack's shoulder in something of an embrace. "When you put it that way, son, I suppose you are correct. I want to be in your life. I would like it if you wanted the same thing."

Then, as usual, he walked away, taking the last word with him. However, as luck would have it, a few moments later, a passing footman came to the rescue. He was carrying a tray of cordial glasses to dispense to the seated guests. Jack took one for each hand and obliged him to return when he had another full tray.

Dutifully, Jack remained in the music room through Piper's performance on the pianoforte. And he was glad of it. She played marvelously. Even though he had nothing to do with her talent, a wealth of pride filled him.

Then, at last, Lilah curtsied before the assembly and took her position at the harp. She'd removed her gloves, he noted. His gaze took in every creamy inch of her exposed flesh. She had elegant hands—something that he hadn't noticed when she'd had them in his hair. And when she closed her eyes and placed her cheek against the frame, he was no longer in Dovermere's music room but in a midnight garden instead.

Every single note hummed through him. Every glissando washed over him. It felt as if her hands were on his body instead of the strings. Drifting off with the music, he watched every flick of her thumb, every graceful sweep of her arms and turn of her wrists. She expressed herself with more passion than even he'd witnessed, her cheeks flushed, her lips parted.

He knew how much this meant to her—not just playing the harp but making her own statement amongst the *ton*. She alone created this music. There was no cousin who could take credit for her success. And no codicil threatening to take it away. It was hers and hers alone. And in that moment, he felt something tender and almost fearful come to life within him.

He drew a breath to subdue the sensation. His chest began to rise and fall rapidly, his pulse escalating. That was when he noticed that the entire assembly was enraptured. Even Ellery sat up straighter, perched on the edge of a gilded chair.

That hard, knotted feeling of jealousy returned. Jack closed his eyes, not wanting to witness this any longer. Not wanting to watch exactly how he was going to lose her.

But how could he lose her when she wasn't his?

Before the music ended, he slipped into the hall and looked for a helpful footman to bring him another glass of kirsch.

When the final vibration of the glissando drifted off, the assembly stayed quiet. Lilah did not even hear a rustle of fabric or throat clearing. Facing the harp and far wall as she was, the guests were seated to her left, but she hesitated to turn her head to address them. Having never performed for anyone other than family, she wondered suddenly if her skill on the harp was lacking. Or perhaps the piece of music she'd played was not in fashion. Nevertheless, she had enjoyed herself immensely.

Standing up from the stool, she turned to the audience, her gaze dropping to the floor as she curtsied. And then it began. The hush abruptly transformed into applause. She rose. Lifting her gaze, she saw the shocked and pleased expressions greeting her. Then several people began to move toward her, congratulating and complimenting her.

She even heard Aunt Zinnia and Mrs. Harwick nearby, telling of how Lilah had always been an excellent harpist but was too modest to play frequently in society. The truth was much simpler—she'd never had the opportunity. However, for the sake of becoming the Season's *Original*, it would behoove Lilah to say that it was modesty alone. Society loved modesty. This comment curled her lips in a wry smile, and she imagined Jack would be smirking at the superfluous attention. Unfortunately, as she scanned the faces in the room, she noted that one in particular was missing.

Piper, who had introduced her before she played, came up to her now and embraced her. "You were simply angelic. I believe the entire room was transported to a cloud in heaven while you played."

"Well done, Cousin," Juliet said, now standing beside her. They shared a look between them, knowing that this was a step in the right direction.

Ellery made his way through the admirers and grinned broadly. "Miss Appleton, my admiration for your accomplishments grows day by day. No, I must correct myself and state firmly that my admiration grows moment by moment."

Lilah returned his smile, though perhaps not with as much enthusiasm. "You are too kind, Ellery."

"I am going to be away for the next few days, but when I return"—he took one step closer and lowered his voice—"I hope you would consider dining with my parents. They are both eager to make your acquaintance."

Lilah didn't know why, but she felt a sudden bout of tears threaten. And not tears of joy. A swift stinging pressure built up behind her eyes, and she had to blink rapidly to keep them at bay. "That sounds lovely." She bobbed a curtsy. "If you will forgive me, I should like to take a breath of air."

"I could escort you."

"No. No. That is not necessary," she said hurriedly, turning toward a side door.

Piper followed close behind. "Are you unwell, Lilah?"

The concern in her tone nearly caused a flood to break free. With the crook of her finger, she dabbed at the corner of her eye. "I feel rather foolish for leaving in such a rush. The attention was a little...overwhelming."

Lilah just needed a moment to gather her composure. This was all happening so suddenly. Two weeks ago, she was practically invisible, completely forgettable, and worried all the time. Now that her hopes were coming to fruition, why weren't her anxieties lessening?

"I know just what you need—the Serenity Room. It's a place where Mother and Father go to...well, keep their sanity, I suppose." Piper laughed, linking arms with Lilah and guiding her down the corridor. "It's quiet, and there is a lovely view of the garden. Since the moon is out this evening, you should be able to see the reflecting pool."

An instant later, however, Lark rushed up behind them. "Forgive me, Lilah, but Mother has requested Piper's presence in the drawing room. The Creightons are leaving, and Mother wants us present to bid them farewell."

Lilah began to turn back, but Piper stopped her. "This should only take a moment. The room is just up ahead. The second door on the left."

If Lilah hadn't needed a moment to gather her thoughts, she likely would have turned back regardless. But the Serenity Room sounded exactly what she needed. She left her new friends and soon found herself at the door.

Stepping inside the dark room, she instantly saw a figure standing at the window, looking out into the garden. "Oh! Forgive me. I did not mean to intrude."

"Lilah?"

Backing out into the hall, she stopped suddenly. "Jack?"

It was certainly his voice, and now that she looked closer, it was clearly his form. She could tell from his distinctive stance, even though he seemed to be listing to one side at the moment.

"Come here," he ordered softly, lifting a hand toward her, even as he turned back toward the window. "You would like this view. I imagine there are hundreds of spiders out there, spinning their webs on a clear night such as this."

Lilah looked over her shoulder at the empty corridor. It would be unseemly to enter the room, knowing that Jack was there. Yet if she stayed only a moment, perhaps she could leave before Piper returned, and no one would be the wiser. Besides, she did want to see the moonlit view from the window.

On a breath, she stepped into the small room, closing the door behind her. That way, if anyone should happen by, no one would make the wrong assumptions. With each step across the room, her slippers sunk into the plush carpet. The dim light outlined the shape of an overstuffed chair and long, sumptuous sofa. There was a table as well and a white stone hearth in the corner but not much else. This room likely served one single purpose: quietude.

She stood beside Jack with little space between them, he staring out one side of the window, and she the other. Somehow, their hands caught and intertwined. She wasn't certain if she had moved or if he had, but she felt all of her anxiety evaporate from that one simple touch.

Still, she couldn't stop herself from asking, "Did you leave the Corbett Ball to go to that other woman—the one you mentioned the night we were in the garden? Have you spent these days apart with…her?"

He chuckled, his hand tightening around hers. "No. Nor with any other woman. And yet while I have remained *ever faithful*, you have been entertaining gentlemen in your parlor."

"Your tone makes calling hours sound indecent," she chided, trying to hide the pleasure his admission gave her. Even though his tone was more mocking than reverent, she knew he would not lie to her. He valued honesty. Therefore, she was honest with him. "I would have been *at home* to you."

"I don't think Lady Granworth or Lady Cosgrove would have approved."

Likely not. "Juliet believes you look at me with a primitive sort of possessiveness. Of course, if that were true, then you would have listened to me play. Why didn't you?"

"I did. I listened, fell under your spell, and then…" He exhaled, the scent sweet like cherry cordial and wine, which made perfect sense because he had been drinking quite a bit tonight.

She faced him, and in the moonlight, she saw his gaze locked on hers. His vulnerability couldn't hide. "And then?"

He tugged her closer, causing her to trip over her own feet and fall against him. His hands curved around her arms, holding her, keeping her secure. "Forget Ellery. He can't have you."

"Jack, you know it is not my choice," she said, feeling those tears threaten again.

Jack lifted his hands to cup her face. "You're mine, Lilah. Ask Vale. He knows. He sent me to you." He nodded as if agreeing with himself. "You're my Christmas present."

Clearly, he was drunk, but still her heart yearned for more of these tender words, more of his thumb's caress against her lips. "It is nearly the end of March, Jack."

He blinked slowly and grinned. "Mmm...then it's high time I opened the wrapping. It would be rude to wait any longer."

She started to laugh until he leaned in closer, forcing her to place her hands against his chest. "In case you have forgotten, we are in your father's house."

"He won't mind. He wants me to be happy, damn him." He started nibbling at the corner of her mouth, along her jaw to the little indentation near her ear. "Don't *you* want me to be happy?"

She closed her eyes and felt her body bend toward his, her resistance fading swiftly. There was something about being in Jack's arms that felt too right to ignore. "Of course, but I do not..."

"Because I want you to be happy. And *oh*, there are things I can do that would make you very happy, my Lilah," he said against her throat, tasting the flesh over her pulse. "Mmm...I can taste your curiosity right here. Your heart is beating so fast. So eager. Do you want me to show you?"

Yes, please. "You've had too much to drink. You don't know what you're doing."

She was feeling a little drunk herself. Little wonder, with his intoxicating kisses over her flesh. It took every ounce of decorum within her to keep her from giving in to temptation and twining her arms around his neck. As it was, her grasp on his lapels was likely holding him closer, rather than pushing him away.

He chuckled, sliding his hands down her back and lifting her hips against his. "I know what I'm doing. I'm very...*accomplished*."

Her head fell back as he opened his mouth over her throat. "I must marry another man."

"*Lilah!*" Juliet gasped from the doorway, the light from the hall spilling into the room.

Abruptly, Lilah pushed herself out of Jack's grasp, which was actually so easily done that she was rather embarrassed that she hadn't put any effort into it before. "It isn't what you think. Well...I mean...it is...but I didn't plan to be alone with Jack."

"The door was closed."

"Yes," Lilah explained. "Because I didn't want it to look like we were...*Bother*. I suppose it looks that way after all."

"It does, indeed," Juliet said as she stepped into the room and closed the door behind her. "And Mr. Marlowe, I asked you to refrain from bringing scandal to my cousin, and you agreed. Now, there are dozens of people headed this way to see the view of the garden from this window."

"What?" Lilah's heart stopped.

"With the family detained by farewells, the housekeeper is leading a tour. It is a good thing I wanted to bring your gloves to you and that Lady Piper mentioned that you were in here, Lilah. Alone." Juliet frowned, wringing the gloves in her grasp. "Doubtless, someone noticed that I walked the corridor unaccompanied. Therefore, none of the guests would believe that the two of you merely happened upon this place by accident. You understand what ruination is, don't you, Mr. Marlowe?"

Lilah felt the ground sway beneath her feet. If she were ruined, she would never become the *Original*. Ellery would not marry her. Nor would any other nobleman. She would be at Winthrop's mercy. And Juliet would lose her wager, not to mention her house. Mother would likely disown her. The disgrace would taint Aunt Zinnia's standing amongst the *ton*. And a scandal was no way to repay the woman who'd offered her a home.

Beside her, Jack straightened, seeming more sober than he had been a moment ago. "I'll climb out the window. No one will know."

That was true enough. After all, Piper knew that Lilah was here but not Jack. Still… "No. You could get hurt. I could not bear it," she whispered to him.

He looked at her, saying nothing, but his eyes were clearer now. Then he turned the latch of the window, swung it inward, and threw a leg over the edge as if he were mounting a horse. "I apologize," he said at last, before slipping down to the ground.

When Lilah turned around, she saw that Juliet was no longer the only one standing in the doorway. Lord Thayne was there as well. And the collective voices of a dozen other people followed close behind.

"Max," Juliet said, beseeching him with a hand on his arm. "Please. Do not speak of this. Do not let this ruin Lilah's life, as it did mine all those years ago."

He stared at Juliet for a moment, his expression grim. Everyone in the room knew that he had the power to both ruin Lilah and to make Juliet lose any chance of regaining her house. But for the first time, an emotion other than loathing crossed his face as he gazed at Juliet.

Lilah wondered if a kissing scandal and animosity were the only things between them or if there was more. Though whatever it might be, she regretted that in asking Thayne for help, Juliet was sacrificing some of her pride in return.

"Close the window, Miss Appleton, and fix your hair." Then he returned to the corridor. "Did anyone bring a lamp? Because it's dreadfully dark in there. I believe we've missed the moon's reflection on the pool already."

His distraction gave Lilah and Juliet just enough time to recover. At least on the surface.

The true damage had yet to be determined.

CHAPTER THIRTEEN

Lilah sat on her vanity stool, seeing the bright eyes and rosy cheeks of her other self in the looking glass. She sighed, worried about the cause. "Nellie, have you ever been in love?"

"Aye, miss," her maid answered with a wan smile, seemingly distracted while she brushed the length of Lilah's hair. "He works on a farm, not far from your father's manor house."

Lilah never knew this about Nellie. Then again, she'd learned a lot about her maid in the past week or more. As Lilah had grown more confident, Nellie had too. It was as if Lilah's worrying nature had been related to her maid's nervousness. Now, after having put more faith in Nellie's abilities, her maid was transforming as well. Although Lilah suspected that Nellie had had a self-assured nature before she'd worked for Lilah's father.

"How did you meet him?" Lilah asked, curious about Nellie's secret life.

"Occasionally, the cook would send me there to collect a cup of fresh milk. But once when Joseph—I mean, Mr. Shalley—wasn't busy, he showed me how to milk the cow myself and welcomed me to return whenever I wanted. Then he started walking me to chapel, and we'd spend our half-day Sundays together."

"Was this Mr. Shalley tender toward you? Kind?" In the mirror, Lilah watched her maid blush.

"Aye." There was a wealth of meaning in that single syllable.

A fresh understanding crept over Lilah, causing her to blush as well. "Do you ever regret falling in love with him?"

Nellie shook her head. "Not once."

Lilah's thoughts drifted off to last night as Nellie pinned her hair. Falling in love with Jack would be terribly inconvenient.

Before long, Juliet entered the room. Their gazes met in the mirror, a shared secret between them. They had not spoken of last night, neither the compromising situation in which Juliet had found her nor the fact that, because of Lilah, Juliet was now indebted to Thayne.

And it was Lilah's fault.

Once again, when in Jack's presence, Lilah had forgotten to worry about the worst thing that could happen.

Juliet lifted a copy of this morning's *Standard* into view. "'*Our fascination with Miss A— increased after last night's performance at the Earl of D—'s soiree. She is certainly one to follow.*'" She placed it on the vanity and patted Lilah's shoulder. "This all but assures your success. It is good news…on many levels."

Yes. It meant that no one had learned of her transgression. And also that no one was paying much attention to the rumors regarding Winthrop. At least, not yet.

Lilah glanced down at the page, skimming the lines to be certain. That was when she saw a mention of Jack.

"In a great disappointment to many curiosity seekers, our Mr. M— made a rather poor showing. Now, one must wonder at the reason M— has ventured into society at all."

"What the devil were you thinking last night? Alone in a room with an unmarried woman of society? Marlowe, even you know the risks." Thayne's shouts could have been heard in Scotland, and with all his stomping around, the floor of Jack's study would soon splinter. "There's no telling what Juliet witnessed."

"Hardly anything," Jack murmured. Even though he wasn't entirely sure what he'd been doing at that precise moment, he knew that it couldn't have been too bad. Certainly not as bad as what he'd wanted to do.

"I do not want to know. Please tell me naught!" Thayne sliced his hand through the air in a cutting motion, likely meant to intimidate. "I'll never forget the way Juliet looked at me. She was so…haunted and lost. Then, because of you, she was obliged to ask me for help. *Me*, Jack! Do you know what that must have cost her? And what aiding her has cost *me*?"

Jack had an idea. He also found it interesting that suddenly *Lady Granworth* had become *Juliet* to Thayne for the first time in years. Because of last night, Thayne and Lady Granworth's past scandal must have bubbled to the surface for them. However, if Jack's own imbecility had caused Lilah's ruin, then unlike Thayne and Juliet, Jack never would have let her out of his sight until they were wed. Damn the consequences and damn her father's will. If Jack had to get Lilah with child for their marriage to have validity, so be it. And if he had to imprison her mother in the same house with them so that she could not disown her daughter, then so be it as well.

At least, that had been the plan he'd formed in his liquor-soaked brain. This morning, however, that *brilliant* brain of his had formed factions—half armed with lances of fire and half with shards of ice. Thoughts were difficult to pinpoint in the ensuing melee.

Jack remembered bits and pieces of last night: a strange conversation with Dovermere, wanting to kill Ellery, and seeing Lilah's face in the moonlight. Her bed-curtain lashes had closed as he'd held her in his arms. Then, they'd sprung open in shock when Juliet had entered the room to find them alone.

Jack pinched the bridge of his nose and squeezed his eyes shut. Even though he was not a drinker by nature, he still knew how to hold his liquor. But perhaps he shouldn't have attempted to hold so much of it. "Think of it this way—now that you have done a favor for Juliet, she owes you a favor in return. This might be the favor that ensures Wolford's victory."

"Ha! Have you even bothered to read this morning's *Standard*? The column states that Miss Appleton is *one to follow*. With the end of the month at hand, Wolford's refusal to be shepherded, and the *Original* sure to be announced, I have little hope of being the victor."

Jack would have shrugged, but he discovered that sitting perfectly still at his desk while carefully holding his face in his hands was the only thing keeping him from becoming ill. "If you leave now, I will make sure that Wolford attends whatever event you have scheduled for this evening."

"Why do you think you'll be able when I have failed?"

"Because Wolford would find it amusing if I went with him."

"Hmm…" Thayne's pacing steps halted near the corner of Jack's desk. "After last night, if there is one person who can make Wolford look good by comparison, it is you."

With Aunt Zinnia visiting Mrs. Harwick, and with Juliet at her solicitor's office, Lilah indulged in a moment of solitude. She played the harp, allowed Nellie to experiment with her hair, and then strolled into the garden to check her azaleas. The buds were the size of her thumb, a beautiful dark-rose color. They would start to bloom any day now. She hoped when they did, she could tell Jack about them. Or perhaps he would come to see her.

Distracted by this happy thought, she entered the townhouse through the garden door and paid no attention to the sound of knocking down the hall until Mr. Wick opened the front door, and in stepped a familiar face.

Then, before Lilah could even say Ivy's name, the Duchess of Vale rushed through the foyer, down the hall, and embraced her. Lilah hugged her back, more than delighted by the surprise. "Ivy, when did you return?"

"Only this morning. North is seeing that his aunt is settled, and I—well, I could not wait to see you." Ivy beamed, her winter-blue eyes shining gaily.

"You have always been impulsive." Lilah laughed. Her dearest friend couldn't have returned at a better time. Right now, she needed some advice. "I thought becoming a duchess might have cured you of it."

"Never," Ivy said with feigned severity before she laughed as well. "Thankfully, North understands my nature. Sometimes he is rather impulsive too."

Together, they walked back toward the parlor. On the way, Ivy untied her hat, revealing a twist of white-blonde hair, before leaving her hat and gloves on the foyer table. After asking Myrtle to bring a tea tray, they stepped into the parlor.

"I have heard that you are taking the *ton* by storm," Ivy said. "How could I have stayed away for an instant longer?"

"Since when do you believe overblown rumors?" Lilah shooed her friend with a wave of her fingers toward the settee. "As you see, I am still very much as I always was."

"No. That is not true at all. You are much changed, and I am not merely speaking of your appearance. Granted, I am surprised. I recall many mentions of a 'vast forehead,' and yet all I see is a lovely expanse of creamy skin. You have a heart-shaped face, Lilah. I have known you all my life. How could I not have noticed this?"

"I took great care to conceal it." Until recently, she'd never had the courage to try anything different. She was already growing accustomed to it. Sometimes when she looked in the mirror, she even forgot what she'd looked like before.

"Yes, I recall your creative fringes over the years and constant wearing of bonnets. I also remember, quite clearly, what your mother would say. Yet in all the years I had asked you to experiment with a new style, you refused."

Ivy's speculative frown forced Lilah to explain the truth. In the next few minutes, she summed up the bargain between

Juliet and the Marquess of Thayne and the reasons for insert-
ing herself into their conflict.

Ivy reached across the settee and squeezed Lilah's hand, a
poignant smile on her lips. "You were always the bravest person I knew."

Instantly, Lilah dismissed the claim. "Brave? You were the
one forever finding yourself in danger."

"And how dangerous was coming home with a dirty pin-
afore when the worst I had to bear from my mother and father
was a tsk and a kiss on my forehead?" She shook her head. "It
was nothing compared with what you and Jasper faced each
day. That is what made you brave. You never ran away, although
I remember encouraging a gypsy tour at one time or another."

Lilah gave a watery laugh, only now realizing the tears
clogging her throat. She sniffed. "I believe you packed a
satchel for me each summer for nearly five years."

"Very true," Ivy agreed. "But I must say that there is something else about you as well. You have a certain confidence
about you. Your cheeks have color and your mouth…This is
strange to admit, but I do not think I ever noticed it before.
Have your lips always been so red and plump?"

Lilah felt her cheeks flush with warmth.

Ivy sat forward, making Lilah wonder if she could see too
much. "And now you are blushing, and my curiosity is piqued.
Could it be that you have fallen in love?"

"Ivy, you are completely incorrigible," Lilah said on a
breath. "How could I possibly be in love with someone when
the Season has only just begun?"

"It took less than a week for me to fall in love. Less than a
minute, actually." For years, Ivy had been in love with Jasper,

but after he'd broken her heart, she'd abandoned any idea of love. At least, until she'd met the Duke of Vale this past Christmas, and his *Marriage Formula* had brought them together.

"Yes, but you had the *Marriage Formula* to aid you."

Ivy glanced away. "Well…not entirely."

"What do you mean?" Lilah asked, grateful for the change in conversation.

"Tut tut." Ivy waggled her finger. "Now is not the time for that. Instead, I want to hear about the man who has stolen your heart and brought such color to your cheeks."

She should have known better. Ivy was rather tenacious when she wanted to be.

Lilah glanced toward the open door to make sure Myrtle hadn't returned with the tea tray yet. "I'm not entirely sure he has stolen my heart."

Ivy pivoted toward her, eagerness in her wide grin. "So it *is* that you are in love—or at least think you might be. I knew it. You have a glow about you that I have never seen."

"Perhaps you are seeing the effects of cleverly applied cosmetics. Juliet knows many secrets of beauty."

"I have no doubt of it, but no. I am not going to be dissuaded. I have heard rumors that a certain gentleman has shown you favor. Tell me, are you in love with Viscount Ellery?"

"Ellery?" Lilah balked. "I do not know him well enough. He has come to call here three times, and once, we went on a carriage ride with the elder two daughters of the Earl of Dovermere. We spoke of Surrey but nothing of consequence."

Ivy frowned and tilted her head in puzzlement. "I've read only one name from your letters. If it is not Ellery, then who could it be? What is his title?"

Lilah drew in a breath. She would never think of admitting this aloud to any other person, but Ivy was the only person who might understand. And the only person who could guide her in what to do from here. "Jack does not have a title."

"Oh, *Jack*, is it? You are using his Christian name?" Ivy lifted a pale brow. "It must be quite serious."

Lilah didn't want to go into depth about their kisses or their meeting in the Serenity Room. Therefore, she censored her response. "Not too serious. After all, without a title, we cannot marry."

Ivy's mouth dropped open for an instant before she collected herself and then grinned madly. "You have thought of marrying him?"

Lilah gulped. Those were only passing thoughts, simple wishes that, if she had the power to choose her own fate, she would want a man just like him. Or not *another* man like him, but him. Only him. As the realization dawned, she slowly nodded. "But it would be foolish—disastrous, even—to fall in love with him."

"My dear," Ivy began, her face a mask of severity hiding the smallest of grins, "I would wager that you already are."

Chapter Fourteen

That evening, Lilah attended a soiree hosted by Baron Tillman-shire. The estate was a sprawling structure of fawn-colored stone, Palladian windows, and a grand centered portico, complete with tall, tapered columns. There were also colorful banners waving from the top of the pediments above each of the main floor windows. Knowing that the baron was Miss Ashbury's father, Lilah wouldn't have been surprised to see tassels on the end of each banner as well.

Inside, the same odd touches appeared on the statues that lined the marble entry hall. The nymphs were each adored with a swathe of brightly colored silk, as if they had been *dressed* for the party. Neither Juliet nor Lilah made a comment. Aunt Zinnia, however, offered a sniff of reproof. There was nothing she hated more than a lack of form and subtlety.

"New money," she said under her breath, casting a scathing glance at the line of footmen dressed in pink satin livery. "Tillmanshire certainly has been busy since he purchased his title last year. It is a shame he did not purchase a little decorum. Otherwise, he might have greeted us by now."

Before the baron bought the estate, it had been empty for three years after Viscount Howe had died penniless and without an heir. Much would have been the same for Lilah's home in Surrey, if not for the estate having been entailed. Then again, with Winthrop left in charge, a dire fate might still befall her home, as well as Lilah. Unless she was named the *Original*.

Fortunately, the matrimonial rumors tying her to Winthrop had died down. Yet she was still worried they would rise once more. If more people learned of the codicil in her father's will, she would have no chance of marrying anyone else. Breaking a betrothal would cause a scandal for anyone involved. What she needed to do was to either find a man who wasn't afraid of a scandal or one who was fond enough of her to risk it.

As if her heart were in perfect synchronization with her wishes, she suddenly conjured a vision of Jack, standing near the doors leading out to Tillmanshire's terrace. In her vivid imagination, he wore a pewter brushed coat that matched the fading light from the sky behind him, and his gaze held the warm glow of the wall sconces.

"I had not heard that Mr. Marlowe was invited this evening," Juliet said, her tone clipped with censure. "One must wonder why he has made so many recent appearances when it was obvious at the earl's dinner that he was not bred for our society."

Lilah's heart quickened in a rapid pizzicato of *he is here, he is here*. Realizing that he was not simply the yearning of her imagination, she blinked, staring at him with fresh, eager eyes. The last time she'd seen him, he was slipping out of a window and down to the ground. She was glad that he did not appear hurt in any way. In fact, he looked quite dashing.

"Perhaps he means to reconcile with his father," Lilah said in his defense.

"I do not believe the earl is here this evening," Aunt Zinnia commented absently as she led their small party toward a gathering of servants pouring tea and wine. "However, Thayne, Wolford, and Vale are all present. So it seems likely that he would have come for them. Does his presence bother you, Juliet?"

"Of course not." Juliet smiled politely, but her jaw clenched. "I'm merely concerned for Lilah's sake. The *ton* is still brimming with eagerness to see where he will turn up next. As you know, I would prefer that all the eagerness were reserved for my cousin."

Lilah did not miss the way Juliet said *turn up*, as if Jack's appearance was akin to something buried rising from the earth after a heavy rain. "I'm certain Aunt Zinnia is right, and he is here with his friends. I, for one, am more disturbed by Wolford's appearance and what that could mean for next week's announcement in the *Standard*."

Just past Jack's shoulder, Wolford stood within a crowd of fawning debutantes and matrons, the cluster of them giggling at whatever he might have said. In this gathering, his was likely one of the oldest titles. That alone earned respectability, despite his reputation.

Juliet's attention abruptly shifted, as Lilah hoped it would. Unfortunately, Thayne chose that moment to step into their line of sight.

He bowed to Aunt Zinnia. "Lady Cosgrove, you are lovely this evening, as always. My mother is near the fountain, talking with the Dowager Duchess of Vale and asked if I would escort you to them."

"I am immune to flattery, young man, but I accept your offer." She tsked at him but with a grin. Then she took his proffered elbow and walked gracefully toward the open doors and stairs leading out on to the terrace, leaving her tea behind.

During the exchange, Thayne had acknowledged neither Juliet nor Lilah.

Knowing the reason, Lilah looked down into her cup. "I am sorry about last night."

"I don't blame you," Juliet began. "And I don't suppose that I truly blame Mr. Marlowe either. It was clear he was in his cups and not thinking of the ramifications. After mulling it over, the sincerity that I witnessed in his expression was enough to persuade me. And the fact that he is here today shows that he is not one to cower or allow you to endure any criticisms alone. Though, thankfully, only four of us are aware of what transpired." She paused to take a breath. "However, as irrational as it may sound, I wish I *could* blame Max."

"I'm sure he didn't mean to slight us just now." Lilah believed ignoring them was likely his way of displaying disapproval toward her and not Juliet.

"Oh yes, he did. Hateful man," she hissed, turning around so that Thayne's retreating figure was to her back. "I firmly believe that—*oh, no.*"

The horror in Juliet's tone startled Lilah enough that she looked up and quickly spotted the source of it. Walking through the front door at the far end of the entry hall was none other than Cousin Winthrop. Even from the distance of thirty feet away, Lilah could see his smarmy, superior grin and glistening, greasy pate. "I hadn't thought he was acquainted with Tillmanshire."

Otherwise, she would not have risked an encounter with him by attending.

"They are too new to society and likely do not realize that not *everyone* deserves an invitation," Juliet said. "And I had just wondered to myself if this night could get any worse."

Lilah shook her head, a dark frisson of fear cascading down her at Juliet's words.

"Worry does not like to be tempted," she whispered. Already, she hadn't wanted to attend this party because of Miss Ashbury's presence here. Unfortunately, Aunt Zinnia had already made arrangements with the Dowager Duchess of Vale and Mrs. Harwick to view the fireworks that Tillmanshire had promised for the evening. Lilah, on the other hand, was not overly fond of loud, booming noises. For good reason.

Together, they deposited their teacups and turned to follow Aunt Zinnia out of doors, a few paces behind. Jack was still near the archway. His hard gaze settled on a figure walking down the hall behind them.

When they neared, he bowed. "Lady Granworth. Miss Appleton. I was wondering if you would permit me the pleasure of escorting you both to the terrace."

"Yes," Lilah said without hesitation and linked her arm with his. Juliet, however, hesitated and eyed her shrewdly until Lilah added, "I was only thinking to avoid Winthrop."

"In that case...Mr. Marlowe, we would appreciate your escort." Juliet took Jack's other arm. Once they were a distance away, halfway to the fountain, they stopped. "Are we mending fences, Mr. Marlowe?"

He grinned at her. "We are making an attempt."

"Very well, then," Juliet said, reluctance lacing her tone. "However, I would prefer if we did not tempt the gossips. I fear that I will not be the only one to notice how you have chosen a limited number of young women to favor with your attention at your few society appearances."

When Lilah saw Winthrop step onto the terrace and look in her direction, her hand tightened on Jack's arm. "Juliet, I would feel easier if Mr. Marlowe were near."

Beneath the sleeve of his superfine coat, his muscles hardened. And beside her, he was a solid source of comfort. "I would prefer to linger as well. After all, I have spoken with Haggerty at length, and I would not want to leave either of you unguarded in his presence."

If Lilah had not loved him before this moment, she would have fallen in love with him now. No matter how brave she might have been, she felt better knowing that she didn't have to be. Her poor heart, however, lay irrevocably in the hands of a man she could not marry.

Juliet looked from Jack to Lilah, her gaze sharper, knowing. Then she closed her eyes briefly before looking away. "The only way to avoid an inappropriate association would be if we were in the company of Thayne, Wolford, Vale, and Ivy as well."

For Lilah's sake, she approved of having all those dearest to her gathered close. There was no telling what horrors that Winthrop's vicious tongue might unleash. Coupling that with Miss Ashbury, who clearly did not like her, Lilah wondered what disaster might unfold.

Jack couldn't shake the overall sense that something dire was about to happen. Several times over the course of the evening, he'd tried to shrug it off. But then, he would catch a glimpse of Haggerty across the way, cozied up to Tillmanshire and his daughter and appearing snug as a worm beneath a rock.

Jack was never far from Lilah's side. However, since she conversed a great deal with Vale's bride, Jack could not remain too close. Otherwise, it would appear as if the four of them had paired off. He understood Juliet's initial reluctance to have him anywhere near Lilah for that reason. His sudden immersion into society had become a matter of curiosity for many, and they would be quick to link his name with Lilah's if he remained exclusively in her company.

Wolford, who had been making the rounds and—surprisingly—gaining admiration, now sidled up to him. "Do you know that Tillmanshire claims to have a collection of gold inlaid etchings from the Orient but refuses to show them? In fact, he even mentioned having sealed off most of his rooms for the party."

"From what I've heard, the baron only recently acquired his fortune. He must be afraid of someone wanting to take what is his."

Wolford grumbled. "Locking doors during a party is bad form. It shows ill breeding. Hell, even you keep your house open, and you haven't always had a fortune."

"No man would dare attempt to take what is mine." Jack's gaze veered to Lilah. When he saw her glance in his direction and smile, that sense of primitive possessiveness tore through him. It was more than the result of jealousy, he realized.

This went deeper. The intensity of what he felt for her nearly frightened him. And he didn't see how he was going to let her go when the time came. The eventuality made him irritable.

"True enough," Wolford agreed. "And with those daggers in your countenance, it is no wonder. Even if you had any treasures to your name, only those who know you would dare stand in your circle, let alone step foot on your doorstep."

"I do possess treasures. However, I see no value in bric-a-brac."

"Or furniture." Wolford chuckled. "It is a good thing you purchased your country estate furnished, or it would likely be as barren as your townhouse. You do realize, I hope, that when you marry, you will have to spend some of your money on baubles and trinkets to satisfy your bride."

Normally, Jack would have issued a jesting retort about never marrying, but the notion struck him more pleasantly than expected. Warmly, even. He could easily imagine Lilah choosing the furnishings for their home. He would give her anything she could ever desire. These thoughts should have startled him, but they did not. Instead, he felt overwhelmed by a sense of impatience.

She wandered over just then, with the duke and duchess in tow.

"What has put that peculiar expression on your face, Marlowe?" Vale asked. "You look as if suffering another moment at this party is more than you can bear. For my sake, I would rather view the fireworks and be gone."

"My husband is rather cross. Tillmanshire did not permit him to examine the explosives beforehand," the duchess said, leaning upon her husband's arm. Vale was forever tinkering with things for a better understanding. "Now, he is determined to make that his next experiment."

"The pyrotechnics were the only reason we attended." Vale nodded, a calculating gleam in his gaze as he was, no doubt, forming a list of ingredients in his head.

Beside Jack, Lilah exhaled a shaky breath. He looked down, noting faint horizontal lines above her dark brows. "Are you not fond of fireworks, Miss Appleton?"

"Only the quiet ones," she said, attempting a laugh.

Yet when her eyes met his, he saw a trace of fear in their depths. He'd witnessed this same expression in the garden when she'd told him about the abuse her brother had suffered. And suddenly, he understood.

In that moment, he would have promised to keep every firework quiet for her. Together with Vale, they could find a way to ensure that each one only issued the faintest crackle, while flaring with colorful, sparkling light.

Before he could make such a vow, however, Juliet came up to Lilah and Ivy and drew them both away for a quiet conversation.

"Marlowe," Vale said, remaining with Jack and Wolford, "I have been wondering all evening why you are here."

"He has become quite the curiosity of late," Wolford remarked.

Jack was confused. Surely Vale noticed Miss Appleton in their midst. Since the duke had always been brilliant, his cluelessness struck Jack as odd. To Vale, he said, "I am honoring the bargain we struck on Christmas Eve."

Yet even as the words left his lips, he knew it was far more than that. From the beginning, it had been more than that.

"Our bargain? Oh, do you mean the flowers I asked you to send Miss Appleton?"

"Of course," Jack said, wondering if his friend had doubted his word. "You wanted my assistance in seeing that she found an alternative to what awaited her in her father's will. I am making certain that she has that."

Vale frowned. "I only wanted you to send her flowers. In fact, I distinctly asked you *not* to make contact."

"What you did was forbid me," Jack reminded, and even Wolford chuckled beside him, as if understanding the likely results. "You had to have known that would have incurred my interest, which led directly to my taking up the banner of her cause…as matter of honor, because we struck a bargain."

"Inciting your interest by forbidding you did not occur to me until this instant." Vale shook his head in puzzlement. "Surely you are aware that she must marry a titled nobleman."

"Yes." Automatically, his gaze drifted over to where Lilah, Juliet, and Ivy stood. But they were no longer there.

Jack's gaze darted around, searching for the three of them. Then, as his heart raced, he found them by the fountain. Lilah appeared to be shaking her head, her hand covering her lips. Jack knew in an instant that something was wrong.

"We must leave here at once. Order the carriage," he said to his friends as he broke from them and started toward her, just as the footmen began to douse the torches.

Dozens of people crowded closer to the edge of the terrace, inadvertently blocking his path. Then, with the first of the fireworks, Jack caught another glimpse of Lilah. Unfortunately, he also spotted Haggerty bow to her in greeting.

"It is true. I heard it from Markham's own lips that he believes you are betrothed already," Juliet said, disbelief in her voice. "He'd heard the news from Miss Ashbury and in the presence of her father."

Lilah shook her head and shivered to the soles of her feet. "No. It cannot be. I thought the rumors had faded."

"Oh, it is true, dear Cousin," Winthrop said, appearing unexpectedly before them, just as a flash of light and deafening boom shook the air. "I see no reason to wait any longer. You are at your prime and never more of a feather for my cap. I sent a letter to the vicar this very morning to read the banns, Sunday next."

"The banns? No," Lilah whispered. *This has to be a nightmare. Or my imagination conjuring a truly horrifying catastrophe. This cannot be real.*

Ivy stood between them. "You have no right, Winthrop. She has been given until the end of the Season before the codicil finalizes."

Juliet stepped forward too. "I've had my own solicitor looking into this matter as well."

"Then you must know that it has always been within my power to exercise my rights," Winthrop said with a frothy, serpentine smile, before turning back to Lilah.

When Juliet lowered her head, Lilah knew he was speaking the truth.

"I wanted you to have a taste of true society so that you would know what I expect from a wife. Surprisingly, you have not disappointed thus far. And now, I eagerly await our nuptials." Winthrop sketched a courtly bow before turning on his heel and leaving Lilah in a state of shock.

More than anything, she needed Jack by her side. She turned away from the horror that was Winthrop and saw Jack's broad shoulders push through a line of guests, his expression hard, his hands fisted at his side. She nearly collapsed with relief. Instead, she staggered a bit, leaning against Ivy for support.

Jack had murder in his eyes as he glanced at Winthrop's retreating form. When his gaze settled on Lilah, it abruptly changed to something so intense that there was no way to describe it.

He stopped directly in front of her, his hands open and ready, as if he were tempted to pull her into his arms right here. And she would have let him. Unfortunately, he didn't. Although it was good of him to know that there was no need to give the gossips anything more to feed upon.

"Miss Appleton, how may I be of assistance?"

Another boom shook the ground at her feet. Lilah felt herself sway toward him, but it was Ivy who caught her by the waist.

"Mr. Marlowe, I fear the night air has given me a headache," Ivy said, sounding very duchess-like. "Would you be so kind as to escort me and my friend to a ready carriage? And Juliet, would you please inform my husband?"

"Thank you, Jack," Lilah whispered as she took his arm.

Beside her, Ivy went still. In the instant that passed, she looked from Lilah to Jack and then back to Lilah again. She lifted her brows as if to ask if this was the man she'd mentioned earlier.

Lilah nodded at this unspoken question. Yes. Jack was indeed the man she loved.

Chapter Fifteen

Lilah did not go to church the following morning with Aunt Zinnia and Juliet. In fact, she did not even sit up in bed when Nellie brought her a tea tray before she left for her day off, along with the other servants.

It wasn't until Lilah heard the final click of a door closing, the hush of rain pattering against her windowpanes, and the house descending into silence that she decided to rise.

Pacing the floor, she felt the weight of the clock and calendar in every step. The outcome she'd been trying to avoid all this time was now upon her. Winthrop had exercised the rights given to him in Father's will. The banns would be read—*her stomach turned*—in one week.

If only he'd waited.

In a day or two, the Season's *Original* would be announced.

In a day or two, Ellery would return.

But it was too late. She had failed. And now, Juliet could lose her house and be forced from town. And the life Lilah had begun to hope for was over. In the deepest yearnings of her heart, she acknowledged that Ellery was not part of it. When she allowed herself to dream, she only saw Jack's face.

A broken sigh left her. Lilah knew only one thing could possibly cheer her after last night. She needed to see her flowers.

Grabbing her wrapper, she slipped into the voluminous sleeves on her way down the servants' stairs. Soon, she found herself in the garden.

Icy sprinkles rained down on her as she gazed at her azaleas. Glossy, dark green leaves splayed out like earthbound stars. In the centers, buds swollen with color were nearly ready to bloom. In a day or two, they would be ready.

A day or two...

Gradually, the sprinkling rain grew heavier, soaking through her plaited hair to her scalp, sluicing down her parted fringe to her temples and into her eyes. Making her way beneath the arbor, she paused to blot her face with the ruffled cuff of her night rail, only to find it wet and dripping. She was soaked through and chilled but felt no urgency to remedy the situation.

Instead, she took a moment to peer down at the silver web between the bench and the arbor post. Small pearls of dew clung to the lovely spiral design. Yet something was different today. There was no movement. No flurry of activity. There was, however, a fat insect caught on one of the outer threads. Surely with such a sizable visitor, the spider would come directly and begin cocooning it in silk, wrapping for later.

Crouching down, Lilah peered closer. She touched the web gently, hoping to alert the spider from wherever she was hiding. That was when she realized what was different.

It wasn't a fat insect caught in the web after all. It was the spider. Only she looked smaller now, her body half its size, her legs shriveled and clawlike beneath her.

Lilah sank to her knees in disbelief. She shook her head. No, this wasn't how it was supposed to be. The spider had tended her web every day. Why did she not have visitors? Why had she been left alone to suffer this fate?

A strange, keening moan filled the arbor. As hot tears trailed down her cheeks, Lilah realized that the sound was coming from her. She was sobbing, mourning the loss of a spider. The idiocy was not lost on her.

"Lilah, darling, what is the matter?"

She didn't even jump at the sound of Jack's voice or his sudden appearance, crouching beside her, his hand at her back. He must have slipped through the garden door as before. Somehow, she knew he would be here, right when she needed him.

She turned into his embrace and buried her face in the damp folds of his greatcoat. "She's dead, Jack. No one came to her web."

"Shh…" he crooned, lifting her to her feet and tucking her into the warmth of his coat. His body was a solid wall of support against her. "It was too early for most insects. It just wasn't her time."

Lilah shook her head, her hands fisting over his chest. "But it had to be her time. She worked too hard to end up like this."

He took her face in his hands and tilted it up to gaze down at her. "I won't let that happen to you."

The determination in his countenance caused a flutter of hope beneath her breast. The fact that he understood her crazy ramblings caused her heart to swell with longing. "Why have you come to the garden this morning?"

"Am I too early for calling hours?" He offered a tender smile as he brushed her dripping hair from her face.

For someone who remembered everything she said, this was an odd thing to have missed. "We do not have calling hours on Sundays. The servants have the—"

"The day off," he finished for her, pressing his lips against her forehead. "The truth is, I was worried about you when I saw your aunt and cousin walk into the chapel without you."

She closed her eyes, inhaling his comforting scent. "Worried? That does not sound like you."

"No. It does not," he said, not elaborating. Instead, he slid an arm around her waist and bent to scoop her into his arms.

She gasped at the suddenness of the motion as he strode up the path toward the house. "Jack! I have strength enough to walk on my own."

"Come. Your feet are bare. You are wet through and need the warmth of a fire before you catch cold."

Left on the latch, the door took only the nudge of his boot before springing open. And he closed it behind him just as easily. She shivered, leaning into him, wanting closer to his warmth, close enough to banish his worry. It did him no good, after all. In fact, worrying served no purpose for her any longer either. The time had come when imagining a catastrophe would no longer save her from reality.

It had been foolish to linger in bed this morning, feeling sorry for herself, hating that she had so few choices and none of them what she wanted. Because if she were allowed to make her own choices, then she would choose a life with Jack.

When he hesitated and looked around without lowering her to the floor, she placed a hand to his chest in reassurance. "As I said, there is no one here. And my aunt and cousin are dining at Mrs. Harwick's after church as well, so they will be gone for hours."

Essentially, this fact left the townhouse under her care. He was her guest. And they would be alone...for hours.

"I wish you had not told me that," he said, his voice suddenly deeper, hoarse. He closed his eyes briefly. Then, after drawing in a deep breath, he started to walk again. "Where is your kitchen? Through here?"

She didn't have time to answer before he'd turned the corner and was already inside the room he sought. Without a word, he lowered her to sit at the edge of the worktable. The moment he stepped apart from her, another shiver sliced through her, making her teeth chatter.

Her hair was dripping through her wrapper, the frigid water making her colder still. She tried wringing out the plait but only saturated her sleeves as the water sluiced down her arms. To her, it seemed the wet outer garment was the culprit. As she untied the strings, she watched as Jack moved around the room, searching cupboards with efficiency, until he closed the last one.

"Where are the drying cloths?" he asked, returning to her just as she slid the wrapper off her shoulders.

"All the clean linens are upstairs. My aunt prefers to keep them in a single closet."

His gaze dipped. "Upstairs."

"Yes. Directly outside my bedchamber." It wasn't until she let the wrapper fall to the table that she followed his gaze downward. Her night rail was damp and nearly transparent. The ruffles down the center did not hide the dark rose color of her nipples or the fact that they were taut and pebbling beneath the fine cotton. In fact, the ruffles weighted the garment so that it conformed to every curve of her flesh. The fabric clung to the swells of her breasts, the tapering of her waist, the flair of her hips, and the dark shadowy triangle between her thighs.

For an instant, whispers of decorum instructed her to cover herself. And she nearly did. Her hands lifted from the table and then hovered in the air on either side of her breasts. But then she looked at Jack again. His eyes were dark, heated, and devouring her. He licked his lips.

"Lilah, order me to leave this instant," he said, his voice more raw than rough, more beseeching than commanding.

"I have few choices that are my own, Mr. Marlowe," she said, feigning vexation, even though it was hard to catch her breath. To ensure he waited until she finished, she leaned forward and splayed her hand over his waistcoat. "I am more inclined to ask you to…stay."

He covered her hand with his and met her gaze. "If I stayed, there would be irreversible consequences. Your choices would diminish even more."

"Then let me have the one that matters most." Determined, she slid off the edge of the table. Lifting her face up to his, she stood in front of him, her feet between his boots. "I don't care about anything else. Whatever happens tomorrow will happen. But today, I am still free. I belong to no one other than myself, and if I want to give myself to the man I love, then I—"

She halted the moment her declaration passed her lips. His gaze never faltered, though his breathing quickened, his chest rising and falling beneath her hands.

"At least, I believe that's what to call it. How do you know, beyond any doubt, when you are in love?"

He lifted his hand to her face, softly tracing the line of her jaw with his fingertips. "It will consume you. Terrify you. Rob you of rational thought. And make you dream of the impossible."

"I thought so." Lilah swayed toward him.

His gaze returned to her body in a blatant statement, like the one he'd made in the Serenity Room. *You are mine.* She felt like his, every part of her humming just for him.

She waited for him to decide. The kitchen fell silent. Only the sound of their breathing and the occasional crackle from the wood pieces beneath the curfew stirred the air.

Then, he lifted her against him. She thought he was going to set her back down on the edge of the worktable, but instead, he turned, heading up the narrow servants' stairs, two at a time. Without a break in stride, he made his way to her open doorway and kicked it shut behind him.

He seemed to know exactly where her bedroom was. "How did you…" and then she remembered their conversation in the garden. "Ah, yes. My window."

Holding her with one hand, he reached behind him and turned the key in the lock. "In case someone returns early."

"To protect my honor?" she teased, remembering her decision to close the door to the Serenity Room.

"There's that and"—he lowered her feet to the floor, his hands flexing on her hips—"I don't want us to be interrupted."

Us. Whenever he said that word, it made her warm, and weak in the knees.

She took a step apart from him and lifted up her night rail—over her body, her arms, her head—until she was stripped bare before him. He growled as he looked at her, shrugging out of his greatcoat. And then, those ready hands hauled her against him.

His mouth descended on hers. There was no moment of hesitation for either of them. He kissed her as he had that first time, devouring her lips, her tongue, as if this kiss was the only thing worth living for. She whimpered, knowing the same was true for her.

Reaching for her hands, he settled them at his waistcoat buttons without breaking contact. She took the hint and began slipping the cloth-covered discs free while he yanked at his cravat and whipped it to the floor. When his waistcoat parted, he removed it, along with his shirt, casting them both to the floor. She only had a glimpse of his body—hard, sculpted perfection—before he pulled her against him again, flesh-to-flesh, the swells of her breasts yielding to the firmness of his broad chest.

He lifted her, kissing her, and crossed the room to the hearth. Yet he didn't stop in front the low fire burning in the grate. Instead, he took her to her window seat and lowered her down. Her plait had come loose, her damp hair falling against her back and causing another shiver.

"Are you cold?" he asked against her lips, his hands gliding over her back, fingers splayed to touch every inch.

She shook her head, arching against his body. "You're very warm."

"Just wait." He grinned, his eyes a gleaming dark gold in the hazy light filtering in through the lattice window. His mouth skimmed down her throat, pausing at the pulse he'd tasted the other night. Then he nudged her back, where he had arranged the pillows behind her.

Gripping her hips, he pulled her to the edge of the seat, her knees on either side of him. Trusting him, she reclined, leaving herself exposed to him.

His gaze simmered over her breasts, her stomach, her sex. He grunted, a primitive sound, one of both possession and approval. She held her breath. His hands followed the same path, beginning at her shoulders, covering her breasts, trailing down her ribs, to her stomach, her hips, her sex, her legs, and all the way to the tips of her toes.

A rush of air left her lungs. She felt claimed. Everything he saw, everything he touched, was his.

Then he ran the same path back up again. After the shock of the first pass, her body was already eager for his touch, responding with quivers and tremors over her flesh and deep inside.

He repeated the sweep, only this time much slower, pausing to linger, kneading her breasts, grazing the taut peaks with the pads of his thumbs. Her nipples responded more and more to each slide until she gasped, her head falling back against the pillows. He leaned over her, closing his hot mouth over the crest. She cried out from the shock and pleasure of it. Clinging to him, her fingers pushed through the thick, damp tendrils of his hair, holding him to her, arching into his mouth.

If she was his, then he was hers as well.

Releasing her, he murmured something that she could not decipher, but the deep, carnal sound flooded her with a warm honey sensation that pooled low inside. He took her other breast, tutoring her flesh in the ways of ecstasy.

His hand coasted down her ribs, her stomach, her hips, and found her sex once more. This time, he did not tease her with a mere touch but cupped her fully, the heat of his hand radiating into her, the rhythmic press of his palm spreading the slick wetness coating her. Then he turned his wrist and caressed her with his fingertips.

He released her breast with a gasp of his own, his head tilting back, his eyes closing. "You're drenched for me."

If it wasn't for the blatant satisfaction on his face, she might have blushed with embarrassment. Instead, she flushed with understanding. This was how he wanted her, wet and writhing beneath his touch.

Boldly, she rose up and kissed him, crushing her mouth to his, tilting her hips against his hand. He pressed against her, stroking the swollen seam of her flesh and then gliding into its warmth, his finger traversing a slow path from beginning to end and back again, over and over until she could hear the wet slide and anticipate the sensation of each touch.

Mouths never separating, his other hand reached for hers, drawing it down to the fall of his breeches. Instinctively, she knew what he wanted. Both of her hands deftly plucked at the fastenings until the flap fell free and a thick column of flesh jutted forth, falling heavily into her palm. That velvety flesh was so hot that she pulled her hand away automatically.

Jack issued a gruff sound, somewhat amused and somewhat pained. "Do you want to stop?"

Yet he chose that moment to slide his finger into her depths, teasing her with slow, languid thrusts.

"*Oh, Jack*" was all she could say for a moment. She could tell by his knowing grin and the challenging lift of his brows that he already knew the answer anyway. Even so, she needed certainty and honesty between them. "I want to know what you feel like inside me."

The heat in his gaze flared. He growled again, slanting his mouth over hers. He shifted between her thighs. Taking her hand, he curled it over his hard length and guided him to her sex. With his hand over hers, he mimicked the slow up and down slide from a moment ago, slipping in between her wet seam, gliding over her flesh, building a sense of urgency that made her back arch and her hips tilt in invitation.

Then he paused at her opening, hesitating in a way that he hadn't with his finger. She wondered if he was waiting for her anticipation to build, and it was. She could feel her body swell and contract in a need she'd never known before. When he released her hand, she settled it over his heart. Their gazes locked. He broke their kiss, his breath against her lips.

"I love you," he said and then plunged inside, stretching her, driving into her body with one hard thrust.

The shock left her stunned. Too stunned to cry out. Her mouth opened but no sound came forth. She gripped his shoulders, pushing him away, then pulling him closer, nails biting into his flesh. Tears stung her eyes, filling them and making his face a blur before she blinked, and they forged a path down her cheeks. She didn't know it would hurt so bad. That she would feel as if her hips were being separated from her body. And yet, he told he loved her…

"Your love is painful," she scolded, blinking away her tears.

He kissed the dampness from her cheeks tenderly. "Yours is as well. Achingly—exquisitely—snug. Your body issues these tiny tremors, gripping me tighter, pulling me deeper. I don't know if I can bear it."

On a groan, he withdrew from her body. She frowned, worried. "But there is more, is there not? It is not just pain. That would be rather unfair." Sort of like her life.

He chuckled and nipped at her lips, traversing down a familiar path to her breasts, suckling and rousing them to ecstasy, making her forget her question as his hand cupped her sex once more. He teased her flesh until she fell back against the pillows, her hips arching wantonly. His kisses trailed down over her stomach and lower still, brushing against the dark curls that shrouded her. Curious, she lifted her head.

He grinned at her. "Do not tell me you love me, Lilah. I forbid you."

She smiled. But the laugh rising from her throat suddenly turned into a moan when his mouth opened over her. His tongue slid between her swollen flesh, devouring her with long, greedy licks. A whisper of decorum filled her head, asking if this was appropriate. Surely not. And she most certainly should not be so eager for every flick of his tongue. She shouldn't be writhing, pushing herself against his mouth.

Jack stilled her frantic movements. Gripping her hips, he murmured those low carnal words to her sex, forcing her to endure the wickedness of his talented mouth. Then his finger slid deeper, thrusting faster, matching the fevered flicks of his tongue. Ten thousand sensations flooded the surface of her skin, tingling, tightening. She wanted to buck her hips, to move with him, but he held her still as his onslaught continued. She gasped for breath, her exhale coming out as a whimper. A plea. He growled, harsh and commanding. The vibration spiraled through her, pulsing deep, fast, consuming her, until…

She fractured, crying out in sharp surprise and then in a low moan of ecstasy.

Pleasure surged through her. His thick flesh was there between her thighs, nudging inside as the wave rippled, following it deep, filling her. This time there was no sudden, searing pain, only fullness, along with that reverberation of rapture still spiraling through her. He matched each wave with languorous thrusts, prolonging her pleasure.

"Yes," he hissed, approving. His thrusts quickened, deepened. With his body grinding against hers, he refused to let her pleasure dissipate but urged her onward as her back arched and her entire universe became the place where their bodies fused.

She cried out again, the sound choked, her tongue repeating his name again and again until she heard him shout. Suddenly, he withdrew and hauled her against him, clutching her, as hot, thick fluid slicked the space between them.

Breathing hard and boneless, she collapsed against him, pressing her face into his neck. "I love you, Jack."

She could hear him grin. Arrogant man.

CHAPTER SIXTEEN

Jack sat in the tufted chair near the hearth, with Lilah curled on his lap and one of her shawls draped over their naked bodies. They drank tepid tea from the same cup and nibbled on cold, stale toast, brushing the crumbs away with kisses.

It was the best meal of his life.

Lilah blinked slowly, a grin on her lush mouth as she twirled her fingertips into the hair at his nape. "Making my own choice has been a revelation. Had I known about all of...this, I would have made demands upon you much sooner."

"Hmm...that first day in the garden? Or later, in Mrs. Harwick's parlor?"

She giggled, sloshing tea over the rim and dripping it on his shoulder. She bent her head, chasing the droplet down the length of his collarbone and licking him clean for good measure.

He groaned. Her wriggling and attentive ministrations roused his desire, engorging his flesh, making him ready to take her once more. Then again, he hadn't lost his desire for her at all. How could a man feel sated and yet yearn for more at the same time? For that matter, how could a man feel so content and yet restless?

Likely the latter was because he knew he couldn't force her to leave with him. But that was all he wanted. She was his, after all. The sooner she accepted it, the better.

"No, indeed," she said, an impish light in her gaze. "I was thinking of that first moment, right outside of Hyde Park, with you on your Destrier."

The image filled his mind, and it took all of his control not to lift her up and settle her down onto his eager flesh. He knew she was tender, her flesh pink and swollen, and he would not allow himself to indulge again until she was healed. "I imagine we would have caused quite the scandal."

"I wonder if such a position would be possible…" She pursed her lips in thought.

His heart, brain, and erection fought for blood. Her curiosity might kill him, but he was willing to make the sacrifice. "We will have a picnic at my country estate when the weather is fine and discover the answer."

She lowered her gaze down to their teacup and sighed. "That would be lovely, Jack, but I am not altogether certain what the future holds."

Their futures were now fused, bonded forever. She should already know that. "Where is the young woman who is determined to make her own choices?" he asked.

"She's here, within this skin, but you have to understand this is all new to me. For years, I cringed when I even thought of disobeying or stepping outside the rules of propriety. My parents demanded perfection—my father, in particular.

Whenever Jasper or I caused an embarrassment, even in front of the servants, he would punish us."

Jack's hands tightened to fists, a terrible violence clawing at his heart.

Lilah covered his hand with hers and lifted it for a kiss. "Not by raising a hand," she continued, "but with shouts and belittling words that struck a deeper blow. I buried mine so deeply that even after my father's death, I strove to be perfect. I never spoke out against my mother, I never fought against the rules of decorum, and I never railed against the codicil in my father's will. I accepted it all out of a longstanding fear that if I was not perfect, then I did not deserve love."

"You *are* perfect," he said fiercely, taking her face in his hands and kissing her brow, her lashes, her nose, cheeks, and lips. "You could yell obscenities in public, spill your tea on the king, break every rule, don a nest for your hat, wear a burlap sack as your dress, and you would still be perfect to me."

She beamed at him, tears leaking from the corners of her eyes. "That is the secret I never knew until now—that love is the only thing that can conquer fear. Love is the only thing that makes me feel powerful and willing to take a risk."

"What risk?" he asked, hoping she was about to tell him that she would leave here with him this very moment.

She reached over and set their teacup down on the small side table before facing him. Tilting her head down, she looked up at him beneath her lashes. "Will you promise me one thing, Jack?"

He didn't hesitate. "Anything."

Yet in the next moment, he wished he would have.

"Do not do anything to save me. I need to fight this next battle alone."

"What?" He shook his head, not sure if he'd heard her correctly. But when he saw her look at him with tender expectation, he knew he had. "Lilah, you don't know what you're asking of me."

She kissed him softly, his mouth firm and unyielding. "Oh, my dear warrior, I know very well, and I know this will be difficult for you. However, I cannot go from never speaking up, out of fear, to hiding behind your shield. I have to try this on my own."

"Whatever your plan is, we both know there is no guarantee that the outcome will be favorable. How can you expect me not to interfere? You are mine. You have just proven it."

She drew back, a frown on her lips. "No. What I have proven is that I am my own person. I thought you, more than anyone else, understood this."

Damn it all! Why wasn't she asking for his help? "Any other woman would be using her wiles to tempt me into marriage. Instead, you seem determined to make it clear that what we shared was little more than an assertion of your independence."

She winced and scrambled off of his lap, leaving him cold and bare. Then she jerked her shawl around her. "Do you really take me for a manipulative sort of woman, even after *what we shared?*"

"Of course not—"

"I thought you valued honesty."

"I do." He stood and reached for her, ever glad when she didn't resist. But she didn't uncross her arms either. He folded her into his embrace nonetheless and was rewarded by the feel of her relaxing against him. Closing his eyes, he pressed his forehead to hers. "You are strong, brave, and determined. I love this about you. But I will hate keeping this promise."

The worst part was that he knew she could survive without him. Yet he wanted her to need him, to want him, so much that she couldn't breathe, couldn't think of a life without him. Because that's how he felt about her.

"What do you expect of me?" she asked softly, her warm breath fanning out over his lips. "There are things I must do myself, not the least of which is speaking to my mother about Father's will. And I would feel much better if I knew we shared this understanding."

"And I would feel much better if I could tuck you into my pocket and take you away with me."

She smiled and unfolded her arms, slipping them around him. The supple pillows of her breasts pressed against him, the heat of her sex nestling against his. "If I were in your pocket, then I could not give you a farewell kiss."

Then she rose up on her toes and did. Only he didn't want it to be farewell. He wanted to remain with her always. Leaving her demanded more strength than he possessed. And he hated feeling this weak. This...vulnerable.

Now, he knew why he'd never wanted to fall in love.

CHAPTER SEVENTEEN

Jack called upon Lilah the following morning, wanting to
settle matters with her.

He did not like the way they'd parted, a few hasty kisses
and him slipping away through the garden. He'd left too
many things unsaid. In the very least, she should have known
his intentions. Yes, he would honor his promise, but that
did not mean he wouldn't try to interfere. And the only way
he saw that he could was through marriage. A plan that he
accepted with open arms. Yet he wasn't certain she would.

Unfortunately, at the door, the butler informed him that
Miss Appleton was not at home for callers.

Jack drew in an impatient breath. "I understand that she
was not at home to me previously, but I believe, if you would
inquire, she will receive me now."

"I'm afraid, sir, that Miss Appleton is not at home," the
butler repeated crisply, enunciating each word.

Jack clenched his teeth and his fists. "You haven't even told
her who is calling."

"Marlowe, is that you?" Vale came up the stairs behind him. "Why ever are you here?"

"I am calling upon Miss Appleton." He made an impatient gesture to the man who hindered his efforts.

The butler bowed to Vale. "Miss Appleton has gone to Surrey this morning, Your Grace."

Jack growled and glared at him.

"Ah, then my wife won't be much longer with her visit," Vale said, inclining his head. "Please inform the duchess that her carriage awaits."

"Very good, sir." And with that, the butler stepped back into the foyer and closed the door, leaving Jack to wonder why Lilah hadn't told him that she planned to leave London.

He knew she'd mentioned a need to speak with her mother, but he hadn't thought she would have gone so soon. A keen sort of panic shot through him at the idea of her traveling alone. He would have gone with her, watched over her…

Vale placed a hand on his shoulder. "Perhaps in the meantime, we could have a chat. There wasn't much time during Tillmanshire's event, not before the unfortunate announcement."

"Yes," he said, distracted as they walked down the few stairs to the pavement. "I came to see if I could offer my assistance."

"Mmm…yes. Which brings me to our topic and how you are under the mistaken assumption that I placed Miss Appleton in your charge."

Jack shook his head in disagreement. "There has been no mistake. You did. Though perhaps you've forgotten. You were rather insensible that night."

Vale stopped, his jaw tight. "I recall the night perfectly, and I believe I asked you merely to send Miss Appleton flowers in order to—"

"Yes, to pique my interest," Jack interrupted, recounting their conversation from Tillmanshire's party.

"No. It was to ensure that Viscount Ellery would take notice."

"Ellery? Why him?" Suddenly, Jack had a sinking suspicion but he hoped he was wrong. *Please don't say the* Marriage Formula.

"The *Marriage Formula*." Vale retrieved a card from a pocket inside his coat that displayed two sets of numbers. "The results of his equation matched perfectly against Miss Appleton's. I'm still hoping that once Ellery finds out about Haggerty's announcement, if he hasn't already, that he will be smitten enough to fight for her."

Jack stared at the card and put his hand over the one in his own pocket. Then, without a word, he turned from Vale before he did something he would regret.

The four-hour trip to Surrey had not prepared Lilah for the wealth of memories that assailed her as she walked into her family home. She could still hear Jasper's irreverent laughter ringing out, like a merry taunt to the dust motes sifting through the air. She could still hear her father's bellows, creaking with each step, demanding to know why the foyer was not in perfect order. She even noticed the letters on the salver, a collection of at least a week. Though they were likely notices from creditors who would never be paid.

Winthrop had let most of the servants go last year, leaving only a maid and a cook for this large house. With the tenants paying no rent and earning a meager income themselves, there was little hope that circumstances would improve.

Leaving her bonnet and reticule in the foyer, Lilah walked upstairs to her mother's sitting room. No matter what state either the house or Mother's life was in, she always maintained her own schedule, which included waiting in her sitting room during calling hours.

As she'd been taught, Lilah rapped quietly on the door. Her mother's cultured voice rang out clearly. "You may enter."

Opening the door, Lilah saw Mother sitting on the edge of her tufted chair, her posture straight as a board. She blinked several times without offering a greeting. Mother was too vain to wear spectacles, and her eyesight had been failing, even before Father died.

"Good day, Mother. You are beautiful, as always." And it was true. Her mother was even lovelier than Aunt Zinnia, her blonde hair still untouched by silver, her eyes a watery blue, and her features perfectly proportionate. Lilah had inherited her coloring from Father's side of the family, but Jasper had taken after their mother. And he'd always looked the part of the perfect son. Some of the time, that had been all that mattered.

Mother frowned. "Lilah, why have you come? Has Zinnia finally abandoned her nonsensical endeavor?"

Of the two sisters, Aunt Zinnia had been the only one who'd read Father's will and saw a different possibility for Lilah's future. She'd taken it upon herself to ensure that Lilah had a chance at a better life. "No, Mother. I have come to visit. Aunt Zinnia sends her best and hopes that you will return with me."

"She knows that I do not travel," Mother said under her breath and then shook her head. "However, the nicety is appreciated. And I imagine she allowed use of her own carriage? I would hope you do not require coin for a hired coach."

As of yet, there had been no single word of affection or gladness that Lilah had come. Then again, she didn't know why she'd expected something more. Holding back her disappointment, Lilah settled into an adjacent chair.

Between them, a needlework square poked out of the top of the narrow basket on the floor. Mother's embroidery had always been exquisite, perfect. Yet this sample did not depict her usual skill. Instead, it revealed the havoc wrought from poor vision. The stitches were large and uneven, the knots tangled at the back. Likely, she wasn't aware of this. Mother never wasted her time on anything other than perfection.

She required beauty and flawlessness in all things, herself included. Her clothes were unwrinkled. Her complexion unblemished. Even her hands were elegant and posed, just so.

Lilah looked down at her own hands, resting in her lap but hidden by gloves. They were identical hands and the only part of Mother that Lilah had inherited.

"Yes, my aunt was gracious enough to loan her carriage," Lilah said. After meeting with the local barrister, she'd given Nellie leave to visit her own family and, quite possibly, Mr. Shalley at the neighboring farm.

Mother bristled. "Surely not alone. Surely you have adhered to the rules of propriety I taught you."

Her mother wasn't worried about her safety, not the way Jack would have been. Those *rules* were—and had always been—more important than Lilah's overall well-being. "My maid accompanied me."

"That sharp tone is unbecoming. I'm certain Winthrop will not tolerate it once you are married."

And here it was—Lilah's moment of reckoning. She drew in a deep breath. "I am not going to marry Cousin Winthrop. That is the reason I have come."

Mother laughed and clucked her tongue in a way that was all too familiar, like the time when Lilah was a little girl, wearing a crown of daisies and preening before her.

"Aren't I pretty, Mother? Ivy says that I am the queen of the forest and will surely marry the king of the meadows."

"Ivy was being kind, dear—which any friend ought, of course," Mother said, her voice pinging sharply with amusement before she shook her head and tsked. "It is a shame, however, that she is so pretty. You would do much better if you were seen next to an ugly girl. Then, you truly could become an imaginary queen."

Mother had never understood the purpose of imagination. Perhaps that had been the reason Lilah had found so much solace in it.

"Of course you will marry Winthrop. The agreement was set in place by your father and is binding."

Lilah's visit to the barrister's office had reaffirmed this. There was no way for her to break the terms of the will as it stood. The barrister informed her that a well-connected husband with a title could do so. As soon as the banns were read, however, such a violation would cause nothing short of a scandal, from which the parties involved would never recover.

"If that is true, then why did the codicil offer me three years and the hope of finding another gentleman?"

"Your father did not want you to do something foolish like your—" She stopped short before she said the word *brother*. Since Jasper's disgrace, Mother had never once referred to him or said his name. "You needed time to understand that Winthrop is your only hope of having a husband at all."

"That is not true. If it weren't for Father's demands that I marry a titled gentleman, I could have found a husband on my own. In fact, I believe I have." She made the declaration more out of rebellion than actually knowing it. Jack had never proposed marriage or even suggested a short future together.

Although he had told her that he loved her. That certainly must account for something.

Mother made that irritating sound again with her tongue and smiled patiently. "You needn't invent stories. Marrying Winthrop is the best option for you and, in turn, you will have a home. The baron has been gracious to allow me to remain here all this time. Now, it is up to you to repay him for his good deeds by upholding expectations and producing an heir."

Lilah grimaced, bile rising up her throat. She swallowed it down and straightened her shoulders. "I am not marrying Winthrop. I am making my own choices."

That smile fell. "You were not born to make your own choices. A young woman adheres to her parents' wishes. Especially one with no…other…options."

"I am not without options!"

"Had you been beautiful, your circumstances might have been different," Mother continued, paying no heed to Lilah's outburst.

"I *am* beautiful…in my own way. I have many admirable qualities. I have even taken to wearing my hair differently. My forehead is not so vast and unbecoming. Have you not read Aunt Zinnia's letters? The *ton* is following my example—" Or at least they had been until Winthrop's announcement. Now, she was uncertain and hadn't been able to bear reading the *Standard* this morning.

Tears gathered along the lower rims of her eyes. She hated having to validate her own worth to her mother. She didn't even know why she was trying. Just once in her life, she would have liked to hear those same words from the woman who bore her. *You are beautiful.*

Yet as Mother had said a moment ago, having children had merely been *upholding expectations* on her part and nothing more.

Mother's gaze narrowed. She angled her head as if seeing Lilah for the first time since her arrival. "Tell me you have not done something foolish and irreversible."

"Like what, Mother? Dreamed of a different life for myself and fallen in love with a man who sees me for who I am?"

"You have lain with him," she accused, recoiling in an apparent mixture of disgust and outrage.

Even though she never would have altered her moments with Jack, Lilah still felt a small amount of guilt. She'd had twenty-three years of instruction on propriety, and it was a hard-etched rule that a woman remained chaste until her wedding. "I have."

"Is he a footman in your aunt's employ? A gardener? Did he promise to marry you if you would lay with him?" She scoffed as she stood and walked toward the window. "If there is one thing you should have learned from your"—Mother broke off and quickly amended—"learned by example, it is that men will say or do anything to slake their lust. They think nothing of ruining entire families, let alone one unmarriageable girl."

"This man did not promise me anything," Lilah admitted with vehement defiance. "I made my own choice."

"That was not your choice!" Her mother's raised voice revealed a crack in her composure. "You only had one thing to offer your cousin and that was your chastity. I doubt he will have you now."

"I would not have him, regardless."

"I cannot bear the disgrace of this. If you were to die in a carriage accident, it would be better for us all."

Lilah sucked in a breath. Anger and hurt sliced into her heart. Still, her mind tried to reject that her mother actually preferred her death to a scandal.

Mother continued. "At least then I would be able to hold my head with some dignity."

"Dignity for whom?" Lilah stood and moved to the window as well, taking hold of her mother's shoulders. "Do you care so much what your neighbors think of you and care so little for your own child—children? Jasper and I deserved more from you and father. We deserved a chance to make mistakes and still find welcome in our parents' bosom."

Lilah embraced her mother, holding on to one last hope of finding the affection she'd always wanted. Perhaps if she just breached this one barrier, the terrible façade would finally fall away and reveal her mother's love.

But it did not come. Her mother remained stiff, unyielding.

After a moment, Lilah released her and stepped back to wipe tears from her cheeks.

"You may leave my presence," Mother said with cold finality, her gaze out the window. "If there is any keepsake in the room that was once yours, you may take it with you."

In other words, this was the last time they would meet. As it had been after Jasper's death, from this point forward, Lilah's name would not be spoken in this house. To her mother, she was dead.

Chapter Eighteen

Jack left London and rode to his mother's house. He needed advice that only her unique perspective could offer.

The hours gave him time to think and time to wonder what was happening with Lilah in Surrey. He hated this uncertainty. He hated not knowing how to proceed. And he hated the news that Vale had delivered—Ellery was Lilah's perfect match.

No. While Jack didn't know the viscount's intentions toward Lilah, he knew Ellery was an honorable man. Yet none of that mattered because Jack felt in his heart that Lilah was his.

But was that enough?

By the time he arrived, dusk had fallen, and Bellum needed a good rest. Exhausted and weary as well, Jack left his Destrier in the care of the stable master.

The fieldstone cottage with green shutters and a cedar-shake roof was a welcoming sight. Jack had purchased this for his mother shortly after leaving school. At the time, he'd made enough money for her to keep a cook and a maid as well.

Now, she could have her choice of any house and any number of servants, but she said she preferred to live a simpler life.

On his way across the lawn, his mother came out through the whitewashed kitchen door, her sand-and-silver-colored hair tumbling out from beneath a matron's cap, her gaze curious, her mouth smiling.

"What gift has brought my son to me this evening?" She opened her arms wide.

As always, he embraced her heartily, lifting her to her toes. She'd grown plump in the past years after he'd begun making his fortune. Her life was easier now, and she always had bread with her broth, in addition to anything else she wished. "I know not. One minute I was in London, and the next thing I knew, Bellum had brought me here."

"Aw...such a sweet lie." As he set her down, she patted his cheek. "Now for the truth. Those worry lines on your brow tell me that you are troubled."

He shrugged. "It was a long ride. Nothing more."

"Very well," she said with a sigh that suggested she did not believe him. But instead of pressing, she merely linked her arm with his as they walked inside.

Then later, as the evening progressed, and he'd had more than his share of wine with his broth, he told her of Lilah. Not of what his intentions were but merely stating that he was acquainted with a young woman whose circumstances were forcing her into a life not of her choosing.

"Would there have been any advice or assistance you would have wanted at that time in your life?" he asked.

Mother was quiet for a moment, her gaze leaving his to stare into the cozy fire. "There is something I am obligated to tell you," she began, her voice quiet. "As you know, the reason that your father and I separated was because he needed to marry an heiress in order to secure monies for the earldom. Up until that point, his family was fine with our arrangement. Yet they would not stand for having the heir to an earldom married to his mistress."

"I remember," he growled, the words bitter on his tongue.

"But what I did not tell you was that your father and I ran away together." She shifted in the chair, seemingly uncomfortable, and eventually met his gaze. "We drove to Gretna Green and eloped in secret."

"Eloped?"

She offered a tentative nod and swallowed. "Within a month, his father discovered what we had done and had our marriage annulled. A scathing letter from the earl arrived, informing us that our union was unlawful. Enraged, your father left to confront his father, but before he could, his father—your grandfather—had a heart seizure and died. With John's mother devastated, and his younger siblings grieving, your father remained behind to see to their well-being."

Jack was trying to wrap his thoughts around this startling news. What his mother had suffered was even worse than he'd imagined.

"By the time John returned, a month had passed. He had not, as I'd hoped, addressed the issue of our marriage to his remaining family. Confessing this, he'd asked me to have patience and wait for a suitable mourning period to pass. I felt affronted. Unimportant," she explained, her voice rising in indignation, even after all this time. Then a pained look crossed her face. "I'd already begun to suspect that I was carrying his child. Yet after the way I'd been treated by my first husband and society after his scandal and subsequent death, I could not bear the thought of your father forcing me to play the mistress in confinement.

"So I demanded that he marry me once more, or we could never be together. And when he asked for understanding, instead I used our love against him. All the secret fears that lovers confess when they believe they are in a safe harbor— I used them as weapons, turning our love into the bitterest hatred. It was no wonder that he chose to leave, and I made him promise never to return," she finished, her voice breaking.

Jack sat forward in the chair, short of breath, and suddenly feeling as if the one person on whom he'd always counted had betrayed him. "If you were married, then that means..."

"You are legitimate. Or at least, you would have been, if not for the annulment before your birth."

Lilah returned to London later that evening, just as Aunt Zinnia and Juliet were donning their hats in the foyer, in preparation to leave and dine with Mrs. Harwick.

"It was a long journey, wasn't it, dear," Aunt Zinnia said, her typically stern voice softer now. "If you'd prefer, we could all stay in and talk about your visit with your mother."

Juliet took notice as well, moving closer and placing a comforting hand at Lilah's shoulder. "We could have cups of chocolate and pieces of cake for our supper."

That sounded truly divine. A night of staying in and drinking cups of warm chocolate normally would have been

Lilah's remedy of choice. Yet at the mention of Mrs. Harwick's, Lilah instantly thought of Jack. There was a possibility that he would have been invited as well. And seeing Jack was the only remedy her heart required.

"Actually, if it wouldn't be too much of a bother, I should like to go to Mrs. Harwick's as well and put this day behind me." Far, far, behind her.

Unfortunately, when they arrived at Mrs. Harwick's, Jack was not there. Nor did he arrive at any time during dinner. Neither did Thayne. Instead, it was just the four of them, chatting away about recent gossip. Though Mrs. Harwick, Aunt Zinnia, and Juliet carefully veered wide of anything relating to Winthrop's announcement at Tillmanshire's party or to the Season's *Original*.

By the time they adjourned to the parlor, Lilah could no longer bear it. She had to know. "Was there anything of note in this morning's *Standard*?"

"Of note?" Mrs. Harwick asked, her eyes blinking for four counts, as if a metronome controlled her lashes.

"There was that fascinating tidbit about the scalloped lace spotted on the cuff of Lady Amberdeen's sleeve," Aunt Zinnia added. "Four tiers of it, mind you. On a *sleeve*. Needless to say, it caused quite a stir."

Juliet remained quiet, seemingly distracted by the tassel at the end of the pillow beneath her arm.

"Was there any mention of the Season's *Original*?" There. She'd said it, and now the question must be answered.

Mrs. Harwick and Aunt Zinnia exchanged a look. Juliet cleared her throat and offered, "There was."

And then the room fell silent again.

Lilah stood and placed her hands on her hips. She'd had enough of politeness, and meanness, and everything else in between.

"I would just like to know who was named." Her voice cracked under the strain of her emotions. "Miss Ashbury?"

"No, dear," Aunt Zinnia said. "No one was named the *Original*."

"What do you mean? The committee always names the *Original* after the first month."

"Usually, yes," Mrs. Harwick added. "But not always."

Juliet brushed her hands over her skirt and lifted her gaze. "The *Standard* announced that the anonymous committee informed them, by way of messenger, that they were delaying their announcement until the end of next month."

"Next month?" Lilah shook her head, not wanting to believe that it was over. She searched the faces in the room, hoping. But it was futile to deny the truth. She'd failed. "Juliet, I'm sorry. I had hoped—albeit foolishly—that I might win for you. That, perhaps, the committee had decided before Lord Tillmanshire's party."

"I never should have let Max goad me into that wager and involve you. It is my own fault." Juliet stood and took Lilah's hand, squeezing it with affection. "You were perfect."

"It isn't over," Lilah said firmly. "I mean, it is for me but not for you. There is still a way for you to win part of the wager. All you need is to make sure that Thayne does not succeed with Wolford." Then, remembering where she was standing, she glanced over at her hostess. "Forgive me, Mrs. Harwick."

"Oh, don't mind me," she said with a laugh. "I happen to enjoy a little rivalry from time to time."

Juliet's eyes brightened to their usual gemlike quality as she nodded. "You have quite the devious mind, Cousin. If all goes well, I can continue to be a thorn in Max's side. Heaven knows he deserves it—one redeeming moment aside, of course."

"What was that?" Aunt Zinnia asked, not hearing the last bit that Juliet whispered.

"Hmm?" Juliet lifted her brows as if she didn't understand the question.

And before Aunt Zinnia could ask again, they were interrupted by the appearance of the marquess in the doorway.

Juliet feigned a gasp. "It is true. If you speak of the devil, he does indeed appear."

"Then what they say about bad pennies is true about you, Lady Granworth," Thayne said matter-of-factly as he stepped into the room, pausing to greet his mother with a kiss upon her cheek. "Good evening, Mother. Lady Cosgrove. Miss Appleton. I hope you don't mind if I eat the rest of the cake. I'm starving."

Mrs. Harwick sighed. "I promise every single one of you that Maxwell was taught proper manners."

"And then he happily slipped free of those chains and became his own man," Thayne said, loading a plate with a tower of little cakes, as if he truly intended to eat them all.

"Maxwell, you wound me." Mrs. Harwick affected a sniff. "I was not overly strict in your instruction. In fact, I was quite indulgent."

He tossed his mother a wink. "Quite right. You were far too indulgent when I needed strictness, and too severe when I required lenience."

Mrs. Harwick grinned. "You have too much of your father's teasing nature. What has put you in such a playful mood?"

After popping another cake into his mouth and licking his fingertips, he sat back against the cushions. "I am pleased to report that I have hired a team of laborers to begin repairs on my recently acquired townhouse."

All eyes turned to Juliet, and hers, in turn, narrowed. "How kind of you to ensure that once this house belongs to its rightful owner, I will be able to move in directly."

"Surely you cannot think to win, even now."

Juliet glanced at Lilah and grinned. "Do not forget, Max, you still have to ensure Wolford makes a good showing before this is over."

The marquess frowned. And though it seemed impossible, Lilah felt immensely better about the events of the day. At least for a moment.

Then Mrs. Harwick changed that with one question. "Where was Jack this evening, Maxwell? I thought he meant to dine with us."

Yes, Lilah thought, eager to see Jack. He should have been here already. Until now, every time she'd needed him, he'd always appeared. That connection should have been even greater now, considering they were both in love. Weren't they?

Apparently no longer hungry for cakes, Thayne set his plate down on the table. "Marlowe is away, out of town, it seems. He did not leave word of when he would return."

Mother's voice made an unwelcome appearance in Lilah's mind. *Men will say or do anything to slake their lust. They think nothing of ruining entire families, let alone one unmarriageable girl.*

And in that moment, a terrible heartbreaking fear crashed over her.

Jack left his mother's home before first light the following morning, his mind weighted. All that he had believed—all the loathing that had spurred him and formed him into the man he'd become—had been a lie. He felt betrayed.

She'd apologized for not telling him the whole truth. She'd even confessed that she'd omitted some of the details out of bitterness but also out of a fear that Jack would leave her too.

There had been truth enough in his mother's circumstances to reconcile her actions. Knowing what she'd suffered and all that she'd sacrificed, he'd forgiven her. But he valued honesty too much not to be angry.

Not only that, but there was one part of the story that still remained a mystery. His father's side.

Once he arrived in town, exhausted, road weary—and yes, still angry—he did not go to his townhouse and mull over all that he'd learned. Instead, he rode directly to Mayfair and pounded on Dovermere's door.

"Why did you not tell me that you had been married to my mother?" Jack asked the instant he entered his father's study.

Dovermere looked up from his ledger with a start and, after a moment, slowly returned the quill pen to the stand. He gestured to the chair. "Good afternoon, Jack. Take a seat. You look like hell." Then he glanced to the door, where the butler waited. "Mr. English, if you would be so kind as to have Cook send a tray, I would be much obliged."

"I did not come here to take tea with you. This is not a social call," Jack said, even as the butler bowed and summarily disappeared. "I want answers."

"You've been to see your mother, I gather."

Jack offered a stiff nod, still standing firm, waiting.

Dovermere exhaled. "I did not even know of your existence until you were ten years old, and your mother wrote to me, asking for your education."

As a child, Jack had known her reasons. Mother had explained that his father had chosen money and other obligations over her. The hollowness that any boy might have felt at such news had been understandable. Jack had filled that empty place with hatred for the aristocracy and with determination to live a better life than that of the man who'd abandoned him. "Why not tell me, then?"

"I wanted to tell you," Dovermere said, a razor's edge cutting into the quietly spoken words. "Your mother did not want to you to be part of the society that had torn us apart. She wanted you to live free and be able to make your own decisions. I honored her wishes."

Honor. They had something in common after all, other than their likeness. "Still, you acknowledged me when you signed the papers at Eton. That act alone informed everyone in society of our connection. You had to know that they would draw conclusions that I was your bastard."

His father smiled. Not in an arrogant manner but more of tenderness. "I was proud to have you for my son, even from that first moment. You were so bold in the way you stood your ground. I already knew you were going to be a better, more determined man than I. And I wanted everyone to know that you were mine. Acknowledging you in a public sphere was the only avenue left to me, after I made my promise to your mother."

Jack swayed on his feet, exhaustion taking over. It must have been exhaustion. Otherwise, he would have been better prepared against the blatant attack his father launched at him. An attack of affection. Up until now, it had been easy to bat away his unwanted visits and constant needling to be part of Jack's life. But this was too much.

He stepped farther into the room and slumped down into the chair. "And now, what does all of it mean?"

"Since our marriage was annulled, it took effort to prove the date of your conception. After that, my solicitor quietly set about legitimizing your birth, just in case."

Legitimate. Jack swallowed down a sizeable lump in his throat. Everything he knew about himself. Every step he'd taken in life. All of it fell under scrutiny. He wasn't a bastard and likely never had been. Oh, but he'd lived like one. He'd fought like one. His identity and his determination both stemmed from that one single fact.

"You are still holding to the promise you made my mother?" he asked and received a nod. "I could still refuse to be named your heir?" Another nod, this one more reluctant.

"You could," his father said as a familiar gleam lit his eyes. "However, that is not to say that it wouldn't become an issue again after my death. Legal papers have a way of surfacing when one no longer has control. Perhaps it would be better to settle matters sooner, rather than later."

Chapter Nineteen

Four days had passed, and Jack Marlowe still had not come to call.

The *Standard* issued the briefest of mentions, regarding a sighting of *Mr. M—* leaving *Lord D—'s* residence earlier in the week but nothing else.

More than anything, Lilah wanted to see him, to tell him that she had broken ties with her mother. When she'd recounted her visit with her mother and told Aunt Zinnia, Juliet, and Ivy of her decision, they had all remained steadfast, promising to stand by her side, even if scandal rained down upon them, no matter what she planned to do next.

The only problem was she wasn't sure what to do next. The banns would be read in three days.

In the meantime, however, she had to pay closer attention to Ellery, who'd arrived only minutes ago, having just returned from his time away.

Aunt Zinnia was not in the parlor, acting as chaperone today. She was across the hall with Juliet, the doors to both rooms left open for a semblance of propriety. Lilah speculated that the reason was because her aunt expected Ellery to make an offer for her.

"If I may be so bold, Miss Appleton. You were in my thoughts a great deal during our time apart." Ellery grinned at her, his gaze searching hers as he sat on the edge of his seat, his body leaning toward hers. "Each day that passed, I was eager to return and even more eager to share my experiences with you. With each of our conversations, I always discover new things we have in common. Such is not the case with any of the other young women I have met."

It would solve all her problems if she could return his sentiment. She did enjoy their talks, but more often than not, she found herself daydreaming of Jack. Yet if she were to attach herself to Ellery, then perhaps that would not always happen. In time, she could grow fond of him. "Your friendship has been most welcome. However, I fear that there has been some news that I must tell you immediately."

He reached out with his hand and settled it over hers. "Miss Appleton—*Lilah*, if I may—if you are referring to the rumor linking you to Lord Haggerty, then I must tell you that I have already heard. In fact, I confess that very news is the reason I cut my travels short and returned to you."

Lilah felt dizzy, the flesh on her brow puckering in confusion. "If you know that my cousin has laid a claim upon me, then why are you here?"

"Because I wanted you to have your choice. I could not simply let this marriage take place without informing you of my regard." Now, he drew her hand into both of his. "I realize there would be quite a scandal involved, should you choose me, but I have already spoken with my parents, and they will support any decision I make. They are still eager to make your acquaintance."

All she had to do was agree, and she could have this man as her husband. He was here before her, leaving her with no doubt of his regard or his plans for the future. He was kind, handsome, honorable, and...

The type of man who deserved a chaste bride, or, in the very least, a woman who loved him.

Lilah slipped her hand free. "Forgive me, Lord Ellery. Any young woman would be fortunate to have earned your regard, but I cannot commit my heart to you when it resides elsewhere."

"Oh." He winced, and abruptly, his posture altered. He shifted back into the chair. Then, when that did not suit him, he stood and looked around the room, as if he'd dropped something earlier. Though Lilah suspected he simply did not want to meet her gaze again. "I was under the impression that your cousin's suit was not welcome."

"It isn't," she said quickly. "Quite honestly, I despise Haggerty."

Ellery slowly nodded. "Then it is Marlowe, as I suspected from the start."

This would have been the perfect time for Lilah to pretend ignorance, but she respected Ellery too much to play him for a fool. Instead, she neither confirmed nor denied his statement. "I have valued our friendship. That will not change. Not for me."

He chose not to respond but merely bowed to her and then turned on his heel, leaving her alone in the parlor.

When the front door closed, Aunt Zinnia and Juliet rushed across the hall. It was the first time Lilah had ever seen her aunt move with such speed that her skirts tangled with her legs.

"Did he make an offer, my dear?" Aunt Zinnia asked, her cheeks flushed, her eyes brimming with excitement.

"He did." Lilah wished she could leave it at that, but with her aunt's hopeful countenance in front of her, she couldn't. "I refused him."

Her aunt's eager grin abruptly fell but then rallied. "If your reason was because of Haggerty's involvement, then perhaps a simple explanation would set matters right."

Lilah shook her head and drew a breath. "He already knew, and he was willing to brave the scandal."

Juliet said nothing, but her tearful gaze spoke for her. Years ago, she'd taken her own path when faced with scandal. Out of respect, Lilah had never asked her about her reasons for it. Yet now, Lilah couldn't help but wonder if Thayne would have stood by Juliet, if given the chance.

Then Juliet squeezed her hand—a wordless display of worry as well as support. Lilah suspected Juliet knew that Jack held her heart. Even if he did not want it.

Just as the cheerless thought formed in her mind, a fearsome knock reverberated against the outer door, filling the foyer and even the parlor with the commanding sound. Lilah felt her heart quicken and her gaze strayed to the open parlor door.

A moment later, Mr. Wick appeared. "Mr. Marlowe to see Miss Appleton."

"Send him away," Aunt Zinnia said with a tired wave of her hand.

"No!" Lilah hadn't meant to shout, but it was more a matter of reflex. It took every bit of decorum to stand still and not rush out to greet him and drag him inside. "Please, Aunt. I would like to see him."

Aunt Zinnia looked at her as if a stranger stood before her. "Is Mr. Marlowe the reason you refused Lord Ellery?"

"Come, Cousin," Juliet said softly to Zinnia, taking her arm. "Let us wait across the hall until this matter is sorted, once and for all."

As they left, Lilah waited, facing the parlor door, shifting from one foot to the other. The thumping of her heart matched the ticking of the clock in the corner. Then, at last, he appeared.

Jack, wearing a dark blue coat with a crisp white cravat and silver satin waistcoat, looked unusually formal for a morning call. He paused in the doorway, his gaze searching her face.

This wasn't like him. He never stopped and surveyed. He always walked with purpose, striding directly to battle or to stake his claim.

"Why are you hesitating?" she asked, her hands cold with trepidation.

"I have some news I wish to discuss, and I am not certain how to proceed." Then, as if he'd made his decision, he entered the room. Slowly. "The first of which concerns that favor to Vale that I mentioned the first day we met."

What an odd way to begin a conversation after they'd been apart. Confused, she frowned. "When he asked you to send me flowers?"

Jack nodded. "I have recently discovered that this errand did, indeed, have something to do with his *Marriage Formula*."

"I remember that you suspected as much." She knew it. All along, Jack was her perfect match. Grinning now, she stepped forward.

Jack shook his head. "Vale compared the results of your equation and came up with a match. The reason he asked me to send you flowers was in an effort for this man to take notice of you, which he did."

She was so happy that she could leap out of her own skin, but Jack, on the other hand, did not look pleased at all. "Did this news not appeal to you?"

"It did not…because you were matched with Lord Ellery." He raked a hand through his hair and frowned. "From what I have heard, he is planning to make an offer for you."

Was that the reason for Jack's chilly greeting? Did the news matter so much to him? Or was it that it mattered so little? "Ellery was already here."

"And?"

"He did make an offer."

Jack's hands clenched to fists. "I had hoped to arrive before him."

"Why?" she asked, holding her breath.

"Because I"—he stared at her, hard—"have found another match for you."

The tension building inside of her came out on an exhale. "You have?"

"Yes." Jack began to pace the room. "Viscount Locke. Have you heard of him?"

"Viscount Locke?" Her brow knitted in puzzlement and then swiftly in anger. She'd been waiting for days to see him, and all their time apart, he'd been trying to find a man who was willing to marry her? "I don't want to marry Viscount Locke. I don't want to marry Lord Ellery either."

Jack stopped pacing. "You don't?"

"No."

Then, abruptly, he looked more like himself. One corner of his mouth arced upward. "Well, that's hardly fair to Locke. You haven't even met him."

Her anger faded under a wave of hurt so deep that she couldn't see clearly. "I thought you loved me, Jack."

His smirk faded. He crossed the room to her, his hands on her arms, pulling her close—almost into his embrace. "I do, Lilah. More than my own life. I just want you to have the freedom to choose the life you want."

"Then I would marry you." Didn't he know this by now?

He released a deep breath and smiled genuinely at her. "I was hoping you would say that. Though I must admit, I feel sorry for Locke. He's…here, you know, and eager to make your acquaintance."

Confused by all this, she wondered why—if he was so pleased—he wasn't holding her closer and making plans to marry. The faint twinge of a headache started to form above the bridge of her nose. "Here? And you still want me to meet him?"

He nodded. "Only if you agree to marry me. Then I'll introduce you."

She felt her cheeks lift and her lips spread into a smile before his statement hit her. When it did, she leapt toward him and twined her hands around his neck. "I agree. In fact, I am nearly ready to march you out that door and drive you to Gretna Green myself."

Of course, their union would cause a scandal. Her father's will guaranteed a great deal of complications as well. But she didn't care about the consequences. She only wanted to be his.

He kissed the tip of her nose and then removed her hands from his neck. "Wait here for just a moment."

He slipped out of the parlor, closing the door behind him. Lilah could hear the murmur of voices, Mr. Wick's and Jack's, in the foyer. Then, Aunt Zinnia and Juliet appeared, their faces mirroring Lilah's confusion.

"Mr. Marlowe has requested that we wait in here," Aunt Zinnia said before her lips pursed in disapproval.

A nervous, excited effervescence filled Lilah. She couldn't wait to become Jack's wife. She wasn't certain, however, how her aunt or cousin would take the news. Aunt Zinnia would need time to adjust, and perhaps Juliet would as well. But Lilah knew in her heart that they loved her and would support her.

While she could never have said the same about her mother, Lilah knew that she had all the family she would ever need in this very townhouse.

Yet before she could prepare her aunt and cousin, Mr. Wick appeared at the parlor door.

He bowed. "Viscount Locke to see you, miss. Are you *at home?*"

"I am," she said quickly, eager to end this introduction. "Please send him in."

"Viscount Locke?" Aunt Zinnia said, looking from Lilah to Juliet. "Why does that title sound so familiar?"

Juliet shook her head. "I don't believe I've ever heard it."

Neither had Lilah, and she knew she had never been introduced to him. At least, not yet.

Then a figure filled the doorway. Instead of a stranger, however, it was Jack. He walked into the parlor and bowed first to Aunt Zinnia, then to Juliet, and finally to Lilah. Behind him, Mr. Wick cleared his throat. "May I present to you, Jack Marlowe, Viscount Locke."

Jack lifted his head and one corner of his mouth. "Now will you consider marrying Viscount Locke? I can vouch for his character. And I do believe he is already in possession of your heart."

What an arrogant man. And Lilah loved him far too much.

EPILOGUE

The Season Standard—the Daily Chronicle of Consequence.

It appears that the new *Viscount L—*'s first order of business was to procure a bride. A report from Gretna Green tells us that our *Miss A—* wore a single pearl on her dress.

In related news, our *Viscount E—* has been spotted in his well-turned-out phaeton. Alone. Although with whispers (of the *Original* nature) circulating about *E—* (among others), we are hopeful for a viscountess in his near future.

There is one pair, however, who are even more eager for the naming of this Season's *Original*. Sources tell us that the rivalry between a certain *Lady G—* and the *Marquess of Th—* is fairly combustible when the two are in the same room.

On the topic of combustion…an odd series of events brings our attention to *Baron H—*. After his recent bout of clumsiness—the sore-slipper debacle in *Dame F—*'s ballroom, the infamous quizzing glass incident at *Sir G—*'s garden party, and last evening's flaming candelabra mishap in *Lord R—*'s dining room—one must wonder if

H— should be dubbed Baron Catastrophe instead. Be on your guard, dear readers!

And for our more daring curiosity-seekers, our *Earl of W*— has not changed his wolfish ways, as his most recent exploits have proven. One must wonder if such a man could ever be tamed.

The end...for now.

Acknowledgements

Thank you to the amazing team of people at Avon/Harper-Collins for giving this book a chance and making it sparkle. Sometimes all it takes to grab a new reader is one look at a great cover, and so my appreciation goes to Tom and the art department for making magic happen. But most of all, I am grateful to Chelsey Emmelhainz—editor extraordinaire—for her incomparable insight, support, and dedication.

Also, thank you to Stefanie Lieberman for helping this first book in a new series find a home.

And a special thank you to Heather and Shelly for the laughs and the advice. Both of you helped the word flow begin again. Wishing you much love.

Want more from Vivienne Lorret?

The Season's Original series continues with

THIS EARL IS ON FIRE

Coming Summer 2016 from Avon Impulse

Can't wait?

Keep reading for an excerpt from
Vivienne Lorret's Season's Original novella

"The Duke's Christmas Wish"

in

ALL I WANT FOR CHRISTMAS IS A DUKE

Available now from Avon Impulse

An excerpt from

"THE DUKE'S CHRISTMAS WISH"

The Christmas Eve Ball at Castle Vale had begun. As usual, Ivy was running late. This time, however, she was not looking for her slippers. She was looking for the duke's study instead.

She hadn't passed a single servant here in the east wing, but when she saw that the hall was lined with paintings of scientists at their worktables, she knew she was on the right track. Hesitating at an open pair of glossy walnut doors, she smoothed her hands over her skirts.

This evening, she wore layers of silvery gray silk organza with little puffed sleeves that rested at the very crests of her shoulders. Her pale, straight hair had been curled, coiffed, and secured by silver combs. Unfortunately, the small oval mirror in the hallway reflected that a few strands had unwound and now lay limply against her temples. Not only that, but her cheeks were flushed as well.

She made a face and shrugged. At least when she arrived later to the ball, her unrefined appearance would only corroborate the story she'd told Lilah about feeling a trifle ill.

Now was not the time to be worried about her appearance, however. Ivy needed to decline the duke's offer for the first dance. What business did she have dancing with him, when she needed to help Lilah win him?

Stepping over the threshold of the study, she prepared to do just that. Yet after a glance about the room, she realized the duke was not here. Disappointed, she was about to turn around when she saw him emerge from a narrow doorway on the far side of the room near the fireplace. For a moment, he stilled and blinked at her, as if he was as surprised as she. Then those creases appeared on the side of his mouth.

He crossed the room, leaving the narrow door behind him ajar. "Miss Sutherland, what brings you to the east wing? Shouldn't you be patiently waiting for the first dance?"

At the word *patiently*, she knew he was teasing her. Yet as he neared, she felt a tremor of apprehension. What if her plan worked too well? Could Ivy's heart bear to see North marry her friend? "Actually, I was hoping to speak with you about that."

"Oh?" He stepped past her and peered into the hallway before closing the door.

Ivy knew that being alone with him, *again*, wasn't at all proper. His closing the door was even less proper. Perhaps she should mention it. Perhaps they should hold their conversation in the open doorway...yet when he gestured for her to accompany him into the other room, she forgot to mention it.

"It was Lilah," she began along the way, "*Miss Appleton's* idea to take the puddings to your tenants, though I'm certain Miss Leeds would like to take the credit." If Ivy had to endure the sight of him marrying anyone, she would rather it be Lilah than that dreadful Miss Leeds. Though neither thought made her happy.

A smirk appeared, looking perfectly at home on his lips. And when she drew close enough to pass through the narrow doorway, something hot and pleased shone in his eyes. "Actually, Mrs. Thorogood told me that the idea was yours."

"Well…it was Lilah who whispered it to me," Ivy said quickly, forgetting all about the cook being present for her idea. *Drat!* Continuing, she tried to make up for all the times she'd missed the opportunity to bring Lilah to his notice. The way she should have been doing all along. "As you might have guessed, I have the propensity to say whatever idea is on my mind, even if the idea isn't mine in the first place. Lilah is incredibly kind and generous. Not only that, but—like you— she is fond of numbers and equations."

"Is she?" He grinned in earnest now as he closed this second door as well.

Most assuredly, *this* was not at all proper. Yet Ivy said nothing to reproach him. She wanted to be here. It was a cozy space, cast in the glow of firelight. Floor-to-ceiling shelves lined the semicircular walls. Unevenly stacked papers and leather books with worn bindings poked out in complete disarray. A few jars were tucked in here and there, along with assorted sizes of microscopes and other scientific paraphernalia. Yet all the clutter appeared to have function and order. There were no plates with half-eaten dinners. There were no forgotten teacups. The room was not a dirty mess. It was a sort of organized chaos. It felt like stepping into the mind of a genius. *His* mind. She realized quite suddenly that this room was an extension of him. "Do you often bring your guests here?"

"Never," he said as he moved toward his desk and leaned back against the one place that wouldn't cause papers to topple. "My aunt has invited herself on few occasions, and Mr. Graves is permitted at my request."

Those intense, magnetic eyes held hers in an unspoken communication that Ivy felt in the center of her heart. She hadn't been imagining the uniqueness of their connection. He felt it too. Which made what she had to do all the more difficult.

"Lilah has quite the head for figures, indeed. Since her brother and father passed away, she's been overseeing her family's estate ledgers," Ivy said, drifting toward his desk, where an assortment of contraptions rested. The first one looked like a miniature ascending room, built out of wood. Picking it up, she toyed with the button-sized pulley and small ropes.

"Hmm…and what other accomplishments does your friend possess?" As he spoke, North reached over and compressed the pulley. The action sent the miniature ascending room on a swift descent, slipping down a few inches until it suddenly caught and held. Then, flipping the contraption over, he brushed his fingertip over what looked like four diminutive clamps.

Ivy beamed. *Brakes.* Somehow he'd come up with a design from her suggestion in only a matter of days.

"That's ingenious. However did you—" Lifting her gaze, she found him staring at her. Another moment passed in silent communication that made her want...*everything*. She wanted so much more than she could ever have.

"I was inspired by a fascinating and brave young woman," he said, setting aside the model to take her hand, drawing her to stand before him.

She cleared her throat and went on with her task. "Lilah is brave. Do you know that I've never seen her flinch in the presence of a spider? She has other fine qualities too."

"I'm certain she does." He expelled a rasp of air that was just shy of a laugh. "Miss Sutherland, I am not going to marry your friend."

"That isn't what I—" Ivy stopped, already seeing in his perceptive expression how easily he'd read her intention. "Why ever not?"

Something tender softened the flesh around his eyes and the creases around his mouth. "I suppose the simplest reason is that Miss Appleton and I are not in the same ledger."

Ledger? Before she could ask what he meant, he reached behind him to a stack of ledgers in three colors on his desk and held them up, one after the other. "You see, for my formula, there are certain people who automatically enter the black ledger—those with high-ranking titles, a good deal of property, and wealth. The brown ledger contains members of the lower-ranking aristocracy and the landed gentry." He stopped then, his gaze fixed on the trio.

"And what about those in the red ledger?"

He shook his head. "They have little, if any, hope of marrying at all."

"Please do not tell me that Lilah is in the red ledger."

He blinked at her. "You needn't worry. If my formula is correct, your friend would find her match among those in the brown ledger."

No. That couldn't be right. Ivy wanted Lilah to be in the black ledger. After everything she'd been through, her friend deserved the very best. "Have you finished her equation? Isn't it possible that her number would pair with yours?"

"I have not, but I already know the answer. And I think you do, as well." He set the ledgers back down. Gently, he took her other hand as well. "Now, tell me the real reason you want me to marry your friend."

She didn't like thinking about the past, and she certainly never spoke of the life-altering incident, yet she found herself wanting to tell North. It would be better for him to understand.

Ivy exhaled. "It's because of Jasper, her brother."

North's brow furrowed. "I don't recall the mention of his name."

"He had an unfortunate…accident and died a couple of years ago." Reluctantly, Ivy released North's hands and turned away. "You see, since we were children, I'd always planned to marry Jasper."

"And he is the reason why you are not married now?"

She nodded even though the answer was more complicated. She began to amble around the room, stopping at a bookshelf full of sideways stacked books and jars filled with all sorts of things. She picked up one that contained a green branch dotted with small white berries that looked suspiciously like mistletoe. "I'd always planned to take care of

Lilah too. Her parents were not very kind. After Jasper died, they became worse.

"Within the year, her father died as well, and for a while I thought she might have a reprieve from the demands put upon her. However, then came the reading of her father's will. After Jasper's death, Lilah's father added a codicil, stating that the line had to be preserved. Lilah has to marry a man of noble blood, or she will essentially lose everything. Worse yet, if she doesn't find a titled gentleman to marry by the end of this coming Season, she will be forced to marry her licentious cousin, who holds her father's estate."

When she turned around, North was there beside her. He lifted a hand to cup her jaw. "I am sorry for your friend. If you like, I will work her equation and find a match for her. In addition, I will introduce her to as many of my unmarried friends as possible. You must know that I would do anything…"

His touch stirred so many sensations within her. She wanted to lean against his hand and close her eyes. Fighting the impulse was next to impossible. "Anything other than marry her yourself."

"I am sorry, Ivy."

He wouldn't marry Lilah. Ivy's entire purpose for attending this party was to save her friend, and she had failed. So then why was joy leaping inside her heart?

"No. I am the one who should be sorry, because hearing those words from your lips fills me with blissful relief, when it should fill me with agony instead." It was no use. She lifted her hand to cover his, to urge him to linger. "I am a terrible friend. I failed Jasper, and now I have failed—"

"How did you fail?" North shook his head, his gaze frank and earnest. "Even in the short duration of our acquaintance, I feel as if I know you. You cannot fail at anything, because you are the kind of person who does not give up when something matters to you. I know you, Ivy, to the very core of my being. You weave the world around you into a fabric of light that blankets anyone who stands near. Your vivacity is as charming as it is infectious. Your heart is warm and open. And your curiosity might even rival my own. There is nothing within you that could fail."

Embarrassed, she wanted to look away so that she wouldn't have to face the truth. She even attempted to step back but found herself against the bookcase. Yet even with North so close, his hand still curled beneath her jaw, she did not feel trapped. Surprisingly, she found his nearness comforting. If ever there was a time to admit her dreaded secret, now was it.

"But I did fail," she said. "For years, I tried hard to be perfect. To let Jasper know that I was the bride for him. I was patient. You may not believe it, but I was. Nearly ten years went by before my impulsive nature finally consumed me. And when I kissed him on that last night we ever spoke, he scolded me and told me that I did not stir his passions."

North slowly shook his head, his gaze drifting to her mouth, lingering. "That is not possible."

"It is true, I tell you. I must have done it wrong. All I know is that I wasn't enough for him. And there you have it."

"Not possible. I simply do not believe it." His thumb swept against the underside of her bottom lip. "Your mouth is far too perfect."

Ivy held her breath. "Apparently not."

"It is a matter of simple mechanics." His gaze lifted to hers. He edged closer by degrees. With one hand propped on the shelf beside her head, and the other sliding to the back of her neck, his fingertip dipped into the hollow at the base of her skull. A riot of tingles traversed her spine, plummeting all the way to her toes. "I'll show you."

And then he kissed her. Her lips parted on a soundless gasp of pleasure. The press of his mouth was brief but warm and pleasantly firm. When he withdrew, the sensation of his lips upon hers lingered. A current zinged through her. She imagined that she knew what an electric coil felt like, all tingly and warm.

Reeling from it, she was almost afraid to ask his thoughts. Instead, she prolonged the moment. She licked her lips to see if she could taste him, and the barest hint of port teased her tongue.

His gaze darkened. The hand at her nape tightened ever so slightly. His nostrils flared and his breath rushed against her lips, but he said nothing.

Surely something that felt so wondrous to her couldn't have been a complete failure. Could it? Ivy closed her eyes before she asked, "Well?"

"I'd say the experiment was a complete success. However..."

Her eyes snapped open. "However?"

"It was only one kiss," he said with a slight lift of his brow, as if uncertain. Yet one of those creases made an appearance beside his mouth. "A scientist must experiment multiple times in order to come to a definitive conclusion. I believe we should make another attempt, for further study, of course."

He hesitated only long enough for her to agree with a nod before he took her mouth again. This time, he angled his head the other direction, kissing her once—*twice*, nuzzling the corner of her mouth. By the time he concluded, she was out of breath and clinging to his shoulders.

"Hmm…" he murmured, the low sound vibrating through her. "Another successful experiment."

She moved closer, her hands sliding down from the breadth of his shoulders beneath his coat to wrap around his torso. This new position molded her body to his. Beneath the solid wall of his chest, his heart pounded. Her breasts ached and her back arched so that she felt the firm rise and fall of his breaths. And lower, she felt the unyielding, intriguing heat of him. "Though…perhaps further study is in order."

"In great depth." His hand abandoned the shelf and settled on her hip. He shifted, his feet on either side of hers. "I must warn you—this may take a while."

ABOUT THE AUTHOR

USA Today best-selling author **VIVIENNE LORRET** loves romance novels, her pink laptop, her husband, and her two sons (not necessarily in that order...but there are days). Transforming copious amounts of tea into words, she is an Avon Impulse author of works including *Tempting Mr. Weatherstone*, The Wallflower Wedding series, The Rakes of Fallow Hall series, *The Duke's Christmas Wish*, and the Season's Original series.

Discover great authors, exclusive offers, and more at hc.com.

Give in to your Impulses . . .
Continue reading for excerpts from
our newest Avon Impulse books.
Available now wherever ebooks are sold.

SERVING TROUBLE
A SECOND SHOT NOVEL
By Sara Jane Stone

IGNITE
THE WILDWOOD SERIES
By Karen Erickson

BLACK LISTED
A BENEDICTION NOVEL
By Shelly Bell

An Excerpt from

SERVING TROUBLE
A Second Shot Novel

by *Sara Jane Stone*

Five years ago, Josie Fairmore left timber country
in search of a bright future. Now she's back home
with a mountain of debt and reeling from a loss
that haunts her. Desperate for a job, she turns
to the one man she wishes she could avoid. But
former Marine Noah Tager has never forgotten
their one wild night and the only thing he desires is
a second chance with his best friend's little sister.

She tried the door. Locked, dammit.

Ignoring the warning bells in her head telling her to run to her best friend's club and offer to serve a topless breakfast, she raised her hand and knocked.

"Hang on a sec," a deep voice called from the other side. She remembered that sound and could hear the echo of his words from five long years ago, before he'd joined the marines and before she'd gone to college hoping for a brighter future—and found more heartache.

Call, email, or send a letter. Hell, send a carrier pigeon. I don't care how you get in touch, or where I am. If you need me, I'll find a way to help.

He'd meant every word. But people changed. They hardened. They took hits and got back up, leaving their heart beaten and wrecked on the ground.

She glanced down as if the bloody pieces of her broken heart would appear at her feet. Nope. Nothing but cement and her boots. She'd left her heart behind in Portland, dead and buried, thank you very much.

The door opened. She looked up and . . .

Oh my . . . Wow. . .

She'd gained five pounds—well, more than that, but she'd

lost the rest. She'd cried for weeks, tears running down her cheeks while she slept, and flooding her eyes when she woke. And it had aged her. There were lines on her face that made her look a lot older than twenty-three.

But Noah . . .

He'd gained five pounds of pure muscle. His tight black T-shirt clung to his biceps. Dark green cargo pants hung low on his hips. And his face . . .

On the drive, she'd tried to trick herself into believing he was just a friend she'd slept with one wild night. She'd made a fool of herself, losing her heart to him then.

Never again.

She'd made a promise to her broken, battered heart and she planned to keep it. She would not fall for Noah this time.

But oh, the temptation . . .

His short blond hair still looked as if he'd just run his hands through it. Stubble, the same color as his hair, covered his jaw. He'd forgotten to shave, or just didn't give a damn. But his familiar blue eyes left her ready to pass out at his feet from lack of oxygen.

He stared at her, wariness radiating from those blue depths. Five years ago, he'd smiled at her and it had touched his eyes. Not now.

"Josie?" His brow knitted as if he'd had to search his memory for her name. His grip tightened on the door. Was he debating whether to slam it in her face and pretend his mind had been playing tricks on him?

"Hi, Noah." She placed her right boot in the doorway, determined to follow him inside if he tried to shut her out.

"You're back," he said as if putting together the pieces of a puzzle. But still no hint of the warm, welcoming smile he'd worn with an easy-going grace five years ago.

"I guess you didn't get the carrier pigeon," she said, forcing a smile. *Please let him remember.* "But I need your help."

An Excerpt from

IGNITE
The Wildwood Series
by *Karen Erickson*

Weston Gallagher is falling hard—
for the wrong woman.

One night of passion has haunted him for years.

Now he's got a second chance to get the girl of
his dreams . . . but there's just one problem:

She hates him.

A knock sounded at his door, startling him and he climbed off the couch to go answer it, pissed that it was most likely Holden ready to convince him he should go out to the bars. He didn't bother looking through the peephole, just unlocked the door and swung it open, launching right into a speech for his little brother.

"I already told you I didn't want to go out tonight," West said, the rest of the words stalling in his throat when he saw who was standing on his front doorstep.

It was Harper, wearing a black trench coat on a warm June night, her long auburn hair extra wavy and flowing past her shoulders, a secretive little smile curving her very red lips.

"You did?" She blinked up at him, all wide-eyed sexy innocence. "Maybe I should go then?"

She started to turn and he grabbed hold of her arm, halting her progress. "Don't go." He sounded eager. Way too eager. Clearing his throat, he started over. "Sorry. I just thought—I thought you were Holden."

"Oh." She turned to fully face him once more and his gaze dropped to her feet, which were in the sexiest, shiniest black high heeled shoes he'd ever seen. "So you don't mind that I stopped by?"

He looked up, their eyes meeting. "Not at all." What was she up to? Her eyes were heavily made up, as were her ruby red lips. And her hair was downright wild . . . all he could think of was fisting it in his hands and tugging her head back so he could plant a long, deep kiss on those juicy lips.

"It's sort of late." She blatantly scanned his mostly naked body, her glossy lips parted, her pink tongue touching just the corner of her mouth. Her gaze lingered on his chest and arms, cataloging his tattoos. She seemed fascinated with them and he was half tempted to flex his muscles just to see if her eyes grew hungrier . . .

Which they seemed to do, without any encouragement on his part. If she didn't stop looking at him like that he might get a freaking boner and that probably wouldn't be good. "Were you in . . . bed?"

The provocative way she just said it made him aware of her close proximity. How her hands tugged on the ends of the belt wrapped tight around her waist. The hollow of her throat was exposed, as was a bit of her chest. She looked practically naked under that coat.

Hmmm.

"No, I wasn't in bed." He paused, wondering what the hell she was up to. Whatever it was, he could appreciate the way she was staring at him, and he was damn thankful she'd come by. He figured he'd blown it for good with Harper. "You want to come in?"

"I would love to." She smiled and he stepped out of her way, the scent of her surrounding him as she walked by. He shut and locked the door and followed her as she moved deeper into the living room. Grabbing the remote from the side table, he turned off the TV, the sudden silence amplifying every move she made.

"So I have a proposition for you," she said, turning to face him once more. "One I'm hoping you'll agree to."

In the hushed quiet of his house, she looked a little less sure, a little more nervous. A lot more like the Harper he knew. He wanted to reach out and reassure her but he also wanted to hear what she had to say first.

"Really?" He rested his hands on his hips, noting the way her gaze dropped to linger on his stomach. He felt downright exposed, what with the way she studied him. Not that he minded. "What is it?"

She bit her lower lip as she contemplated him, her straight white teeth a bold contrast to the deep red coating her lips. "Last night, when we talked, you said you weren't boyfriend material."

He winced. Did he really need a reminder of the stupid things he'd said?

"And I told you I wasn't looking for a relationship, which is true. I don't want one. But I do want *something* from you, West." She reached for the coat belt, slowly undoing it. "I'm hoping you want the same thing."

An Excerpt from

BLACK LISTED
A Benediction Novel
by Shelly Bell

Years ago con artist Lisa Smith fell in love with
her mark, then vanished without a trace . . .
but now he's found her and he's not going
to let her slip through his fingers again.

An Avon Red Romance

He sucked in a breath, the tightening in his chest becoming more pronounced as he watched her glide across the dance floor with a glass of champagne in her hand. She'd changed since the last time he'd seen her. Gone was her halo of white blonde tresses that spilled down her back and those round silver irises that looked at him with what he'd believed was love. Like a chameleon, she'd adapted to her environment, her chestnut hair cut into a sleek bob and an air of sophistication clinging to her designer-clad body.

With a smile on her face, she had everyone at this wedding fooled, but he knew the truth. She was a con artist who had stolen millions from unsuspecting men and women. At the drop of a hat, she could become someone else, fade into the crowds until she turned invisible, only to return moments later as someone new. And no one would ever guess the truth. She'd mastered the art of disguise, her ability to convince someone of her love and devotion worthy of an Academy Award. Just when she had you wrapped completely around her finger, she'd disappear without a trace, taking your money and your heart with her.

But she'd grown careless when she'd allowed herself to be

photographed, the picture on the front page of every major newspaper. She'd been in the background, barely discernable to most. But not to him. Never him. He'd know his chameleon anywhere.

She had no idea he was watching her.

Stalking her.

Hunting her.

His chameleon had forgotten to use the reptilian sense that warned her of impending danger. She might believe she was a predator, but she was now the prey.

His prey.

Sweat dripped down the back of his neck and black spots flickered in his vision. He shook his head as if clearing the cobwebs from his mind. Didn't she understand he needed her? After everything he'd done for her, she owed him. It was time for her to repay her debts.

Time and fate had kept them apart for far too long. But now that he'd found her, he was never letting her go again.

She loved to play her games.

He smiled.

A game was what they'd play.

Walking away from her friends, Lisa Smith took a sip of wine and headed toward where she'd last seen the caterer. Not spotting him, she stopped and scanned the crowd.

"Lisa!"

Lisa turned and caught sight of her friend Rachel Dawson walking toward her with two men by her side.

It took only a moment for it to register.

The long blond hair she loved to tug on during rough sex.

The stubble lining his jaw that used to scratch the skin of her inner thighs as he worked her over with his mouth.

The roguish and lighthearted appearance he maintained in public and the dark dominance that lurked beneath the surface.

It was him.

He was here.

Her *Master.*

He had found her.

She blinked a few times, trying to see if maybe she was imagining that the man she'd run from five years ago was suddenly only feet away and talking with her friends as if he knew them. Which was impossible, right?

Her heart galloped a wild beat and the sounds of the crowd disappeared under the roar of her pulse.

She wanted to run *from* him.

She wanted to run *to* him.

All the sorrow and regret she'd buried deep down inside came rushing back with a force that nearly bowled her over. And when the ghost from her past stood right in front of her and looked at her like a stranger, the glass of red wine slipped from her shaking hand onto the green grass, the liquid pooling beneath her heels.

Seemingly oblivious to her shock, Rachel smiled, a twinkle of mischief in her eyes. "I'd like to introduce you to Logan's friend, Sawyer Hayes. Sawyer, this is Lisa Smith."

"Hello," Sawyer said cordially, standing so close she could feel his body heat radiating off him and smell a scent that reminded her of the best days of her life. "It's nice to see you again, Annaliese."

Her mind was a jumbled mess.

Like she was prey caught in the sights of a hunter, she became entrapped in his eyes.

She couldn't breathe.

Couldn't speak.

Couldn't move.

"You know each other," Rachel said, her brows wrinkled in confusion.

"You could say that," Sawyer said slowly, still holding Lisa captive with his eyes. "She's my wife."